MONSTER SQUAD
RETURN OF THE
PHOENIX

HEATH STALLCUP

RETURN OF THE PHOENIX

A MONSTER SQUAD NOVEL

BOOK 1

HEATH STALLCUP

DEVILDOG PRESS

SWANVILLE, MAINE

For my grandchildren. Hopefully one day they will be able to pick this up and realize that their grand-father didn't just dream of writing, but had the tenacity to see it through at least once.

Acknowledgements

You know, you see these acknowledgement pages and as a writer you ask yourself if anybody ever reads these or do they skip straight to the meat and potatoes and jump into the story? Well, regardless, I want to take the time to thank some people who, without their help, this story would never have seen the light of day.

First off, I need to thank my wife Jessie. Without her encouragement and understanding, this project would have ended up like the fifty or so others that were started and never finished - >DELETED< from my hard drive, just another idea that was never seen to fruition. All the nights that she went to bed alone so that I could have a few hours of peace and quiet at the computer without distraction has finally produced this, the first in a short series of stories that she has continued to encourage me to finish.

You know, there's a whole long list of people I should thank that influenced me as I grew up. From my high school English teacher Sandra Mantooth, all the way to the authors that I read today, but I'm told that I need to keep this short. I'm naturally long winded, so I'll end here. But, if you look Ms. Mantooth…I *did* get your name slipped in there!

-Heath

Return of the Phoenix
A Monster Squad Novel
By
Heath Stallcup

Mankind has always suspected that he wasn't alone at the top of the food chain. Since time immemorial, he has had an innate fear of the dark, a fear of the unfamiliar, a fear that something evil lurked just outside his field of vision. Whether he lived in a cave, a mud brick house, or a Tudor mansion, man has been afraid of that noise in the darkness that signified that he was not alone, that something might be waiting to attack him or his family. Grown men could tromp into the woods and play hunter by day, but once the sun set and the moon lit the sky, the unfamiliar snap of a twig or rustling of a bush could make the deadliest of hunter's blood run cold. Something was out there. He didn't know what it was, but the hair on the back of his neck stood on end for a reason. Man's sixth sense that warned of an unseen danger was alive and well and screaming at him; his fight or flight instinct was kicked into high gear.

If that same man experienced nothing, he would of course laugh it off as simply 'nerves' or too much coffee. Perhaps it was just an overactive imagination playing tricks with him. But sometimes things would occur that simply could not be explained by the ordinary. Sometimes people would get hurt or attacked by things that defied rational explanation. Sometimes people would simply disappear...never to return again.

Those who did survive, if they dared speak of the horrors they experienced, were often ridiculed by others. Some were institutionalized. Some— the truly unfortunate ones—enter into a special level of Hell reserved for survivors of attacks that can only exist in dime store novellas or bad science fiction movies and horror comics. These poor souls were left to deal with the consequences on their own, all the while asking, 'why couldn't somebody do something about the monsters that were out there?' Why can't somebody do something to protect the innocent? Why can't somebody do something to stop the things that go bump in the night?

Somebody has.

This is their story.

1

"OPCOM, this is Team Leader. We are approaching now. One click to target," the disembodied voice whispered across the overhead speakers. "Zero tangos."

Colonel Matt Mitchell was bent over the operations console observing an overhead view of the heat signatures of his assault team as they approached an abandoned farmhouse outside of Brownsville, Texas. The command center had switched to red light and all non-essential personnel had vacated the center. Communications techs, logistics personnel, weapons and tactics specialists and OPCOM's lone civilian government representative, Laura Youngblood, sat anxiously near their respective stations waiting for the fecal matter to hit the atmospheric oscillator. "Keep your head about you, chief," he answered back. "Just because you can't see them doesn't mean they can't see you."

"Copy that," came the whispered reply.

"Be safe out there Phoenix," Mitchell whispered to himself, a creepy feeling crawling up his back and settling in the base of his neck.

Mitchell turned to peer at a countdown clock over the shoulder of one of his communications techs. The mission team had only been "feet down" in Texas for forty-three minutes, but it felt like this mission was already taking too long. The heat in this piss-ant border town was so intense during the day that it played hell with their satellite infra-red observation. Reading heat signatures in this type of heat, you actually watched for cold spots for your men. The colonel had practically begged for a bird with microwave visual capability, hoping that he could at least borrow one that had true-eye visibility, but none of the alphabet soup groups would loan him one regardless of the risk involved. He was stuck with the only bird he had, and tracking body heat was all he could do.

Mitchell cursed again as his men faded in and out of view. "Those asshats promised me everything I needed to make this unit work, and I have to send my men into the meat grinder with antiquated equipment." Mitchell glanced up at Youngblood. "Any chance those assholes you used to work with would return *your* calls?"

"Colonel, I tried to call in every marker I had," Laura replied, her eyes not leaving her monitor.

"What did those limp-wristed spooks say?"

Laura sighed and finally made eye contact with him. "They laughed at me, sir."

Although Laura was still technically a civilian and didn't have to refer to Colonel Mitchell as 'sir', she did so out of respect. Mitchell was a tough SOB, but he treated her as one of the guys rather than a know-nothing civie, and after all the grief she met climbing her way through the ranks at the CIA, she knew the caliber of man he was simply in the way he treated his people and the way he treated her. When

4

she was assigned to him, he didn't piss and moan about her being a woman or her being weak, he simply reviewed her file, accepted the accolades of her superiors and her mental, physical, and shooting scores for what they were and assessed her as he would any other member of his team. He placed her based on her merits. And she was now his second-in-command. Nobody ordered him to do it, nobody suggested he do it. Nobody pulled any strings and nobody coerced him because of who her family was. Hell, nobody *knew* who her family was, she had seen to that. And over the years, Mitchell had become much like a father figure for her. A brother in arms, but one she could go to if she felt she needed to air a personal problem that she didn't feel comfortable sharing with anyone else.

"I all but begged them, sir. I tried to express the importance of this particular mission without going in to details, of course, but it was like butting heads with a brick wall." Half-Irish and half-Native American, Laura Youngblood stood a solid 5' 11" with long mahogany hair. She looked to have a permanent tan, and her dark eyes gleamed with intelligent mischief. She was her father's only daughter, the youngest of six kids. With five older brothers, she knew how to roughhouse with the best of them. She could definitely give as good as she could take.

"Bastards. Let them hope they never need us to come clean up a mess for them or they'll wish they had played a helluva lot nicer with us," Mitchell swore out loud. "And yes, lieutenant, you can record that comment into the hard copy. Maybe when the powers-that-be sees that we aren't getting the support

5

we were promised, maybe...just maybe...some-body's head will roll over this!"

The communications officer cut a shit-eating grin at the colonel and simply uttered a "Yes, sir."

"Approaching the outer perimeter," the disem-bodied voice whispered again.

Mitchell returned to his post. Laura couldn't help but notice that every time he assumed his duties in the command center, his stature seemed to grow. A Green Beret, Mitchell was an Army Special Forces soldier and a large man by nature. He kept himself in shape despite his age, but when his troops were 'in-the-muck' as Mitchell would say, he seemed to grow larger. Almost as a defensive move, like a mother hen fluffing her feathers to appear larger to a predator when her chicks are threatened.

"Go easy, Phoenix. It's daylight, so it should be like shooting fish in a barrel. But we know they'll be somewhere deep and shadowed, and hopefully asleep. If they wake, cornered rats tend to bite."

"Copy that, OPCOM. Slow and easy until bingo," the speakers responded.

"Colonel, they still have four hours until dusk. No discernible weather noted. Blackhawk dispatched to LZ for pickup," the logistics officer stated.

"Noted and marked," Mitchell responded. "Team Leader, you are T-minus four hours until bug-out."

"No problem, skipper. We should be mopped up long before that. We're almost to the farmhouse. We'll soon be going radio sile—" static hissed across the secured channel and was amplified through the command center.

Mitchell stood instantly. "Sitrep! Now!"

The command center was suddenly abuzz with activity. Techs were adjusting the contrast on their screens trying to discern their operators from the heat of the day. Unfortunately, it was nearly impossible in the scorching Texas sun. Communications techs were trying every frequency, adjusting their equipment, going for every band available for any kind of signal. Suddenly one of them cried out, "I have them!"

"Big screen!" Mitchell barked and the operator switched his monitor to the overhead screen so that all could observe the team's heat signatures in the dry Texas scabland. But rather than seeing the seven special operators, they saw dozens of higher heat signatures running rampant at high speed, three and four attacking individual heat sources at a time, literally tearing it to shreds, then moving to assist another group that was tearing up another target.

Through the overhead static that nobody had thought to turn off, a gurgling voice tried to yell 'trap' but it sounded as if the owner of the voice had gargled with broken glass. Automatic gunfire could be heard, but the static made it sound as if it was just a bad connection and it didn't last long. The heat signature picture indicated why.

The attack didn't last long; the heat signatures all scattered in different directions and left the scene. Quickly.

"Good lord...what was that?" somebody asked quietly.

"Get me that Blackhawk. Redirect them to a half click from that site. I want my boys picked up. Tell them to look for survivors," Mitchell's voice was calm and even though spoken through clenched teeth. He knew there were no survivors. He could tell from the quickly cooling pieces of what once was his team on the screen above. "Tell those chopper boys to look for *any* kind of evidence of what might have done this. No matter *how* crazy it might appear. I want it. All of it. Every hair, scrap of clothes, everything."

"I'll scramble the clean-up team as well, sir," Laura didn't sound well as she said it.

"Make it so," Mitchell turned to leave the command center.

"Sir?" Laura asked as he turned to go.

"What is it?"

"Where will you be, sir?"

"I'll be in my office. I have some calls to make. There are some answers I need and some heads I want. And I won't rest until I have them."

"He said *what*?" Laura asked, shooting up from her chair in Colonel Mitchell's office.

Mitchell poured her a short glass of single malt scotch. His brow furrowed in deep thought. "Yeah, that was my reaction, too." Mitchell said, reclining behind his desk. His eyes probed her, reading her reaction and wondering if she would have beaten the shit out of the congressman, then choked the very life out of him had he been here in person. That was the colonel's first instinct. "When he placed the blame on our training and lack of preparedness, I was pissed. When he said that I was inept and shouldn't be in command, I went past pissed and straight to livid. But when he said that my biggest mistake was making you my second…I told him that if he ever darkened our door again, I'd personally gut him and mail his balls back to his kid."

Laura paled. "God, you didn't really say that, did you? He's on our appropriations committee, Matt." Though she was glad that Mitchell had stood up for her. She knew that Senator Franklin had never liked her and often doubted her ability to lead. She just didn't know if it stemmed from her record with The Company or because she was a woman.

"The man's a political hack. He's hated us from the git-go. The only reason he's on the committee is so that the others will have somebody to keep them in check and so that the president has somebody he knows will go whining to him with *everything* that is decided when they're in session. Besides, I had already called the other three congressmen and they assured me that heads will roll for us not having had the support from NSA and CIA that we were supposed to have. We also got heartfelt condolences for the men and their families. But the *honorable* Senator Franklin was the only one to go off the deep end." There was obvious venom when he said 'honorable' and that was one thing that Franklin would *never* be.

Mitchell had dealt with enough politicians over his career to know that there are bad ones, there are mediocre ones and there are damn few good ones. The one in question here was a certifiable nutcase;

9

laughed at by his colleagues, ridiculed in the press, and somehow re-elected by his constituents. Franklin had been rumored to have gone off the deep end a long time ago, but that didn't stop someone from putting the dumbass on their Oversight Committee and making him a permanent pain in their ass.

The 'Monster Squad' as they were known, had an oversight committee of four politicians who could either make them or break them at a whim. They approved their budget, appropriated the equipment, manpower, support personnel, and made everything possible for their entire operation to exist. Their operation was, for all intent and purpose, a 'black op', meaning that nobody outside the four man oversight committee and the president himself even knew that they existed. Oh, their records reflected that they were military or government employees, but they 'officially' existed as clerks or cooks or field officers, not here in the center of the United States working out of an old defunct hangar at Tinker Air Force Base in Oklahoma City protecting this end of the world from things that go bump in the night and that mommies and daddies tell their little kiddies don't really exist.

Placing the command center here at Tinker was JC Watts' idea. It was, pretty much, the center of the continental U.S., and it did provide a pretty good cover. The team could deploy from there and traverse the country easily and in equal time from this location. Nobody would expect a group of monster hunters to operate out of an unassuming hangar that used to be used for overhauling old aircraft.

The hangar itself, to the odd passerby, was still just an old hangar. But underground, it was a state-of-the-art command center. Not huge, by any stretch of the imagination, but efficient and equipped well. Three of the four congress-critters, as Mitchell often referred to them, saw to it that the men stationed there had their creature comforts. Tinker was well equipped for recreational activities as well, and Oklahoma City, though not known as a Mecca for the arts or being a thriving metropolis, still had a down home quality of goodness to it. Good food, good people, and good clean fun. Just don't expect more than triple A baseball if you're a fan. At least they finally got an NBA team to settle there. *Still*, Laura often thought, *it would have been nice to settle someplace a bit more lively*.

At least it's not Montana.

Laura sighed with relief. "Thank God. You had me scared we were shut down for good."

"Nope," Mitchell answered. "In fact", he continued as he refilled his scotch, "you and I are to start recruiting for a new monster squad right away." Mitchell leaned back in his chair again and held the scotch glass to his forehead. "How in the hell are we going to replace a team like that on such short notice?"

Laura shook her head as she thought of the many months of training the team had put in; the physical augmentation, the boosters…everything that made up being a member of the squad. She thought of each member and how 'alive' they had been as they packed their gear just hours before in preparation for this op.

"Any word from the Blackhawk or the clean-up team on what attacked them?" Mitchell asked.

"Not yet, sir. Preliminary reports just indicate a lot of tracks coming in and out from multiple directions. But the area is soft sand, so they can't get impressions or even pour castings," Laura glanced at her notes. "But whatever it was, some of them had a running gait of over twenty-five feet. So they were covering some serious terrain at a very high rate of speed."

Mitchell wished again he could have gotten the technical support he had requested. Even an unmanned drone with video capability could have given his squad enough fair warning to prepare for the onslaught. Imagining the last moments of his team's lives was not something he wanted to do, but he knew it was a nightmare he wouldn't soon be rid of.

Mitchell reclined in his chair and held the scotch to his chest. "How soon before Squad One returns from England?"

"They're supposed to be training for the next three weeks, but I can have them on the next flight home."

Mitchell rubbed his eyes, debating what to do.

"I know this is probably going to go over like a lead balloon…but I do have an idea," Laura offered.

"Right now I'm open to anything," Mitchell waved her on without opening his eyes, letting the iced scotch ease his ache.

"Maybe we could contact the other squads? See if they could each offer up one member. We could mold them into what we need them to be?"

Laura watched the colonel carefully for any movement. If she didn't know any better, she'd think he had fallen asleep, but she knew him well enough to know his mind was carefully weighing all the pros and cons of this possibility. His gears were turning and she could almost tell when the light came on over his head.

Mitchell commanded Team Four which covered the U.S., Canada, and most of Mexico. The team was made of two small squads of seven men each. Team Five covered South America and was based out of Brazil. Teams One, Two and Three covered Europe and Africa. The teams were really a modern solution to a very old problem: Monsters.

Monsters are, by the simplest definition, things that go bump in the night. If it is a threat, then the Monster Squads take them out. Period. So far, the most common monsters that the squads had really encountered were vampires and very rarely the occasional zombie uprising. But considering that the monsters have had centuries to hone their hiding skills and the squads have only been around for a few generations, it wasn't hard to understand why, *IF* there were other kinds of monsters out there, the squads weren't running into them.

Teams of experts scoured the papers, internet blogs, news reports, any source of information looking for key words that might indicate a monster or group of monsters in an area. If something is triggered, a scout is sent out to verify the findings. If the scout sends back positive intelligence, then the squad is mobilized and the monster is taken out. Once the threat or threats (plural) are taken out, a clean-up team is sent in to remove any evidence of the monster ever being there, or the squad having entered. The world goes on its merry way never knowing that what goes bump in the night might eat you and pick its teeth with your bones.

"Make it so. Call who you have to and get who we can. We'll probably get their bottom of the barrel squad members…if anybody is even willing to part with some…but it beats the shit out of going out in the field and recruiting from raw recruits."

"You got it, boss." She got up to leave but stopped and turned back around. Mitchell opened his eyes and gave her a questioning look. Laura picked up the rest of her scotch and downed it. Setting the glass back on his desk she said, "Never leave a good scotch behind." Mitchell gave her a rare smile.

"I couldn't agree more." He followed suit. "You know, he's right about one thing."

Laura paused. "Sir?"

"Franklin. The son of a bitch is right about one thing."

"What's that?" Laura asked, not really sure she wanted to know.

"In the end, I'm still the one responsible for their lives." And Mitchell knew that they would haunt him for the rest of his.

Jack Thompson moaned as his body screamed at him in pain. Everything was dark, but his body was on fire and every movement made him painfully aware of every nerve ending firing double-time. He was being jostled, bounced uncaringly and with the sounds surrounding him, it sounded as though somebody was carrying him. Quickly.

Slowly he became more aware and current memories began to return to him. His team was approaching the old mud-brick farm house when suddenly dark, hairy creatures attacked them from every direction. They were blindingly fast. And strong. Good heavens they were strong. And they were vicious as hell, too. Teeth! He remembered teeth as long as his fingers, and claws at the end of paws that looked a lot like a man's hand. They looked a lot like dogs…good, Lord! Wolves! They were attacked by some kind of mutated wolves.

Jack's mind was spinning and he could feel himself beginning to lose consciousness.

Could it be? Could they have been attacked by werewolves? During the day? A sudden jarring sent a pain so intense through his body that Jack passed out, but the last thing to go through his mind was an image of a black wolf face snarling at him wanting to tear out his throat.

2

"Problem, Matt." Laura had barely stuck her head into Mitchell's office. He knew something was wrong because she *always* knocked before opening his door. It was like an unwritten law for her, and for her to break it now, even under these circumstances, something must be really haywire.

"Report." Mitchell dropped what he was doing to give her his full attention.

"You know that we don't usually keep in contact with the other squads, right?" Mitchell nodded, urging her to continue. "Three other teams were hit at almost the exact same time as we were. Same M.O., same results."

Mitchell paled. He stood up slowly as the information sunk in. Out of five teams that covered the world, only *one* remained untouched? "Holy shit," he whispered. He turned to look at Laura. "Which team is still kicking?" Mitchell knew a lot of the operators personally, and he couldn't choose any one team to root for to have survived this coordinated attack.

"Team Five. The Brazilians got the same kind of report of a large cell of vampires in a southern area, except their scout couldn't verify anything. They're going back now to look to see if he missed something that was *supposed* to be there to bait the trap—"

"Which would make him inept," Mitchell finished for her. "What of our boys with the Brits?" Matt's eyes couldn't hide his concern.

"No, they're all safe. But you know the Brits have three squads with Team One. They lost eight men when one of their squads was hit. I've sent word to send our boys home," she said. "Whoever coordinated this attack may not have baited their trap good enough for the Brazilian scout to catch it."

"Or maybe they didn't want to take out all of the squads…for whatever reason," Mitchell added.

"To what purpose?" Laura asked, puzzled.

"Think about it, Laura. If you have a group like ours, small, tight-knit, everybody pretty much knows everybody else, and you take out four of the five, and you leave that fifth team totally unharmed, it could cast a shadow of suspicion on that fifth team."

"How so, sir?"

"Like they're in cahoots with the monsters."

"Surely you don't think the Brazilians would team up with the monsters, Matt. I've known Pablo and his team since you brought me on here and—" Laura began to argue, but Mitchell cut her off again.

"No, I'm not saying that is the case at all. I'm saying that the monsters might be trying to make it look like that." Mitchell sighed and reached for the scotch again. "All I'm saying is, to the Europeans, it might not look so good that the SA team got off without a scratch. We might have to keep our eyes and ears open for a bit."

Laura nodded, thinking through his thought processes.

"Meanwhile, start reviewing active duty personnel files and get the trainers and detailers geared up for work. Let's get 'em with doc for the enhancement protocols and their inoculations. I want you to look at SEALs and Green Berets first." Laura shot him a questioning glance. "I've learned from personal experience that those two groups make the easiest transition to the squad. Just get me the best candidates in here. Tomorrow!"

"Yes, sir!" She turned and was out the door before he could add any other demands.

Mitchell sat at his desk and considered the ramifications of this attack. Whoever was behind this knew their tactics. They knew what it would take to get squads from all four of those teams out at the exact same time, and had something strong enough and fast enough to take out and destroy armed operators in broad daylight. Their previous intel had said vampires were in the area, and the scouts had confirmed evidence of vampire attacks. Mitchell hand-picked his scouts so he knew his men were trustworthy. If the evidence was faked, then it was a damned convincing fake.

But vampires that could attack in daylight? Not unless they wore lead-lined clothes and sunscreen with an SPF of, oh, about 10,000. So, what does that leave? Zombies are slow moving and they don't leave a heat signature, and it would take a horde of literally thousands to overtake a fully armed squad. Werewolves? They're night creatures as well, and so far, no squad had reported evidence of werewolf activity in those areas. Besides, the next full moon was two weeks off.

Whatever this new attacker was, they needed to start coordinating with the other teams to ensure that this never happened again. Losing a squad member was horrible. Losing a whole squad was a fucking tragedy. But losing four squads from five different teams? In one night? That is totally unacceptable.

Elsewhere, across the world…

The heat was unbearable. The wind just made it worse, blowing sand into places that sand was never meant to be. Insects in the desert were never your friend. For them, it's eat or be eaten. Same thing goes for reptiles. If they weren't venomous, they had some form of defense or attack that made them very unpleasant and not good bedfellows. The nights are cold, the days are sweltering, and even the brushy cover that provided the shade from the unrelenting sun barely allowed movement for the two man sniper team sent to this insurgent camp buried in the shallow valley below.

The mission: assassinate one terrorist leader. Cut the head from the snake and allow the insurgents to feel the terror of knowing that they, too, can be stung in the same manner in which they sting others. In other words, a taste of their own medicine.

"I've tasted this shit before," Lamb muttered softly.

"When's that?"

"Yesterday." He spat the desert sand out of his mouth. "And the day before that. And the day before that."

"And the day before that." Jacobs added. "I think I've heard this bitch before."

"Nothing like sand to make your gum taste good."

"Yeah, nice and crunchy. That's why you don't chew it with your mouth open, moron." Jacobs grinned at him, his face crusting as he smiled, the dirt lines around his eyes making his Asian features look even more exotic.

"Hand me the water before I become jerky." Lamb sipped the lukewarm water wishing he had something cold and alcoholic. Four days in the desert takes its toll on everybody but this mission sucked worse than the others. Being a sniper team lets you travel the world, take you to ALL the fun places, meet new and exciting people…and kill them.

"I've got motion at ten o'clock," Jacobs barely spoke.

Lamb shifted the reticle of his scope towards the ten o'clock position and saw two people moving between barrels in the compound below. From their perch on a hill overlooking the compound below, they had a good view of everything in plain sight, but there was still a lot of the camp that was blocked from view. The heat of the day kept most of the camp's occupants inside, and at night, their female entertainment meant that few wandered around then either.

"Tell me again how lucky we are to get tagged for this mission," Lamb muttered to Jacobs.

"Oh, we're lucky all right. In fact, if we were any luckier, I'd buy a damned lotto ticket."

Lamb adjusted his scope to magnify higher, bringing the men's faces in clearer. "It's not him."

Jacobs sighed audibly. *Four days of sweating our balls off in this heat, under cover, eaten alive by sand fleas, eating dehydrated food, sipping piss warm water and for what? To take down ONE guy?* "Personally, I think we should just call in an air strike and napalm the place. That would guarantee his ass was fried."

"Boss man wants a positive ID on this turd. He wants to know for sure that the name on the toe tag matches the occupant. He doesn't like matching dental records," Lamb explained.

"We suffer so the forensic coroner doesn't have to earn his check? That's rich."

"Movement," Lamb whispered.

"Is it him?" Jacobs asked as he slipped closer forward, bringing his spotting scope up and scanning.

"Not sure yet, but maybe." Lamb adjusted the scope again, zooming in on the man's face. *Yes! Finally!*

"Bingo! We got him!" Lamb whispered.

"Then take him out and let's get back to some type of civility. I need a shower as bad as you do."

"I plan to but he's moving." Lamb watched the man talk with another of his cohorts, then stomp off toward a small outbuilding. "Looks like he's going to the head."

Lamb adjusted for range, windage, and elevation as Jacobs read them off to him. *Level. Steady. Breathe. Hold.* Both men studied the target, waiting for the pink mist that would have once been the man's head, but he quickly opened the door and stepped inside.

"I got a good look at the innards of the shitter. Think I can make a good estimate of where he is." Lamb grinned at Jacobs.

"Leave it to you to kill a man while he takes a dump," Jacobs muttered. "One thing's for sure. Nobody will notice the smell if he doesn't come out after a couple of days."

"The suppressor on that fifty will still be heard. Want a little diversion?" Jacobs asked.

"Go give 'em an atta-boy and fire a few out of that AK you've been dragging around."

Jacobs grabbed a small robe to toss on and pulled on his shumagh turban. With the dirt encrusted on his face and his three weeks of beard growth, he shouldn't be recognized as anything other than a random goat herder from this distance. He crawled out from their cover and made his way about eighty yards down from where Lamb was set up for the kill shot.

Approaching the edge of the sheer drop, he waved his arms and shouted in Arabic, "Good hunting, brothers! Death to the infidels! *Allahu akbar!*" and fired his AK-47 into the air. The recoil from the .50 caliber was definitely felt, but the noise was much quieter since the sound suppressor took the majority of noise out of the picture. From the shallow valley bellow, a few armed men waved back and returned Jacobs greeting.

Lamb had focused his shot on the center of the latrine door. The round splintered the wood and left a jagged hole, but it appeared that nobody noticed the shot. Lamb waited to see if the target would stagger out of the shitter wounded or pissed off that somebody had shot at him. Nothing near the latrine moved. Lamb adjusted the scope on his rifle and zeroed in at the bottom of the door. Blood was flowing out from under the door at an alarming rate.

Jacobs approached the makeshift cover and scooted in next to Lamb. "Anything?"

"Bottom of the door."

Jacobs verified dark arterial blood mixed with bits of debris. Far too much blood to have been a mere wounding. "Confirmed. We're out of here."

Both men quickly scooted back from the edge, grabbed their gear, and hauled ass away from there. Three clicks from the camp they had a small military SCOUT vehicle camouflaged and waiting to take them further from what would surely be a camp crawling with very pissed off bad guys just waiting to cut the nuts off of whoever had pissed in their Post Toasties once they found the body of their leader.

Three hours and four dozen kidney jarring bumps later the two men disembarked and trudged into their own camp. "There was a couple of bumps back there I think you missed. Wanna go back and hit 'em again?" Lamb asked, pushing Jacobs with his rucksack.

"Nah. I'll hit 'em twice next time. Wouldn't want ya to think I was going soft on ya or anything," he chuckled. "Shower or debrief first?"

Lamb raised his eyebrows and gave Jacobs a 'duh' stare. "I've been microwaving in the desert for four days and shot across sixty clicks of the driest litter box God ever created. You tell me."

"Catch you in twenty then. I'll check in with the LT first," Jacobs said, then tossed him his go-bag.

As Jacobs entered the headquarters tent, his eyes adjusted to the gloom. He pulled his sunglasses off and scanned the interior. A young Navy lieutenant raised his head and met his gaze, a smile playing across his face. Crossing the room, the man met him with a hardy arm grasp.

"Damned good to see ya again, Jake! I was starting to worry."

"Me, too, LT. I hate silent ops, but we got the bastard," Jacobs replied.

He had to admit that, although Lieutenant Andrews was fairly young, he held himself like a much older and more experienced officer. The LT, as his men called him, was an Academy Man, football player, and Navy SEAL who now commanded the elite team; but he was still one of the guys. He drank with them, played cards with them, went shooting with them, chased women with them, and treated them equally. Commission or not, he fraternized with his men as if they were brothers…because they were. He bled with his men the same as any other spec op warrior, and yet he would take all the blame if somehow an op went south. And for that, his men held even more respect for him. The big blonde man with blue eyes stood out here in the Middle East, but so did most other Americans. As the LT was fond of saying, *'We're not here to win their hearts and minds, we're here to win a war. Otherwise they'd send the friggin' Boy Scouts.'*

"Where's Lamb?" Andrews asked, glancing around.

"Showers, sir. He stunk to high heaven. I felt it was a necessary precaution prior to debriefing."

Andrews smiled. "Just tell me you got the bastard and that's all I'll need for my report."

"One shot, one kill, sir. Positive ID," Jacobs replied. "Shot him through the latrine door."

"Good enough for me, Jake. I'll write it up, shoot ya a copy in an e-mail." He clapped the man on the back. "Now go get some R&R. You and Lamb both. You got a special op coming up."

Jacobs face fell. "Sir? Already? We just got back off a four day in the melt…"

The LT didn't look happy. "I know, Jake. This one is from Pentagon Special. I don't even know what it's about, but it isn't here. You're flying out of here tomorrow at 0600 hours."

Jacobs was confused and he obviously didn't like being away from his comrades in arms. "What about the team, sir? What will they do without us as backup?"

"The detailer is sending replacements to cover for you fellas until you return," Andrews answered flatly. Jacobs could tell by his tone that he wasn't happy. Their well-oiled machine was about to have some monkey wrenches tossed into the gears.

"Sir, do we know the duration of this op?"

"May be permanent, Jake." Andrews paused. He was obviously upset but trying not to show it. "Maybe you could break the news to Lamb for me? I don't think I can do this twice." Jacobs remembered the times that the LT and Lamb had covered each other's asses in the thick, the friendship shared, the

bond formed just being team mates and he understood completely. It was like losing a brother.

"Are we being kicked out of the Teams, sir?" he
had to ask.

"What? Good God, no!" Andrews replied. "You
boys' records are exemplary! You're the best I got."
The LT shuffled, seemed a bit uncomfortable, then
he sighed, "Hell, if I didn't know any better, I'd think
somebody else was trying to recruit you boys out
from under me. Maybe CIA or some shit. But to be
completely honest, Jake, I just don't know what's going on. I've made inquiries up and down the chain of
command, but I get blocked at every level. I can't get
any answers."

"I guess we'll find out when we get there," Jacobs
said, scratching at his chin in thought.

"When you do, let me know what the hell is going on, wouldja? I hate being left in the dark when it
comes to my boys." Andrews' eyes bore into him. His
Southern drawl kept slipping out when he spoke of
his men. It was how his men knew they were close to
him. Whenever he spoke of his family in Alabama,
his accent would come slipping back, and before anyone could truly point to it, the man was speaking
'fluent redneck'.

"You got it, LT." Jacobs snapped a crisp salute.
He spun a quick about-face and marched out of the
headquarters tent and double-timed it back to the
tent he shared with Lamb.

Lamb was standing in front of his locker inspect-
ing what few clean uniforms he had left, a towel
wrapped around his waist when Jacobs came into the
tent. "I got news from the LT!"

"Yeah? Wazzat?" Lamb asked without looking up.

"I'll tell ya about after I wash the grit out of my ass."

Lamb followed Jake to the showers. "What's the news? You can't hold out on me, bro."

Jake tossed his towel over the edge of the shower door. "Another op. Wheels up at 0600 tomorrow."

"What?" Lamb was aghast. He turned on Jacobs. "What do you mean another op? We just got back off four days in the microwave!"

"Don't blow your top at me, brother. It's from DC, not the LT. And he doesn't know any more than I just told you. He tried pulling in what few favors he had to find out. We're all in the dark on this one. Hell, with our luck, we're going from this hellhole to the friggin' Antarctic!" With that he turned back and hit the shower valve letting the cool water flow over him.

"Fuck!" Lamb threw a boot across the tent and knocked over his shave kit. "Shit!"

"Throwing a hissy-fit won't do any good," Jacobs' voice called from further out.

"Fuck you and the white horse you rode in on."

"Hothead!" Jacobs retorted.

Thirty minutes later, as both men lay on their cots, they contemplated the ramifications of their new orders. Both men had exemplary careers. Lamb had come from the East Coast originally, but being an Army brat and having no real place to call home, he joined the Navy to piss off his old man. The only thing that redeemed him in his old man's eyes was when he became a Navy SEAL. The old man had been an Airborne Ranger and had spent the majority of his time barking orders both at work and at home. Lamb had been raised by his mother to be respectful not only of his father's position, but of his temperament. But teenage boys tend to rebel and rebel he did. In spades. And when that fateful day came, Lamb was on the receiving end of the beating of his life. For a brief moment he actually thought he would hold his own until it became painfully obvious that the old man was holding back, taunting the younger Lamb into fighting harder, to prove himself to be worthy of the name.

"You may be a Lamb, boy, but you'll never be a Lamb led to slaughter!" his father said as he backhanded him across the face. *"I'll make a man out of you if I have to beat you to death."* And he nearly did. Had his mother not gotten between them, he might nearly have paid for his pride with his life. The old man was many things, but smart enough to know when to quit wasn't one of them.

Thankfully, one thing Sgt. Major Lamb would never do was raise a hand to a woman. And when Mrs. Lamb stepped between father and son, the beating stopped. She helped her son to his room and nursed his broken body as best she could. The next morning, Ronald Lamb was gone. No note, no good-bye, no 'kiss my ass', not even a thank you for his mom. He just packed a change of clothes into a small duffel and left. When the bank had opened the next morning, Ronald cleaned out his accounts and left town. It was three years later when Mrs. Lamb received her first letter from her only son, telling her that he'd joined the Navy and had just graduated BUDs. Her son was a newly minted SEAL. He was requesting permission to return home for Thanksgiving. It truly was a heartfelt reunion. And the first time in three years that his father hadn't felt that his son hadn't run *away*, but *to* something. Manhood.

"You reckon we'll get stateside?" Lamb asked.

"Beats the dog shit outta me, brother. Like I said, we could end up in Antarctica. Or shoot, even Australia for all I know," Jacobs replied.

"Oh, wouldn't that be the shit? Australia! Koala bears and kangaroos and shit. And what are those sticks you throw in the air and they come back to you?" Lamb asked.

"What? You mean a boomerang?" Jacobs shot him a sideways look, wondering if he was serious.

"Yeah, that's the thing. And those funky ass tubes those little pygmies blow in to make that weird ass noise."

"Okay, moron, your brain has had too much exposure to the sun." Jacobs stood up and stretched.

"Asshole, I'm *not* Australian, and it's not like I ever played with one," Lamb shot back.

"You don't have to be an Aussie to know what a boomerang is, and they aren't *pygmies* in Australia!" Jacobs accused.

"Oh yeah?"

"Yeah!" Jacobs tried not to think of leaving the team behind. "I can't wait to get stateside and crawl inside the biggest, coldest beer I can find."

"Not me, pal. I haven't had a drink since we got here and my system is cleaned out. I'm giving it up for good. I'm sick of the hangovers and bumming money from ya."

We'll see how long this one lasts, buddy. You got more demons than Lucifer himself, pal. Jacobs lay back down on his cot. Although the shower had really helped to cool him off, the heat was still there, and he knew it was going to be rough trying to sleep tonight. Especially not knowing what tomorrow might bring.

3

Robert Mueller pulled his Jeep CJ-7 into the driveway of his ex-wife's house. *His* house before the divorce. He stared at the front yard, the porch, the mailbox, the awnings over the windows. He remembered how happy they were when they first found the house and how hard he and Barbara had worked as they practically rebuilt the cottage from the ground up. *Somebody tell me again what I did wrong? All I did was try to love you, Babs,* he told himself.

He practically had to force himself to step out of the Jeep and reach into the rear to retrieve his son's birthday present. Bobby was turning six today. Practically a carbon copy of his father, Bobby had sandy blonde hair, blue eyes and a cheesy grin that cut straight to his mom's heart. Both looked like they would be more comfortable along the beach with surfboards in hand. Her 'beach boys' was Barbara Mueller's pet name for them before the divorce. Now, she rarely said anything nice to Robert unless Bobby was present, and even then, she was barely able to keep a civil tongue in her mouth. It took Robert a long time to realize that she finally cracked under the pressure of being an Army wife. Her husband could be called out at any time, and not knowing when or *if* he would come home was just more than her fragile disposition could handle. So she did the only thing she knew to do. She turned on him. And in doing so, she all but destroyed him. She took the two things he held most dear. His wife and son.

Robert approached the front door cautiously. For one of the military's fiercest warriors, one might find it odd that he was trembling as he reached for the doorbell. Just before he could push the button, Barbara opened the door and stood staring at him accusingly with her hands on her hips. "Late again, I see." The bitterness wasn't missed in her voice.

"I wasn't sure of the time," Robert said sheepishly, handing her Bobby's gift.

Even though he knew she was acting like a territorial bitch, she still looked beautiful to him. Her slender body fit perfectly in her shorts and tank top, and her short black hair kept her shoulders bare, and oh-so-kissable.

"The party is almost over." *So you might as well leave.* Robert assumed she meant. Her demeanor was anything but inviting and she made no move to invite him in to what once was home to both of them.

"Then I guess I can just drop this off and leave. I was just hoping to see Bobby again," Robert said, his eyes gazing into hers. "It's been so long." *She isn't budging.*

Barbara didn't move. She kept herself wedged in the doorway, a veritable shield between father and son and his sixth birthday party. Robert waited for her to say something. Anything. But Barbara was stone. Just like her heart was when she met him at the door with the divorce papers. *Fine. You want to be a bitch, be one. But I WILL see my son if I have to hire a lawyer to do it.*

"Here. Just please tell him it's from me." Robert pushed the gift at her so that she had to let go of the screen door to grab it and he turned to leave. As he approached his Jeep he felt Barbara's hand grab him from behind and pull him around.

"This isn't fair to Bobby or to me for you to just show up whenever you feel like it and disrupt our lives." She was shaking with anger, and Robert could tell that she was itching to bring back all of her previous arguments to stir up one doozy of a fight. But this was his son's birthday and he simply wasn't in the mood.

"I don't have a choice when I'm going to be in, you know that. And I don't think you should be so *shocked* that I should show up for his *birthday*. Common sense would tell ya that it's a parent's right to be there to celebrate the birth of their offspring," Robert replied, trying not to lose his temper.

Barbara took a deep breath and rose to all of her five-foot, two inches and puffed up her ninety-eight pounds to point at his chest. To any passersby it might appear like a toy poodle dressing down a St. Bernard, but Barbara Mueller used to rule Robert with an iron fist, and she wasn't going to stop trying to exercise that control now. She stood up to his six-foot, six-inch, two hundred and sixty pound muscle bound self without fear. "He's your *son* not OFFSPRING!" she yelled.

Robert sighed. "I'm not going to fight with you, Babs." Robert turned and started to get in his Jeep.

Barbara all but yelled at him, "My name is Barbara. You will address me as Barbara from now on!"

Robert turned on her very slowly. For just a fleeting moment, Barbara felt a moment of panic thinking that she had actually pushed him too far and that he was going to hurt her. And she also felt, for that same fleeting moment, that she actually *deserved* it for the way she had been treating him and for the way she had been using Bobby as a tool to hurt Robert. But when Robert turned and she saw his face, she saw the twinkle in his eye and the cheesy grin on his face. He slowly closed the gap until there was barely a breath between them.

He looked down on her and said softly, "You will always be *MY* Babs."

She barely had time to see his hands move as they wrapped around her waist and he picked her up to meet him eye-to-eye. He pulled her close, and before she knew what he was doing, he kissed her. Hard at first, then softening into the tender deliciousness she had almost forgotten. In shock, she wasn't sure what to do. She had divorced him! He wasn't supposed to do this! She began to hit at him, but it was like striking a stone wall. All she was accomplishing was hurting her fists. When he softened his kiss, she remembered why she married him in the first place. His grip lightened and he slid her slowly to the ground, her fists went from beating his chest to wrapping around his neck and how she ended up kissing him back, she doesn't remember. How long they stood in the driveway kissing, she doesn't know, but she knew that this was where she wanted to be. She felt safe again. He made her feel that way. Her mountain of a man holding her gently, kissing her, making her feel like she is the only woman in the world…this is what she truly wanted. The fight in her drained away as she let down her guard and opened her heart to him once again.

Robert's pager went off and she cursed softly beneath his mouth. *No! This can't be happening again. This is why I had to divorce you the first time. You can't do this. You can't. Don't look at it. If you choose that damned pager...*

Robert pulled away from her to look at the pager. He cursed again and hung his head low. "I'm sorry, baby. I have to."

Barbara didn't even know she was crying, but Robert reached up to wipe the tears from her eyes. The sadness in his eyes bore through to her very soul. *If I could make it all better, I would.* He cupped her face and reached in for another kiss. She kissed him again, this time more desperately, her arms wrapping around his neck again holding on and squeezing herself against him.

The pager buzzed again, and this time Barbara practically choked out a sob. "I love you so much, Babs. Tell Bobby I love him, too." He kissed her once more on the tip of her nose.

He mounted his Jeep and started it up. He looked out at her standing in the driveway and she stood staring at him, tears streaming down her face. "You bring your ass home safe, Robert. Or I swear to God, I'll dig up your corpse so I can kill you myself," she whispered as his Jeep pulled from the curb.

Jimmy 'Tango Down' Wallace didn't appear to be much of a threat to the bikers in the bar, but there was still something about the little man that made them uneasy. TD, as he was known to his friends, was just trying to enjoy a cold beer and maybe shoot some pool, but the majority of the patrons in this shit-hole dive were already so inebriated and rowdy that he knew there would be trouble.

At 5'8", TD wasn't large in stature, but he carried himself with a surety that was unmistakable. He was a no-nonsense kind of fellow made of tougher things than most could endure. He just *looked* like he was tougher than shoe leather, and the jagged scar running from his right brow and down his cheek added to the intensity the man carried. An Air Force Combat Controller for the last eight years, TD had spent as much time in the muck as any other spec ops warrior. He had fought evil all over the globe – from the Columbian drug lords to terrorist cells in Iraq, TD had seen or done most everything there was to do and still be able to walk away from it. He still recalled when the flight surgeon promised they could make him pretty again, he said, 'Fuck it. Pain don't last forever, and chicks dig scars.' It may have been an old expression, but it definitely held true. TD was never much on looks prior to the incident that left him scarred, but afterward, the chicks certainly seemed more interested.

Draining his beer, he took one last look around the bar to see if any patrons were sober enough to offer a game at the pool table. Satisfied that there were none, he slid off his barstool to leave. Counting out his bar tab and allowing for a tip, he dropped a small wad of bills on the bar and was turning to leave when his pager went off. Glancing at the number, he knew he had to return to base as soon as possible.

The drive to the base was shorter than he expected, and he arrived at the station chief's watch post. TD checked in, signed the log and was headed to the locker room when he was intercepted by his commanding officer. "Tango, I got orders for you. My office, five minutes."

"Yes, sir," TD responded. He loaded his bug-out bag and was checking his gear when Dave Marshal came sliding through the door. TD and Dave had pretty much spent all of their time together. Having enlisted at the same time, gone through boot camp together, Security Forces school and Combat Controller training together.

"You get paged, too?" Dave asked.

"Yup. I figured it was a full deployment and that we'd all be paged, no?" TD answered, glancing around the locker room and noticing that nobody else was coming or going.

"Nope. I called Marley and Pride to see if they might need a ride in and they said they weren't paged." Marshal had that look on his face that always made TD's guts spin. Something wasn't right.

"Cap wants us in his office. Maybe we'll get the low-down on what's going on."

Marshal poured a cup of coffee from the mixer stand. "All I know is, if we're bugging out tonight, I'm gonna need some go-juice to keep my butt from dragging. We were supposed to have a three day R&R and I haven't slept since Cap cut us loose."

TD stood and headed towards the CO's door. Marshal held his 'cup-o-mud' but followed. After knocking and Cap clearing them for entry, both men entered and waited for acknowledgement. Their CO was going through papers and told them without looking up, "Take a seat, boys. I've got new orders for you."

Both men sat simultaneously and waited for Cap to tell them what the hell was going on. Cap finally looked up at both of them and sighed. "Orders just came in. You're both taking off first thing in the morning."

TD had to ask, "But, Cap, we just got here a couple of weeks ago. We were supposed to start training nubs in less than two weeks. Surely they can't send us back to the sandbox already?"

Cap cleared his throat and hiked his eyebrows at them. "Boys, I don't have a friggin' clue *where* you're headed. All I got was this set of orders sent out from the Pentagon telling me to release the two of you for follow-up commands. It doesn't say where you're going, what you'll be doing, or who you'll be doing it with. It just says to have your butts on the tarmac at 0600 for sendoff."

Marshal looked up from his coffee. "The Pentagon, sir?"

Cap gave him an exasperated look. "Yes, Dave. The friggin' Pentagon. You know what that is? The big five-sided building in DC where all the higher ups sit around with their thumbs up their petunias and try to second guess the men in the field! *That* Pentagon!" Cap cleared his throat and sat back in his chair, studying the two men. "Either one of you put in a request for a change of scenery lately?"

TD and Marshal exchanged glances, shaking their heads. "No, sir," TD replied. "I've been looking forward to instructor duty for some time now. Actually thought of it as a bit of a break, to be honest."

Cap nodded his head. "You both have earned a little down time, that's for sure. But orders is orders and mine are telling me to cargo you boys outta here. I don't like it. I don't like it one bit." Cap reached into his bottom drawer and pulled out his 'hidden' bottle of cheap rotgut and three shot glasses. "But I figure if you boys are leaving, then we might as well have at least one drink together so I can wish you boys all the luck in the world...for whatever the hell it is they're going to do with you.

Cap poured the three shots and handed the men theirs. "*Salud,*" he offered.

"*Salud,*" they responded and tossed back the hooch.

Cap grimaced slightly. "Whew. That will put some starch in your shorts, I tell ya."

Marshal, gasping for air, stuttered out, "Real smooth, sir."

"Bullshit. I can't afford the 'smooth' stuff. This is rotgut in a fancy whiskey bottle." Cap sighed heavily.

"I hate to get in new instructors and then have them pulled out from under me like this."

"So this has happened before, sir?" TD asked.

"Nope. First time. Usually once the detailers send you boys to me, I have you for two years." Setting the bottle back in the bottom of his drawer, Cap said, "This is honestly the first time I've had guys pulled out from under me after just six weeks."

Cap handed the men their orders and wished them well. Both men walked out of their CO's office confused. Their orders had no destination on them. Just the flight and tail number of the plane they were supposed to board the next morning.

"Something isn't right here, Dave. I got this eerie feeling," TD said as they headed to pack their gear.

"Well, the Air Force hasn't screwed us yet, have they, pal?" Marshal always had a way of at least trying to find a silver lining. "Whatever they have in store for us, I guess we'll find out tomorrow."

Gus Tracy took one look at the orders he had been handed and stated simply, "You're shitting me, right?"

"Sorry, Tracy. These came in for you just an hour ago. Hot off the printer," the young specialist said. "No idea what your final destination might be, but these are the weirdest orders I've ever seen issued."

Gus looked it over again. Surely there was a typo somewhere. In his ten years in the Army, he'd never received transfer orders that didn't have a destination, a command name and at least an *offer* for using some annual leave in getting there. "Where's Colonel Baird?" Gus asked.

"He's in the procurement office. He should be back shortly, though."

Gus looked at the departure time again. He had less than twelve hours to pack everything he could and be ready to leave. Sighing to himself, he turned to the specialist assigned to the Colonel's office. "Is he aware of this?"

"To my knowledge, yes. He was confused as hell when he left here. Told me to contact you and make you aware of it as soon as possible." The specialist turned and retrieved Gus' service record. "I went ahead and brought everything up to date for you. Your medical and dental records are on their way over here now. Should be here within the hour."

Gus took his service jacket and tucked it under his arm. "This sucks balls, ya know."

"I know, Tracy. I'm really sorry. I wish I had answers for you."

"Jeez. Less than twelve hours to pack up everything and make ready. That's bullshit. It took me two months to *un*pack all my crap." Gus looked at the orders one more time. Nothing had changed, but he hoped there was some small piece of information he had missed. "Fine. Tell the old man I'm getting my shit together. If he needs me, I'll be in my barracks."

Gus Tracy, Army Airborne, Green Beret and all around nice guy, once the terror of Baghdad, now being treated like a mushroom; kept in the dark and fed bullshit when all he really wanted was a few simple answers.

Gus took no care while shoving things in his duffel bag. He paused only briefly to admire the SFG pin on his uniform. "Say goodbye to the Fifth, Gus. I guess they don't need you anymore." He muttered to himself. The Fifth being the Fifth Special Forces Group, the only real home Gus had known in his twelve year stint in the Army. A career military man, Gus Tracy had been under a lot of commands, been to many foreign places, met strange and exciting new people... and killed them. Yet he never questioned the Army. He never questioned those in authority over him. To him, these men were like gods. They had gone through the ranks, earned the same rights and respect that he had, yet they had the ability to not only serve, but to lead as well. The Army had always taken care of Sergeant First Class Tracy and he wasn't about to question them now.

Although Tracy's mind was turning about on where he might be headed, he diligently packed up all of his belongings. Much to his surprise, nearly all of it fit in the single duffel. What little that didn't, he soon realized he could easily toss out and replace when he got to his new command. Coming from nothing, Gus never was one for acquiring personal things that didn't pertain directly to his job. The closest thing to a personal belonging that he owned was his father's straight razor. Gus never tried to actually shave with it, but the shiny metal folding blade

42

brought him a small bit of comfort. He may be alone in the world, but at one time he had family who loved him.

But that was a long, long time ago…during another life that he could never return to.

Gus quietly shifted the duffel over his shoulder, scanned the area one last time to make sure he hadn't forgotten anything then wordlessly left the building. He would just as soon wait at the airport than to sit here and argue over something he had no control over. Besides, most airports had bars in them and Gus really felt the need for a drink.

Maria Consuela Rosalea Sanchez had just come on duty at LAPD. As she finished changing in the locker room and headed to the shift office to log in, her lieutenant approached her. "Sanchez. Captain Rodgers needs to see you ASAP."

Sanchez paused a moment. *Who is Rodgers?* "LT?" she asked. "Who is Rodgers again?"

"Admin. She works in personnel."

Sanchez took the stairs instead of the elevators to help keep in shape. She was one of the first females to make it onto LAPD's illustrious SWAT teams, and she prided herself on her fitness and shooting skills. Anything and everything she could do to help keep herself in shape, she would do, including taking the stairs to the top floors to the administration levels.

Once reaching the upper levels, she scanned the names on the closed office doors. When she found Captain Rodgers office, she knocked and stepped into the office. "You wanted to see me, captain?"

"Sgt. Sanchez, please have a seat." Captain Rodgers was shuffling through a pile of records and pulled a thick one out as she sat down behind her desk. She slipped on a pair of reading glasses and began going through the record, nodding and smiling. When she was done, she closed the file and took off her glasses. She looked directly into Sanchez's curious eyes.

"Have I done something wrong, ma'am?"

"What? No. Not at all, Sanchez," Rodgers replied. She turned her chair to cross her legs. "But tell me, have you ever served in the military?"

"No, ma'am."

"I didn't think so. Your record states that, after high school, you attended UCLA where you obtained a degree in criminal justice, applied to LAPD, went through the academy where you scored in the upper ninety percent of your class."

"Upper ninety-five percent of my class, ma'am," Sanchez corrected.

Rodgers turned to her again and smiled. "Of course. Upper ninety-five percent of your class." She opened the file again and using her finger as a marker, "You've always scored in the upper percentile on the range. You applied for SWAT...how many times, before being given a chance to try?"

"Eleven, ma'am," Sanchez stated.

Rodgers stared at her. Her face was unreadable. "That is either stone-cold perseverance or stupidity, I'm not sure which," she said.

"I'm one of the first female SWAT members in the nation, ma'am."

"Yes, you are," Rodgers stated. "Is this something you're proud of?"

"Very." Sanchez replied. "Is this going somewhere, ma'am?"

Rodgers inhaled deeply and closed the file again. "No. But you are. You are being transferred."

Sanchez was floored. She couldn't possibly imagine what she could have done to deserve being transferred. Her record was perfect. "Ma'am?" she asked, "Is this a mistake?"

"I'm afraid not, Sgt. Sanchez. Despite your exemplary record with our department, your presence is *strongly* requested elsewhere. And it's signed by the governor on behalf of our military."

Sanchez was shaking her head, clearly not understanding what was going on. "Ma'am, I have no idea what you're talking about."

"Sergeant, somebody, somewhere at some time has taken notice of you and now, for whatever reason, they want you to come and work for them. I tried to make a few calls to see what this is about, but I've been stonewalled. All I can tell you is that we have been strongly urged by the office of the governor to see to it that you accept this offer." Rodgers was not smiling.

"Wait a moment." Sanchez was still trying to piece this together in her mind, "*Someone*, but we don't know who, wants me, but we don't know why, to come work for them, but we don't know what it is."

"Correct."

"Well, doesn't that make a whole hell of a lot of sense?" Sanchez exclaimed.

"I couldn't agree more," Rodgers stated. "However, let me say this...although you don't *have* to accept this offer, when the governor's office strongly suggests you take something..." Rodgers let that hang for a moment. Sanchez digested the ramifications of going against the governor's office. "And who knows? Girl, this could be the job of a lifetime!" Rodgers said with a smile.

"I suppose it could be," Sanchez said, thinking to herself.

Rodgers leaned forward on her desk, "You know, this all seems rather 'cloak & dagger' to me." Sanchez raised her eyebrows on that one. "Either way, you are expected to catch this military flight tomorrow morning at LAX at 6AM." Rodgers handed a sticky note to her with a flight number and gate on it.

"Well," Sanchez replied, "I guess I have some packing to do."

4

Jack Thompson opened his eyes and looked around the darkened room. His wounds had been bandaged and he was covered in an ornate, silken throw. As his eyes slowly came into focus and adjusted to the low light, he began to notice very old looking tapestries on the walls, plush pillows and throws scattered across a divan and European style antique furniture. He felt like he had been transported back in time to 17th Century France or England.

Jack tried to sit up, and pain shot through his lower back. He hadn't realized he moaned until he heard it with his own ears. The sound had shattered the deafening quiet of the room. He lay there in the overstuffed bed almost panting from the pain, listening to his own heartbeat reverberate through his head. Opening his eyes again, he took stock of the room. One small candle flickering in the corner, a bedside table with a bowl of clear broth and a spoon, a side table covered in a lacey material. An upright chair sat at the far end of the room. He couldn't find anything other than maybe the spoon to form into a makeshift weapon. Perhaps he could break a leg off the side table.

The four-post bed had a heavy canopy over it made of dark red material. Perhaps velvet?

Jack's mind spun as pain shot through his body. He tried again to pull himself to a sitting position, but this time, he moved more slowly and deliberately. He felt the sweat pop out on his forehead from trying to overcome the pain and a sitting position in this over-stuffed bed was more than uncomfortable. Taking a mental assessment of his injuries, Thompson figured his ribs were broken on both sides because each breath felt as if a crushing weight was sitting on his chest. His forearm may have been broken, but was now set with splints and wrapped in thick gauze. His legs felt heavy, and when he lifted the silken throw, he saw that they, too, were splinted.

Damn. I'm messed up, he thought. *No quick escape anytime soon.*

Jack heard footsteps approaching the door. Light in weight and echoing on a hard floor. They stopped outside his door, and he could hear the tinkling of flatware or glass as if a tray was set aside. The sound of a solid bolt being released and the heavy oak door opened slightly. More tinkling as the tray was picked up again and the door opened.

In the murk of the room, he couldn't see who was approaching his bed, but he could tell the form was small and fragile in appearance. A woman, most likely. As the visitor approached the bed, the small candle brightened her features and Jack could just make out her face. Most striking, indeed. Large almond-shaped eyes wrapped around the deepest blue he had ever seen. Her pale features and blonde hair made him think of photos he had seen of Nordic women. Small in stature, with long, flowing blonde hair, she approached the bed and sat the tray on the side table near the bowl of broth.

The visitor turned and gave him a quick assessment. "You look a lot better than when you were first brought in," she stated as she turned and poured water into a large wash basin. She soaked a thick cotton towel and wrung out the water. Jack stiffened somewhat as she approached him and began wiping the sweat from his forehead. "You're in pain, yes?" she asked. Her accent lilting slightly. He couldn't quite make out her origins from her voice.

"I'm a bit uncomfortable, yeah," Jack replied, his breath coming in short pants.

"Perhaps you should lie back down. It will help to relieve the pressure on your chest." She reached to help him slide down the pillows, but Jack held her hands.

"No thank you. I'd like to sit up for a while." He couldn't help but notice the depth of her eyes as he spoke to her. "Something tells me that I've been laying on my back for a bit too long."

His visitor simply nodded with a slight smile. "I brought you some sweet milk and toasted bread," she stated simply, motioning towards the tray. "I was hoping you'd be awake enough to transition to solid foods." She reached under the bed and brought up a tray table and positioned it across his lap. Setting the tray on the table, she then picked up the bowl of broth and turned to leave. "If you need anything else, simply call for me. I will do all that I can to aid in your recovery and to make you comfortable during your stay with us."

49

She turned to leave when Jack seemed to snap out of his haze and back to attention. "What do I call you?" He asked.

His visitor stopped and turned, dazzling him with the brilliance of her smile. "Nadia. My name is Nadia." Then she turned and was gone.

Jack thought for a moment. Her accent was strange. Almost Russian, but not quite. Perhaps a satellite country of the former Soviet Union. He let out the breath that he hadn't realized he had been holding and almost panted as his body ached, the pain ebbing through him.

He pulled the tray table closer and ate what he could. He didn't realize how tired he was or how much energy it took just to ingest food. The bread was toasted sourdough and appeared to be hand cut from a large loaf like French bread. The milk was sweet, but with a slightly gamey taste to it. Unlike any he had drank before, he thought maybe it was goat milk. It was very rich and he could see little globs of cream beginning to rise. Farm milk, just like he grew up on. Except theirs was from cows and wasn't nearly as flavorful.

Jack ate what he could then pushed the tray table back. Carefully, he pushed himself back down and lay quietly in the room, his mind racing. Why hadn't he thought to interrogate her as to the nature of his surroundings? *Where am I exactly? How long have I been here? Do my people know I'm here? Am I a prisoner? Who are YOU?* Questions ran through his head until his mind began to fog. His body needed sleep to heal. And sleep was slipping up on him. With the warm, sweet milk and the bread in his stomach, he could feel himself slipping, the darkness coming on him.

And when it did, his dreams were vivid and frightening.

Robert Mueller followed a small woman in black BDUs to a room and she opened the door for him. "Have a seat, fill out the forms in front of you, and we'll get you settled in shortly." She motioned through the door and Robert stepped in. His eyes instantly scanned the room, taking note of everything. Most surprising to him was that the room already had five men and one woman in there, sitting in small groups or by themselves, filling out paperwork. Eyes raised to assess him when he first entered, then dropped back to their task.

Robert entered and took a seat near the rear. He noticed insignia from Navy, Air Force, Army, and was somewhat surprised there weren't any Marines in there to round out the group. Hell, even the Latino chick was dressed in dark blue cop overalls with SWAT patches. Taking his seat, he opened the folder on the desk and began filling out personal information. It only took a few minutes and he found himself sitting alone, observing the other men in the room. The SEALs had sat at the front of the room and were whispering to each other. A couple of Air Force guys were passing thoughts back and forth on a piece of notebook paper and chuckling. The woman seemed bored. In the far corner of the room sat a very large Army Green Beret and Robert felt a bit better knowing a brother in arms was there with him. The large man sat quietly with eyes forward, sitting almost at attention.

He heard the SEALs chortle and snort and glance over their shoulders at the other men in the room. Then they burst out laughing. One of the Air Force soldiers finally took notice. "What's the problem, squid?"

The dark haired Asian SEAL turned around in his chair with a shit-eating-grin and asked, "Do you Air Force ladies really wear lace bras under those cammies?" he asked, and the sandy haired one burst out laughing again.

The Air Force men weren't going to take the bait. The smaller one simply said, "Naw, we wear Navy-issue thongs. You know the kind…like they give those SEAL pussies when they graduate from SEAL school."

"Ooh, deep cut there, Airedale." The SEAL laughed. "Too bad the Air Force doesn't have any real spec ops like the other branches. Jealous much?"

Before things could escalate, the large man in the corner said simply, "Can it, boys." His voice was deep and loud and everyone could tell he wasn't trying to project his voice. It simply was the way the man spoke…with authority.

Before anybody could offer a smart assed retort, the door opened and a full-bird colonel entered. The SEALS jumped to attention and shouted, "Attention on deck!"

All of the men were on their feet at attention when the colonel stated simply, "At ease, gentlemen. And, umm, ma'am."

The man strode across the room and pulled a podium towards the center. He pulled some papers from his folder and spread them over the surface of the podium. The colonel glanced through the papers and then raised his eyes to settle on the group of men seated in the room. He seemed to grade each of them as his eyes took them in. Almost as if studying them, assessing their strengths and weaknesses.

"Folks, my name is Colonel Matt Mitchell. I will be your commanding officer while you are assigned here. Shortly you will be meeting Laura Youngblood, your new Executive Officer." The colonel seemed to pause as if trying to decide exactly how to proceed. "You've all been hand-selected to take part in this venture because you are, quite simply, the absolute best that this nation has to offer."

All of them listened carefully, waiting for the colonel to explain to them exactly what each of them were doing here. Each man was career military and understood that everything comes in its own time, but the enigmatic way they were brought here had them all a bit anxious. Sanchez, on the other hand, wasn't used to beating around the bush.

"I'll be honest with you. This is the first time we've had Air Force Combat Controllers in this program, but from what my XO has told me, you men will become an integral part of our new squad." The two Combat Controllers simply nodded at the colonel. "This is also the first time we'll be incorporating a female into one of our squads. Other teams have used them and they work quite well. I've gone over your record, Sanchez, and it is quite remarkable. I think my XO did a fine job in recruiting you." Sgt. Sanchez gave a slight nod, still unsure why she was here.

"Historically, this program has run very smooth using Army and Navy spec op warriors because, quite frankly, they are used to being parts of a team. And that is exactly what we are here. One team." The colonel paused to let his statements soak in. "One team with one goal. One mission. To defend the people of this country from the nastiest monsters you can possibly imagine."

Matt shuffled his papers and pulled up a roster. One by one he called each person's name and each responded with either a 'here' or by raising their hand. Mitchell stepped out from behind the podium and picked up a remote from the far table. When he clicked it the lights lowered and an overhead projector came on. A sword and shield logo with 'MS4' came up on the screen. Clicking again, the image changed to a global map with different areas shaded different colors. Each sector had a different 'MS' number and all of America, Canada and northern Mexico were under a blue shading with 'MS4' written across the area.

"This is our coverage zone. As you can see, we cover the continental U.S., Canada, northern Mexico and usually cover Alaska as well. And before you ask, we are *exempt* from the *Posse Comitatus* Act. We are mandated to act within the borders of the United States and these other zones with the permission of their respective governments," Mitchell stated.

He then went through each slide, covering the history of each squad, the area they cover, their duties and responsibilities and the size of each unit. Mitchell went over their black budget, the gear that they would be required to learn, support equipment and personnel. He soon reached the 'augmentation' slide and paused. When he spoke again, he observed each one to judge their reactions to what he was saying.

"You will each be going through a process of augmentation. You will receive a series of inoculations, injections and other oral supplements that will increase your strength, your speed, and your ability to heal." Mitchell was somewhat surprised that the biggest reaction was simply a raised eyebrow from one of the SEALs. "This is not only to protect you from the various diseases you may encounter in the field, but also make you impervious to the virus that causes transition in most every human on earth."

It was at this point that one of the men raised a hand to interrupt Mitchell. "Yes, petty officer?" Mitchell asked Lamb.

Lamb's face held a confused look when he asked for clarification. "Sir, what sort of virus are we talking about here? Bio-warfare?"

Mitchell's face stayed stoic when he answered, "Vampirism, petty officer. Vampirism."

None of them said anything, but one could tell that the mix of emotions went from disbelief to being unsure they heard what Mitchell had said. "You all need to understand a basic fact before I go any further. When I say 'Monster Squad' I mean real-life monsters. Honest-to-God boogers that go bump in the night." He let his statement soak in a moment before continuing. "We fight monsters. We hunt them down, destroy them and then clean up any evidence that they were ever here."

One of the Combat Controllers snickered. "Yes, sir. Understood, sir." A lopsided grin spread across his face.

Mitchell's features hardened. "I don't think you read me, soldier."

Some of the men straightened and thought that perhaps Mitchell was serious. Matt clicked the next slide and began to run through a series of photos of examples of exactly what the men were expected to battle. As each slide came up, the men began to sober more and realize that he wasn't joking. Pictures of 'people' with fangs, elongated, reinforced nails, and pasty skin ran across the screen. Mitchell gave a brief narrative of where each was killed and the risks involved. "The virus is spread through scratches, spittle, other bodily fluids and of course, bites. The augmentation is designed to give you a resistance to the virus and prevent 'turning' if you come in contact with the pathogen."

When he reached the last slide, Mitchell set the remote down. "There are a lot of other types of monsters out there that we deal with, but the most common and by far, the most virulent, are vampires." He gave each person a good long stare square in the eyes. "Historically we have faced down and destroyed everything from zombies to griffins. We have dealt with gargoyles, with trolls, with ghouls, goblins…hell we even had a team in Europe that had to take down a dragon." The colonel stood straighter and announced, "In fact, they even had to deal with one of 'the wee people' in Ireland, and I don't mean a damned midget either." The men sort of looked at him suspiciously. When Matt realized nobody understood what he was talking about, he clued them in. "A leprechaun."

This was followed with 'ohs' and nods of understanding.

"If you gentlemen will follow me, I'll let you see an undead example of what we're talking about. I would say a living, breathing example, but just like the lore and legend, these things are NOT alive. They are animated, but they are not alive in the sense that medical science considers biological creatures to 'live'."

They all rose from their seats and followed Mitchell down a series of hallways to a reinforced cell with a pitiful looking man huddled in the corner. When the soldiers came closer to the cell, the creature sprung forward and tried to attack. When it struck the bars of its cell, its flesh began to smoke and char and the creature shrieked in pain, then pulled back to its corner. They all stood their ground, but were amazed at the feral nature of the creature huddled in the shadows.

"The bars are coated in silver. Apparently that part of the legends are true. These things have a very serious anaphylactic reaction to silver. If the silver gets under the skin or into the bloodstream, death is almost instantaneous." Gesturing toward the creature, Matt continued, "We captured this one in New Mexico about seven years ago. Originally we intended to study it and see if we could come up with a cure to the disease. Perhaps an antibody that we could then inject from a distance so that our men wouldn't have to come into contact with it. Obviously, those efforts failed."

"Are they all this crazed, sir?" Jacobs inquired.

"Negative. When our efforts failed to find a cure, we decided to take a different route." Mitchell sighed. "It was decided by those much higher than me that our new goal was to see how long it took for these things to starve to death when their food source is removed."

This time Mueller felt the need for clarification. "How long has this guy been without food, sir?"

Mitchell seemed to be lost in the creature's eyes. Robert thought that perhaps he didn't hear the question, but Mitchell finally inhaled deeply and said softly, "Nearly three years." The creature sat in its corner snarling and gnashing its teeth at the intruders, primal hunger forcing it closer than the burns on its shoulders reminding it that the food couldn't be had. "He didn't used to be like this." Matt sounded almost sad.

"Sir?" Lamb asked.

"When he was first captured and we informed him that we were researching a cure, he was actually very forthcoming and agreeable to the efforts. He was a biologist in his former life and had a photographic memory. He actually assisted in a lot of the weapons' research. When efforts failed and the decision was made to starve him to death, he was slowly overcome by 'the thirst'. Now he's just a shell of what he once was."

"Did you know him, colonel? Before, I mean," Jacobs asked.

Shaking his head, Matt responded, "No. But he was quite civilized when we were feeding him, and he was quite the gentleman." Mitchell sighed and continued, "I've hated monsters my entire life, but this man...excuse me, this *creature*, taught me that not all monsters embrace what they are. Not all of them want to be infected." Mitchell turned to address the group as a whole. "And that is exactly what this is. An infection. It affects the mind, the body...and yes, the very soul. It is my firm belief that the body is truly dead and, therefore, the soul has left. But if a man is decent prior to infection, then there is a chance he will still be a decent 'being' afterwards. If they have a dark spot in their soul, the infection amplifies it. They revert to the most basic of instincts: food, sex, and destruction."

Mitchell turned and walked out, leaving the creature to its solitude. The soldiers all turned and followed. When Mitchell re-entered the briefing room, the men followed and took their seats again. "From this point on, you will all be receiving a promotion, combat pay, hazardous duty pay, and we will do everything in our power to prepare you for doing battle with these...*things*. However, you will all be stripped of rank," Mitchell stated.

The men exchanged looks of confusion. Mitchell continued, "We are mixing different branches of our nation's military, and now, one of our finest police forces into one unit, and maintaining rank and title can become confusing, especially when we are in combat. Therefore, you will be issued new uniforms, new insignia and after you've each finished your training, we will be assigning combat enumerations. These will in no way have anything to do with ability, rank or privilege. Each of you will be tested on your actual strengths, weaknesses, and ability. Your strengths will be amplified via the augmentation program, your weaknesses will be assessed and turned into a strength either by unit billet or by training, and your abilities will improve vastly by program's end."

Gus Tracy raised his hand to interrupt. "Sir? What can we, as operators, expect to see during this augmentation? I mean, what sort of improvements?"

"Good question," Mitchell responded. He pulled out a graph from his folder and used it as a guide. "These numbers are not set in stone, but they are a rule of thumb from previous subjects who underwent and successfully completed the regimen."

Matt cleared his throat and stated, "Strength increases, on average, to nearly four times that of when the subject began the program. Speed increased to nearly two and half times. Visual acuity increased nearly threefold, not to mention a remarkable increase in depth perception, night vision and speed of acclimation to light changes. Hearing increased nearly threefold. Subjects were able to hear sounds that only canines could detect. So as far as you are concerned, it will be like steroids, *on steroids*. You will feel like Superman." Matt smiled at the group. "Only without the flying."

Putting up his papers, he asked the group, "Any questions?"

"Yes, sir," Lamb responded with a cheesy grin. "How fast can we get started?"

5

Senator Leslie Franklin sat behind his desk when the call came in from his aide. The call that nobody would have wanted to make, but being the senator's aide, it had to be done. The Monster Squad not only was *not* being disbanded, they were to receive an increase in funding and had already gotten new recruits to replace the lost men. Senator Franklin was beyond mad, he was livid. His secretary took it upon herself to cancel the rest of his appointments when she heard the man using words that she hadn't heard since high school and heard the crystal decanter that the senator used to store his favorite cognac shatter against his office door.

"What do you mean they already have replacements on the ground? That simply can't be. It's only been thirty-six hours since half of them were killed!" he screamed into the telephone.

"Yes, sir, I realize that. B-but Ms. Youngblood already had a list prepared. It was pushed through the Pentagon and the men re-allocated within hours. They've already began training, sir," The aide responded.

Franklin wanted to slam the phone down, but somehow, his energy was simply drained. He laid it carefully back into its cradle and sat back in his plush leather chair. He propped his head in his hands and wanted so desperately to weep, yet he held himself in check. He couldn't allow this to happen. There had to be a way. He just needed to think of it. There *had* to be a way to stop the Monster Squad for good.

Jack Thompson woke feeling slightly better, but his body still ached. There was a new candle burning by his bedside and fresh linens stacked near the bed. He noticed two more wet washrags near the wash basin and realized that Nadia must have come to him during his sleep and tended to him once again.

He tried to rise from the bed, but his ribs and back protested in pain. His legs throbbed and he knew that he was damaged far worse than he originally thought. Flashes of the battle came to him and he remembered seeing his men being torn limb from limb. He pressed his eyes closed tightly, trying to rid his mind of the memories, but they wouldn't leave. He knew he was lucky to have survived, but he wished now that he hadn't. For a fleeting moment he questioned himself, 'Is this survivor's guilt'?

He slowly rolled to his side, and a small cry escaped his lips. Then he heard movement from the darkened corner of his room. "You're awake. Excellent."

It wasn't Nadia's voice. Definitely male, but not very masculine. At least, not very macho sounding like most of the soldiers he was used to dealing with. Again, a slight accent, but he couldn't quite place it. "Forgive me if I startled you. Nadia and I were taking turns looking after you while you slept." With that, the figure stood and stepped out of the shadows and closer to the bedside, bringing an antique French-styled chair with him. Setting it near the bed, the man took his seat again and sat facing Jack.

"There now. That's better." He reached out and fluffed a pillow and placed it under Jack's head in an attempt to make him more comfortable. "And how are you feeling today?"

Jack could tell at first glance, this 'man' wasn't human. *Vampire*, was his first thought, but something just isn't quite right. He couldn't quite place his finger on it, but somehow he knew. And if he wasn't a vampire, he was something *very* close to it.

"Who are you?" Jack asked, clearly defensive.

"Forgive my rudeness," the man replied, standing slightly and bowing. "I am Rufus Thorn. Owner of this castle and, at the moment, your host." With that, he took his seat again. "And, how are you feeling today? Better, I hope."

Jack pulled back slightly to get a clearer look at this Mr. Thorn. "You're not human," he stated bluntly.

"No, I am not," Rufus replied with a slight smile. "Quite perceptive of you." Rufus sat back in the high-backed chair and gave Jack a studying look. "Of course, I suppose I should expect as much as someone who spends as much time of their life as you do hunting down my kind and exterminating them. But you are correct in your assessment. I am most definitely *not* human. And I haven't been for centuries." Rufus cleared his throat and gave Jack a rather pleasant smile.

"Is this where you kill me? Or are you going to heal me up so you can torture me? Or…"

Rufus appeared genuinely shocked. "My God, boy, I should say not! We are…how do the dime store novels say? Vampire vegetarians. And I must say, for those who risked their very lives to save yours, you have a rather odd way of giving thanks."

Now it was Jack's turn to appear shocked. "Vege-what? You're a vampire. How can you be a vegetarian?" With his outburst, Jack began coughing and could not quite get it under control. Rufus stood and poured some water from the pitcher into a crystal glass and offered it to him to drink. After Jack got his coughing under control, Rufus retook his seat.

"It seems to me that you and I have much to talk about. It would appear that you really do not know all that much about who…or what…you are hunting when you go tromping through the night and shoot at anybody with fangs. Do you, old boy?"

Although Jack was more than just a bit skeptical, he had to admit to himself that he was more than just a bit intrigued. Why would a vampire bother to save a human for anything other than a snack? Especially one that had been given an anti-vampirism cocktail? Or maybe the bloodsucker didn't know that? Wouldn't he be in for a surprise when he tried to get a little SOCCOM snack in the middle of the night! Still, if that were the case, wouldn't they both be dead right now?

64

"Let me tell you a little story about vampires. And not the story that mummies and daddies tell their kiddies to keep them from going outside at night either…"

"Squad One is in the briefing room. They're up to date, and as expected, it hit them hard," Matt said as he slumped into his chair.

"I can only imagine what it must be like for them," Laura said, reliving the deaths of the other squad again in her mind. "Have you figured out yet whether to incorporate the newbies into the existing squad or keep them together?"

"I haven't decided yet," Matt replied. He poured a cup of coffee and turned back to his desk. "Part of me thinks that breaking up the existing squad would be harder on their morale, but another part of me thinks that the best way to train the new members and keep everybody alive longer will be putting old with new."

"Well, the training reports are looking really good, sir," Laura said as she dropped a stack of papers on Matt's desk.

"How are they coming along?" he asked, looking up from his daily scheduling.

"Actually? Better than previous efforts. The Air Force guys were a better fit than I thought they'd be," she replied, taking a seat. "Like always, once the

Army and Navy guys got through trying to see who's dick was bigger, they fit like cogs on a gear. I was a bit leery of mixing in the Combat Controllers, but with all of the air support we've been using lately, I really felt they'd be necessary. And Sanchez is more than pulling her own weight. Plus we've got three qualified snipers, all have been taught hand-to-hand, they've all…"

"You don't have to sell me on them, Laura. I trust your judgment, remember?" the colonel replied.

"Yes, sir." She answered back feeling less defensive. "They're all fitting in nicely. And the augmentation is working quicker than with the other teams. I think the new formula really has it down to a fine art."

"Good news." Matt allowed himself to smile for the first time since the attack. Since losing his team, he hadn't allowed any good news to truly lift his spirits, but this was the turning of a new leaf. "So what's on the agenda for today?"

"They've finished up the new hand-to-hand techniques. Not too tough for most of them as you'd expect. We're moving on to firearms and armaments."

"All the FN stuff. Gotcha. Is Jay Wolf coming in for this again?"

"He should be arriving within the hour, sir."

"Let me know when he gets here.

The colonel had his men prepare the briefing room and indoor shooting ranges for Jay Wolf, owner and CEO of Elite Ammunition based in Harvard, Illinois. Although the team was used to some pretty heavy firepower in the field of battle, this new battlefield was almost always close quarters battle or CQB. This sort of scenario called for an entirely new breed of weaponry and the Monster Squad liked to keep things simple. If you can use the same caliber cartridge for both your sidearm and your carbine rifle, that made it a definite plus.

The unit decided on FN's lineup of 5.7X28MM weapons for CQB and the SCAR-H 17 308 for sniping. The US military had a very good working relationship with Fabrique National de Herstal and procuring the weapons wasn't a problem. Getting the proper ammunition *was*. Enter, Jay Wolf of Elite. Mr. Wolf was a specialty ammunition manufacturer and when Matt went searching for other ammunition suppliers besides FN for 5.7 ammo, there was only ONE. That one was Elite. Being that they were a small company, and the fact that Mr. Wolf was ex-military, Matt knew that Wolf could keep a secret. If Matt needed umpteen rounds of silver hollow point ammunition, then Mr. Wolf would see to it. The problem was getting the bullets. Matt actually had to have another bullet manufacturer make the bullets, ship them to Elite, and then have Elite make the rounds for the squad.

What made Elite's rounds 'elite'? The fact that they spent thousands of man-hours finding the maximum ft/lbs that could be safely pushed through both the handgun and the carbine for maximum carnage, whereas, FN, in an effort to appease the populace, and facing unfounded rumors that the FiveseveN pistol was a cop-killer gun, had begun to water-down their factory produced rounds. Not the kind of ammunition you wanted to use when hunting a monster with a really thick skin.

When Jay Wolf entered the compound Laura met up with him and escorted him to Matt's office. It was as if two old Army buddies had met again after many years apart. Scotch was shared, war-stories swapped, and condolences given for the loss of the squad. Jay knew some of those guys personally and would feel their loss later once it had really sunk in. He knew the news would be devastating to his wife and business partner, Lisa once he got home and broke the sad tale to her. Although bound by secrecy, the agreement had to include her. There was no way one could produce tens of thousands of rounds of silver ammunition for the federal government and not include your wife and business partner especially when she was an integral piece of every part of the business.

"Jay, we got these new boys out here training to replace that squad," Matt said, staring out the window of his office at the guys running obstacle courses or practicing their hand-to-hand skills. "I'd like you to go over the importance of the weapons and rounds." He turned to face Jay, his face obviously holding something back.

"Okay, Matt. I guess I can do that," Jay said. "But don't you usually have your smiths go over the weapons systems with them? I'm sure they'd have a lot more input than I would—"

"On the weapons themselves, perhaps. But you know the nuances. You know these rounds. Hell, you hand load each one to match specs." Matt drained the remaining puddle of his drink. "Besides, these guys are still of a mindset that bigger is better. They don't understand the concept behind the firing rate, the faster, smaller bullet, ft/lbs of energy and all that crap." Matt sat on the edge of his desk and gave Jay a good hard look. "You're not military anymore. You're a real person in the real world with real world results. You brought the presentation with you?"

"Of course."

"Then let's do this." Matt stood and opened his office door. "I just want somebody who won't let these guys walk all over them, and I figure a tanker like yourself is just the man for the job."

In the briefing room Jay went over the weapons systems and the rounds he created for the squad. He explained how a smaller bullet travelling at a higher rate of speed could give as much kinetic energy as a larger bullet at a slower rate of speed, but still have armor piercing capability. And while the team was not likely to meet up with anything out there wearing body armor, they were likely to meet up with something whose skin was as tough as armor, if not tougher.

Jay ran through his slides and videos showing how his 'hot loads' could pierce car doors and still remain lethal. He gave graphs, slides, and photos showing the end result of pig cadavers shot through windshields and the dissection of the remains and the damage caused by the tumbling bullets when they entered the bodies and struck bone. He explained how the 5.7 was, in all actuality a .224 bullet with a much smaller grain weight; that when it struck a body would tumble and leave a wound cavity very similar to that of a .45 caliber bullet. Ballistic gel videos showed a cavitation effect that was down-right frightening for such a small projectile.

When his presentation was finished, he asked the men, "Any questions?"

Dave Marshal was the first to raise his hand. "If you can get this kind of result from a souped-up fuckin' .22, why can't you just soup us up some *real* rounds like a .40 or a .45?"

This brought a few chuckles from the other men and few nods. Matt averted his eyes and simply sighed. He was afraid of this.

"I guess you weren't paying attention during the presentation, were you?" Jay refrained from calling the man a dumbass. Knowing that he had begun his augmentation regimen, the man could probably tear him in half already with little effort. "The FiveseveN is a high-capacity, low recoil firearm with dead on accuracy and a reputation in the field second to none. With a recoil less than half of a nine millimeter, you can reacquire your target in a fraction of the time."

"Meaning…what, exactly?" Marshal goaded.

"Meaning you can put all twenty rounds dead on the bull's-eye in less time than it takes to put eight rounds on the bull's-eye with a .45," Jay stated flatly. "Plus you will also have the P90 carbine that can empty fifty rounds in 3.3 seconds with deadly accuracy in close quarters, and they both share the same ammunition." Jay walked around the podium and approached the table that the men were seated behind. He placed both hands flat on the table and stared directly into Dave's eyes. "In a shit-hit-the-fan situation, it's a damned good thing to be able to use the same ammunition for both your sidearm and your carbine, wouldn't you think? Not to mention being able to reacquire your target in a fraction of the time of any other weapon platform available on the market, especially when the things you are going to be shooting at has reflexes ten times faster than a cheetah." He allowed a moment for the statement to sink in.

"Now, when you consider that this '*souped-up fuckin .22*' – as you call it – has the kinetic energy of a standard .40 caliber, leaves the wound channel of a .45 due to tumbling, and about half the recoil of a 9MM, not to mention the standard magazine holds twenty rounds with one in the pipe, it sounds to me like a pretty nifty little fucking weapon, wouldn't you agree?" He left little argument for them as he turned back to the podium and turned off the overhead projectors. "Now. Are you boys ready to start seeing just what these weapons are actually capable of first hand? Or do you want to sit here and keep making dumb-assed assumptions?"

This brought a few more snickers as Marshal lowered his eyes and simply nodded. He heard a few affirmatives come from the men, but they didn't seem quite as excited as he would have liked. "Trust me, gentlemen. Once you get the feel for these weapons, you'll wonder why you ever questioned them. Many federal agencies have made the switch to this platform including the United States Secret Service, the FBI, the Air Marshal's Service and a whole slew of sheriffs and police departments. And they aren't even using *my* ammunition."

6

Senator Franklin's car pulled into the parking garage, circled its way up to the roof, and parked in the far corner away from any of the other cars and as deep in the shadows as it could be placed. The honorable senator from Illinois sat in the back and waited to meet a man he had never met before and knew only as a voice on the phone. Put together by a mutual friend who needed some sensitive work done, the senator had hired the man to do some investigating for him. *"Dirt digging,"* the private investigator said. *"Fact finding,"* the senator corrected him. The subject, Colonel Matt Mitchell.

Leslie Franklin knew that if he couldn't get the other men who sat on the oversight committee to shut down or defund the black operation, then they had to be destroyed from within. The only way he could think to do that was to destroy the leader. Laura Youngblood was an untouchable. She was CIA and her records were sealed. Her past destroyed, her new existence written so perfectly that the truth couldn't be found, and if anybody was found sniffing around her, he or she would simply disappear never to be seen again. But Mitchell was another story. Career military men always leave a trail of destruction. Ex-wives, drunk & disorderly charges, brawls, something. Anything. It just had to be found. Nobody was clean and anybody who climbed to the top usually did it by stepping on someone else. He knew that from experience.

As the senator sat nervously, he would glance at the watch on his wrist, then out the window of the car. Then at his driver, then back to his watch. From the shadows a hand appeared and knocked on his window and the good Senator nearly wet himself. He had no idea why he was so nervous, but he literally jumped when the knock came at his window. Hitting the button to roll the window down, he was about to go into a tirade about how the man was late, but a large manila envelope was suddenly shoved in the window and the shadowy figure was gone as suddenly as he appeared.

Franklin had dropped the envelope in the floor of the car, but picked it up and set it in the seat beside him. He stepped out of the car to speak to the investigator only to find himself standing alone in the parking garage. However the man had gotten into the corner of the garage where the car was, he was gone now. *Spooky sonofabitch*, he thought as he stepped back into the car.

Ordering his driver to take him back to his office, he opened the envelope and perused the contents. Not much here that he couldn't have found on his own. Birth certificate. Copy of college transcripts. Highlights of his service jacket. Operational records. Locations of service. Dammit. Nothing of use as far as he could tell. As he was about to put the contents back into the envelope, he happened to notice the last page: a summary and conclusion sheet. Although on paper Matt Mitchell appeared to be an exemplary officer and had done nothing wrong worth reporting, the man had never had so much as a speeding ticket. No credit rating other than a single Visa with a $5,000 limit and had never been married. Conclusion, he was manufactured. Unknown by whom, but manufactured, nonetheless. Anybody who lives long enough to attain the rank of colonel in the United Sates military leaves a longer paper trail than Matt Mitchell had. Most college-age kids left a longer paper trail than Mitchell had.

Well, this left more questions than answers. But at least the investigator appeared to be on to something, even if that something was actually a whole lot of nothing. Or, rather, less than enough.

Franklin sat back in the soft leather of the Lincoln and pondered the ramifications of a manufactured officer running a clandestine group of black op SOCCOM soldiers in the middle of America's heartland. "At least it's a first step," he said.

"Sir?" the driver asked.

"Nothing. Just thinking aloud," Franklin answered absent-mindedly. Either way, bringing down Mitchell alone still might not be enough to destroy the entire project. *I'm going to need more than this. A lot more.*

After ensuring that Jack Thompson was comfortable and had some solid food in front of him, Rufus took his seat next to the bed again and settled in for a chat. "It would seem to me that you and your comrades may well have been misinformed on quite a bit concerning we vampires," he started. Jack simply hiked a skeptical eyebrow. "I can tell by that look that you aren't sure of what I'm about to tell you, and while I can't very well *prove* everything I'm about to disclose to you, I can assure you that it is all the truth."

Jack swallowed the bite he had been chewing and asked, "And why am I supposed to care?"

"Ah. Therein lies the true question, doesn't it?" Rufus sat forward and pulled the chair slightly closer to the bed allowing the candle light to highlight his face more. "You see, it is my sincere hope that once you are fully healed and are capable of leaving here, that you will return to your people and explain what it is *really* going on out here."

Jack stopped eating for a moment and allowed himself the slim hope that he not only would survive being a prisoner of the monsters, but that he would actually be allowed to leave. "You mean to tell me that I'm not a prisoner here?"

Rufus sat back with a look of shock, and Jack honestly couldn't tell if it was feigned or real. "Good heavens, man! Why would we have saved your life and risked our own only to keep you a prisoner here? To what end? I've told you that we're vegetarians. We don't feed on humans. We certainly don't imprison them. What's next? You expect me to torture you as well? Perhaps place you on the rack as they did in the medieval days?"

"Well forgive the shit out of me for thinking that a bloodsucker might want to actually suck my blood…" Jack replied, instantly regretting it.

Rufus laughed; a deep, hearty laugh that actually brought a careful smile to Jack's own mouth. "My dear boy, you have a lot to learn. A very lot," he said, still chuckling, as if there was an inside joke that Jack was unaware of. "Firstly, we are vegetarians. We may be old, but we still remember what it was like to be human. And we cherish life. All life. But human life above all else." Rufus paused to allow his statement to hit home with Jack. "We have taken a solemn oath to take no human lives in order to sustain our own." Jack raised his brow again on that one, obviously not believing him.

Rufus stood up and slowly began pacing the room as he began his tale, "Many, many years ago, I was very close to death. I was born with weak lungs and had many problems as a child. My parents moved me from Britannia to France and from France to many other areas, all in the hopes of either finding a cure or an environ that was more suitable for my breathing. When I was but twenty-three years and approaching my twenty-fourth birthday, I had a series of attacks that left me bedridden. I really wasn't sure where we were at this time. You see, I had been very ill the previous year and my parents had moved us again. My father owned a large estate in Britain and my mother was a Duchess, so money wasn't a problem for them. As a last ditch effort, they tried a

Romanian doctor, who, I believe, infected me with vampirism.

"I was never actually bitten by a vampire, nor was I drained, or seduced, or...well, whatever it is that you are taught. No, I was actually purposely injected by a so-called physician selling my parents on the hope of life." Rufus paused in his pacing and turned to face Jack, his head bowed, and Jack saw the pain in his eyes. "The first nights were horrible. The nightmares, the pain, the thirst...more than I could bear. By the time it had taken hold fully, I was stronger and completely out of my mind with hunger. I tore through my restraints and murdered my parents," he stated softly.

Rufus sat back down and cleared his throat. "For many years afterward, I ran from what and who I was. Eventually, I learned to control many things. My hunger, though, always tore at me. Then I encountered a much older vampire who took me under his wing, so to speak. He taught me that we didn't need to hunt humans for food, although it took a while to develop the taste. Cattle and other livestock could be substituted, and the vampirism doesn't transfer to them.

"With time, we developed ways to bleed a little from the livestock and keep them alive. Much the same as you might 'milk' your livestock. Keep the stock alive and simply take what was needed to survive. It sustains us, but we *are* weaker than our brethren who still feed on humans for sustenance."

Jack set his tray aside and tried to get a bit more comfortable. "So why don't more vampires do this whole 'vegetarian' thing like you do?"

"To them, it is a sign of weakness. It makes you weaker and slower to feed on anything other than humans and to other vampires, it is not only offensive, it is practically heresy," Rufus replied. "It is the cause of our own civil war."

"Civil war?" Jack asked, in disbelief.

"Yes. You see, there are more and more of us converting to what we call 'The New Way' and fewer and fewer of the those who absolutely refute it and demand we convert back to the 'Old Ways'…the way it was meant to be. It has become the main political point in what has become the Great Vampire Civil War."

"Okay. And where exactly do we fit in to this scenario?" Jack asked, not sure he was going to like the answer.

"That is what I was hoping to speak to you about," Rufus said as he sat on the edge of the chair. He paused as if gathering his thoughts, choosing his words wisely. "Many of the vampires you and your team have hunted down over the past few years have been '*Lamia Beastia*' that were set up to appear as Hunters." Rufus peered into Jack's eyes to see if he was catching on. "The Hunters are 'Lamia Humanus' and they are those who feed on humans. They are cunning, ruthless and vicious in their attacks against both humans and us."

"Wait a minute!" Jack interjected. "You mean to tell me that of the two sides of vampires, we've only been killing the so-called 'good guys'? And that you and your goat-suckers are the good guys and we should just leave you alone?"

"Well," Rufus replied, "yes, and no."

"What the hell? I'm supposed to just believe that—"

"No, please, you must understand something, first," Rufus stated, putting his hands up to stop Jack's outburst. "Firstly, yes, you are correct that there are two sides in our civil war. Secondly, you haven't *only* been killing our side, but you have been *mostly* killing only our side because the other side has been laying the proverbial bread crumbs to our doorsteps. And thirdly, there was no way for any of you to know or realize that there were any vampires out there who weren't a threat to humanity."

Jack stared at Rufus for quite some time before simply saying, "Right."

"I realize that this is a lot for you to try to take in. And I do understand that you are not yet prepared to believe what I say. I can only hope that as you heal and become more mobile, that I can show you more proof and perhaps convince you that what I say is true."

"And if you can't?" Jack asked.

Rufus shook his head as he stood and replaced the chair in its original position. "Then, I'm afraid you will leave here and tell your friends that you were saved and given medical treatment by a bunch of crazed vampires who tried like mad to convince you to assist them in their cause. Either way, you will leave here unharmed…as promised.

"I mean it when I tell you that we mean you no harm, Mr. Thompson. I only wish for you to understand the situation that we are in and the situation that you and your team are making worse for us by killing our kind when the real threat is still out there trying to destroy us and using you as their weapon." With that Rufus turned and left Jack alone in his candlelit room to ponder the possibilities.

Senator Franklin put away the summaries of the upcoming bills that would require his vote and pulled his keys from his trouser pocket. Unlocking the lower drawer of his desk, he pulled an old cigar box out and sat it gingerly on his desk. Opening the box, he sifted the contents and ran his fingertips gently across each item, studying them, his heart breaking all over again with loss. He pulled from the box a cell phone and dialed it. Placing the phone to his ear, he listened again to the message that he had long ago memorized, only to hear the voice that he had not heard in years. A lonely tear ran from his eye along the base of his nose to the edge of his lip and he choked back a painful smile. When the message finished playing, he turned the phone off and placed it and the other contents of the cigar box back and locked it away in his drawer.

The senator sat quietly in his office, staring at the framed picture on his desk, gently rocking in his overstuffed leather chair. His heart slowly hardening once again. His face slowly turning bitter again. Mitchell had to be stopped before it was too late. He had no idea what he was doing and Franklin couldn't do it without the support of the rest of the oversight committee.

An assassination was out of the question. They'd simply replace him. The best PI in DC couldn't find enough information to hang him. His contacts in the FBI and the CIA were trying to dig up more as quietly as they could, but he wasn't hopeful. He had no contacts in the Defense Intelligence Agency, or he'd have called in that marker as well.

The man would have to be ruined. The Monster Squad would have to be ruined as well. This latest fiasco wasn't enough to do it and half of the entire team was decimated. What more would it take? The entire base in Oklahoma City leveled to the ground? That wasn't exactly likely.

Although Franklin was considered a very powerful man in Washington, in matters like this, his hands were pretty much tied. He was beating his head against a well-liked wall. Well-liked by the people who knew about it and who made things happen.

Then a creepy smile slowly spread across Senator Franklin's thin face. *What if the Monster Squad and all of their actions were to somehow become public knowledge? What if it appeared to be a leak in their own organization, as well?'* He was beginning to like the sounds of this idea. The more he contemplated the idea, the more the idea began to take shape, and the easier it seemed it would be to place all the blame on MS4, use the public pandemonium to his full advantage, and with the blame and responsibility resting fully on Mitchell's shoulders, use the full force of the senator's power to shut the squad down for good.

The problem will be ensuring that whatever is leaked can never be traced back to this office, he thought. Franklin knew he was hardly literate in computers. He could barely check his own e-mail. It was time to hire the best hackers that his barely earned money could buy.

Laura had double checked to make sure that Mitchell and Wolf were well occupied studying the new team as they ran through their drills. Wolf oversaw the men's check-out on the weaponry, and when he felt the men were adequately familiar with the hardware, Mitchell let them loose on live-fire drills. Once the shooting started, Laura slipped out the back and through the dark, unguarded hallways to the holding cell holding the facilities lone prisoner.

There, in the darkest corner, huddled as though protecting itself from the cold, was the vampire Mitchell had shown the men. Laura squatted next to the cell bars and called to the being that once was a biologist assisting the team. "Evan? Are you still in there?"

The creature stirred, raising its head. Sunken eyes peered over its arm that was crossed over the legs that it had drawn close to its body. They watched her intently, but she couldn't tell if there was any recognition behind them.

She checked the hallway again and then pulled four expired IV bags of human blood from under her shirt and slid them across the floor toward the creature. It didn't stir. Laura had expected it to attack the bags of blood and devour them, yet when it didn't move or make any attempts at the blood, she almost started to panic. She knew the blood was to be destroyed and couldn't stand the thought of Evan suffering because some idiot on the oversight committee wanted to know if the creatures could be starved to death. That thought process made no sense. In order for them to be starved, humans would have to be extinct. Or a vampire sealed up for who knew how long? She truly thought that Franklin was behind the torture, but the rule came down and Evan was placed behind silver-plated bars to be tortured for whatever was left of his natural (or unnatural) life. She hadn't slept right since.

"Kill me please," the voice was soft and dry, almost raspy.

"Evan!" Laura exclaimed, not sure she even heard him. She stepped closer to the cell. "Please, tell me you're still in there. Tell me you have control over whatever this is that has you!" she practically sobbed.

The eyes simply lowered and the creature lowered its head back to its resting position, ignoring her.

"Evan, wait. I brought you blood. I know it's not fresh, but it's human. Not animal blood. The clinic was about to throw it out and I salvaged it for you." She sounded desperate. "Please, drink it. Regain some of your strength," she pressed herself against the bars and pleaded with him.

"To what end?" came the soft still voice again, the head not moving.

"I don't know," she cried. "Just please. At least it's something. Perhaps I can convince Mitchell to release you and you can carry on your work. Maybe I can get more and at least you won't have to starve any longer." Tears were flowing freely down her face now. She lowered her eyes and cried; her body began to rock with the sobbing. She never even sensed him move, but she felt his leathery hand stroke her hair through the silver bars, careful not to touch the metal lest the flesh burn.

"Don't cry," was all he could say.

She looked up at what was left of him and the only part of him that didn't look like a monster was his eyes. They were still as blue as she remembered. In his other hand he held the IV bags.

"What do you think, Jay?" Mitchell asked as the men ran their drills.

"I think I'd like some of that go-juice you got them on, that's what I think," Wolf replied, still awed at the speed and accuracy of the warriors going through the live-fire drills.

Mitchell chuckled. "I know. But you also know that without the constant monitoring by our docs and the ongoing regimen, your heart would explode in less than a month. Lisa wouldn't like that and something tells me she'd have my ass on a platter over it. No matter how good you might *think* you were feeling prior to that. If it were a one-and-done type of thing, I might would consider it, buddy."

Jay nodded, but he was still jealous of the abilities of the squad, and they hadn't yet reached their full potential. "How long before they're ready to hit the streets and rid the world of hobgoblins and ghoulies?"

"We're looking at probably another couple of weeks of intense training," Mitchell said. "They're still breaking out of their old training ideas and embracing the single squad ideal." Mitchell headed up a flight of stairs to a control room with live video feed screens. "In the past we only used Navy SEALs and Army Rangers or Green Berets. This time we're incorporating Air Force Combat Controllers and an LAPD SWAT sniper as well."

"Why break from tradition, Matt?"

"We're starting to see a lot more air support in our strikes and the Combat Controllers have more than proved themselves in the operations in the Middle East. Ya know, they were the first in to coordinate air strikes the first time we went over there."

"I do now."

"Since we're using more air support, they seemed a natural. And they seem to be mixing in well. They have the hand-to-hand and small arms training that we expected, and they have nerves of steel. A good mix. So far, they're proving more than capable." Mitchell seemed quite proud that this group had meshed as well as they had.

"And to be completely honest, it was Laura's decision to include them. She hand-selected the entire team," he stated proudly with a wave of his hand, displaying the wall of monitors showing the helmet cams during the live fire scenarios. "And that little gal from SWAT was one of the first females to ever make it as a SWAT officer. Tough as friggin' nails, too."

A moment later a claxon sounded and a red light went off indicating the end to the timed run. Mitchell escorted Wolf down to the training grounds to get input from the men. Once they were both down on the training floor, the men had already began tearing down the weaponry and cleaning them.

"What's your take, boys?" Mitchell asked as he approached them.

Tracy looked up from the table of weapons with a lopsided grin. "To be honest, sir? I'd like to have one of these little bastards for myself. Hell, I think I could hide one of these P90s in my boxers," he said with a chuckle.

Someone else muttered under their breath, "There'd be plenty of room for one." Although it brought a round of laughs, nobody was man enough to admit who it was.

Mueller offered constructive input in that he would like to see a both-eyes-open type of scope on top of the P90. Perhaps an Aim point or EOTech and do away with the factory ghost ring sight. Mitchell assured him that once they were familiar with the weaponry, the men would have their choice of optics for the weapons.

Jacobs asked if the FiveseveN had night-sites available. He didn't like the answer. The factory did have them available, but they weren't adjustable. Jay's company, however, did offer adjustable night sites and he told Matt that if the men wanted them, he could have his smiths expedite as many sets as needed and their smiths could install them without much problem.

Marshal, Lamb, and Sanchez were all checking out the SCAR 17. They had yet to actually get to use it during the drills since the weapon would be set up primarily as a sniping platform. They were really hoping to convince the colonel to allow them to install the shorter barrel and use it as a CQB weapon as well. Both of the men felt that the weapon could be used as a short range sniping weapon and a close quarter battle rifle effectively if the colonel would give them a chance to play with the platform and prove it. Wolf and Mitchell weren't sure about it, but both men agreed that if the two snipers were that confident, they would at least give them the opportunity to prove their theory. Sanchez liked it just the way it was.

Once the Q&A session was over, Jay took his leave and, with the bottle of single malt that Colonel Mitchell sent as a gift, headed back to Illinois to manufacture up more of the 'special' rounds that the squad would need.

7

Jack Thompson tried once more to get out of bed, but his legs were hurting too much to take any weight. He almost cried out from the pain and collapsed back onto the bed when the door opened and Nadia rushed in to collect him and help him back under the covers. She berated him for attempting such a foolish move when he was obviously so hurt, that's when she noticed that most of the bruises and cuts on his body were healed completely – far too quickly and far too completely for a human to have healed. Many of his wounds should have left deep purple scars, yet he had none.

She gave him a cool sponge bath and dried him with a soft towel, searching the entire time for the marks and scars that had been there when he first arrived, yet finding very little physical remains to indicate what he had been through other than the broken bones that had yet to knit. She brought him his meal and fresh bedding and excused herself rather than sitting with him to keep him company like she had the last few nights she had brought him food.

Jack felt alone in this place and missed Nadia's presence. He didn't feel like eating tonight. She had brought him more of the toasted sourdough, sweet milk, and this time some roasted meat that looked very much like rabbit. It smelled wonderful, but he just didn't have the appetite. Probably from the pain he caused himself from trying to get out of bed. Or perhaps from the chiding he received from his blonde haired caretaker. He wasn't sure anymore.

As he sat and pondered his circumstances, there was a gentle knock on his door and it slowly opened. Rufus entered with a troubled face. "May I speak with you, Jack?"

"Yes, of course," he replied.

"Nadia brings me her thoughts and concerns and I felt I must share them with you. For your own good, if nothing more." Rufus was uneasy, and Jack could tell that something was troubling him, but he had no idea if perhaps he had somehow upset Nadia more than he knew by trying to get out of bed, or if it was something else.

"She, of course, has been your nursemaid since you arrived here. She has changed your dressings, given you bedside baths, seen to all of your needs, so she alone would best know things," Rufus began.

"Okay." Jack wasn't sure where this was going, but a sudden thought of a doctor trying to tell his patient that he was about to die from an ingrown toenail suddenly came to mind.

"She tells me that your wounds have almost healed. Well, except, of course, for your bones, which will still take some time."

"And this is bad, because…"

"Because humans do not heal this quickly," Rufus stated rather bluntly. "Or this completely."

Jack looked confused. "I don't understand."

"Jack, you should have bruising. You should still have open wounds. And, had they healed, you would have scars," Rufus explained. "You've been here barely a week and your outward appearance is one of complete health."

Jack's mind still wasn't quite grasping what Rufus was getting at. "I still don't get it. What are trying to say?"

Rufus sighed heavily. "Jack, we know from a rather thorough examination when you were brought in that you were not bitten by any of the lycans during the battle. Therefore, you could not have contracted viral lycanthropy from them. You could not have been infected by any of us. You still have a heartbeat, and you did not heal almost immediately, therefore, you have not been infected by a vampire…"

"So?" Jack still wasn't following Rufus' line of thought.

"You are obviously infected with something," Rufus stated. "Otherwise, you would not be healing so fast."

Jack smiled. "Oh. I get it. You wanna know why I'm getting better so quick?"

"*Exactement*," Rufus stated.

"Simple, really." Jack stated. "You see, when we enter into the squad, we go through an augmentation process. It speeds us up, makes us faster, helps us hear better, see better, stronger, increased reaction times, *et cetera*. It also makes us heal faster *and* we get inoculated against vampire bites." Jack was smiling now. "So if you and your buddies *had* decided to make me into a midnight snack after you brought me here, you'd have thrown up everything you ate since kindergarten and I still wouldn't have gotten infected."

Rufus was obviously thinking. Hard. If there was an inoculation against vampires, there could be a cure. Or something similar. Or, perhaps not.

But, IF there was an inoculation against vampirism, why not just give it to the masses, and prevent all vampires from feeding. Something wasn't right. Either Jack wasn't telling the whole story, or someone wasn't telling Jack the whole story.

"Jack, if I may be so bold? May we have a small sample of your blood? Simply for testing?" Rufus asked.

Jack smiled. "Why would I care? It's not like you could make an anti-anti-vampire shot from it." He laughed. Then he sobered. "Could you?"

"Somehow, I doubt it. *Non*, my dear boy. I simply want to have it tested. Believe it or not, we have some of the best hematologists in the world right here. We are always looking for a cure to this damned disease," Rufus stated. "I'm not about to hope that your blood might help us find that, but I have a wicked feeling that someone isn't being completely honest with you. I'd simply like to get to the bottom of it all and find out what is true."

"Knock yourself out, Rufus," Jack said. "Just leave me enough to keep the old ticker pumping."

"Er, *oui*. We won't be needing that much. Perhaps, just a vial will do. Thank you, though."

Evan Peters drained the last of the IV bags and could feel his mind clearing. The fog of mindless hunger that kept him trapped behind the veil of feral ferocity was slowly dissipating. He watched as his skin began to regain its luster, his hands and arms filling out again like a slowly filled water balloon. He lifted a strand of his limp and lifeless, dull hair and watched as the color slowly came back to it and a light sheen returned to it.

"Like the fountain of youth," Laura murmured, still sitting behind the bars of his cell. She had observed his transformation with total awe. He knew that she had to dispose of the bags, lest they both be caught.

"I only wish it hadn't been human blood. It will only make the transition to animal blood later that much more difficult," he replied. He lifted his eyes to meet hers and she saw once again the man she had admired for so long. The man that she had grown to care for. The man she had fallen in love with. She knew she was risking everything by doing this and could only hope that if she were found out that Matt would understand. "That is assuming that there will be a transition allowed," Evan continued.

"We won't get caught," she said, hoping she sounded convincing.

"Perhaps. Perhaps not." Evan handed her the empty bags carefully through the silver bars. "But in the event Colonel Mitchell decides to check on his prisoner, how am I supposed to explain my sudden increase in good health?" he asked her. "Stray rats?"

"Not funny," She replied, stuffing the empty bags into her shirt. "I don't have an answer for that. I'm hoping that I can breach returning you to your duties with him in the very near future."

Evan eyed her carefully. "That could be dangerous for you. Career wise, anyway."

"If we're found out, I just washed my career down the tubes anyway," she replied.

"So why would you do this?" he asked, the answer already tickling the back of his mind. Still, he hoped she would say what he had longed to hear.

"Oh, I don't know." She said, not making eye contact. She glanced down the hallways again to make sure the coast was clear. "Maybe so I could start sleeping at night again." She smiled at him as she got up to go. "I'll try to get more, but I can't promise when." Laura turned to leave when Evan slid his hand between the bars and held her shoulder. She turned to face him once more.

"Thank you," was all he could bring himself to tell her.

Laura simply nodded before she slipped down the hallway.

93

Mitchell sat in his office reviewing the progress reports and approving requisition forms for the next quarter. MS4 had a four-man research and development team that specialized in sniffing out the newest in body armors and next generation protective gear. Although they tested it as best as they could, and felt confident that it was the best that could be had, the stuff didn't come cheap. Laura was more than capable of making the decision to procure the stuff, but Mitchell liked being a hands-on kind of CO. He wanted to know exactly what his men were counting on to bring them back from every mission. He observed as the R&D team put each new prospective item through its paces and ran every possible scenario conceivable. Light weight, durable, and strong enough to withstand teeth, claws and projectiles was the name of the game. Fire proof was a plus, but no matter what, it could not, under any circumstances, limit their range of motion. That's a tall order to fill, but with due diligence, the best of the best was found.

Mitchell just didn't like having to pay for it. The 'toys' as the oversight committee was so fond of calling their equipment, were getting more and more expensive, and with the devastating blow MS4 took in south Texas, their return on investment wasn't looking too great. He kept hoping that they could find a 'cure' shot...an anti-virus to their main enemy

– the vampires – that, when shot, would either kill them instantly or return them to their previously human state. That was what Doctor Peters was working on before the morons on the oversight committee demanded he couldn't be trusted and decided he should be starved to death. *Starved to death! Hah! How do you starve something that is already dead?* Mitchell thought. He had half a mind to start feeding the man himself…correction, the creature. Peters stopped being a man the night he was infected. Yet, there was something about him that Mitchell found agreeable. Matt couldn't explain it, but he did trust him. Laura trusted him. And he felt that Peters was close to finding them a usable weapon against the blood suckers.

A knock at the door broke his chain of thought. "Come," Mitchell stated.

Laura walked in and made straight for the single malt. She poured herself half a glass and sat in the chair facing Mitchell. Matt waited for her to give a clue why she was there, but she never met his eyes. She simply downed the glass and allowed the amber liquid to burn her throat and warm her belly. She waited a moment to see if it would give her more courage, but she found that it didn't. If anything, it made her slightly more nervous. Matt sat back in his chair, slightly intrigued at Laura's unorthodox behavior, yet he still waited. He knew his ex-CIA officer well enough that she would tell him whatever was on her mind when she was ready, but this behavior was definitely not her usual.

She stood to pour another glass. While her back was still to him she asked, "Care to join me?"

"What's the occasion?" Matt asked, not sure he really wanted to know.

"Maybe the end of my career," Laura stated cautiously, her back still to her Commanding Officer.

Matt was silent for a moment. Then flatly he said, "If that's the case, make mine a double." Laura poured him a glass to match hers and handed it to him. They both sat in silence a moment longer. Neither drank the scotch she had prepared, but Matt allowed her time to prepare whatever it was she was about to tell him.

"I fed Evan," she said softly.

Matt sat quietly, staring into the amber liquid in his glass. He surprised her by not exploding instantly. Rather, he took a drink of the scotch and leaned back in his chair. "What happened?"

Laura finally made eye contact with him. He didn't appear angry at all. Rather, he seemed more curious. "The clinic was tossing outdated IV blood. I offered to take it to the incinerator. Instead, I gave it to Evan. I just couldn't bear the thought of him being…like…that anymore."

"And…"

"And…he got better. With just four bags of outdated blood he looks almost as well as the day we escorted him in there."

"What am I supposed to do with this information, Laura?" Matt swallowed the rest of his drink to give her a moment to actually think about the position he was now in. "If I allow him to start being fed, I go against the OC. He'd still be in prison." Matt stood and paced his office, his own thoughts fighting with him. "If I were to authorize his release, who's to say he wouldn't be totally pissed at us and go on a rampage for having him locked up for these past years? I know I would."

"I don't think he—" Laura tried to debate, but Matt cut her off again,

"And there's no way in hell I could get livestock blood in here again without the OC finding out about it."

"The guy at the clinic said that they have blood sent to the incinerator daily."

"And you think the OC wouldn't find out?" Matt asked.

"Matt, he was *this* close!" she cried. "You know it. I know it. And I think that's why the OC shut him down." She stood up and walked to the window in his office overlooking the facility. "His lab is right there. It's still equipped. It's all been mothballed. The only thing missing is HIM!"

"And any asshole from the OC can pull a surprise visit at any time."

"And they wouldn't know him from Adam," she stated. And Matt knew she was right. With a spray-on tan and a lab coat, Evan could pass for anybody. Hell, cut his hair and put him in uniform and he could pass for any of his soldiers.

"So what do we report to the OC?" Matt asked. "He's assassinated? Escaped? What?"

"Nothing," she stated. "They've never asked to see him before. What would change that?" Laura went back to her chair and sat down. She swallowed the rest of her drink and sighed. "We simply get him fed, make sure he understands the circumstances that got him put there, and let him get back to work.

That's all he wants anyway." She looked at Matt and they both knew that she wanted him out more than Evan wanted out. "He wants to be human again. And if that simply cannot happen, then he wants to help us find a way to take them out with the lowest risk to our men. Period."

"Fine. But before I put both of our heads on the chopping block, I'm talking to him. Personally," Matt said.

"Agreed." Laura tried her best to sound completely business-like, but inside, her heart was jumping with joy.

"No. I'm talking to him alone. Man to man," Matt replied. "Well, man to, er…well…vampire."

8

"Is it just me or have you guys been eating like a race horse, too?" Ing Jacobs asked the other MS4 members as they went through the chow line.

"Dude, I don't think I ate this much in high school when I was working out like crazy and playing football," Robert Mueller responded. "Seems like I'm always hungry. And craving meat."

Gus Tracy sat down at the table with a huge pile of pork chops on his tray. "One of the nurses said that it has something to do with the enhancements they give us to make us stronger and faster. Its like 'roids but better. Anyway, it makes you really hungry and you crave tons of protein. Especially meat." He picked up a chop and started gnawing on it. "Still, being told that is one thing, but it's another to actually go through it. I feel like I could eat a whole cow."

Dave Marshal tossed in his two cents as well. "I'll tell you what really sucks nuts. I used to *live* for coffee. I mean, I'd still kill for an honest-to-God cup of espresso. But either my buds have changed, or the stuff they serve here is recycled dog hike. I mean, seriously, it doesn't even smell like coffee. Still, these other 'regular joes' go on about how great the coffee is here, but Jebus, I catch a whiff of it and it stinks like sewer water!"

Lamb kicked in his thoughts as well. "It's not just you, pal. Ya know how they cut us off the junk food, right? One of the gate guards smuggled me in a Coke. A flippin' Coke for cryin' out loud. I mean…it's just a soda, right? Stuff stunk to high heaven and tasted like it had lemons in it. I think this stuff they're pumping through us has changed our taste buds or something." He picked up another beef rib and ripped off a mouthful. "But I gotta tell ya, I don't care how strong they make us, or how fast or whatever. If they make beer and cheese doodles taste bad, I'm gonna be so pissed off."

Jimmy 'Tango Down' Wallace listened to them all while he was eating. Although he was the smallest of the bunch, he had packed on a lot of muscle over the time he had been there and watched his speed, agility and strength go through the roof. "I can't say for Cokes or coffee, but so far, the chow here ain't too bad. Lots of good lean meat, green veggies, and plenty of complex carbs. I'm a happy camper." He smiled as he chewed.

Tracy nudged TD with a grin. "We got us a regular Jack LaLanne here, fellas!"

Most of the guys just looked at him with a goofy confused expression. Finally Lamb asked, "Who the heck is Jack LaLanne?"

"Are you freakin' kiddin' me? He was like the original fitness nut. He had the very first TV show on exercise and shit when I was a kid. He's like ninety-five years old and still in better shape than most guys half his age!" Gus said, totally shocked that none of these guys had ever heard of Jack LaLanne.

"Jesus, Tracy, you're such a weirdo," Jacobs said as he grabbed some of the food off Gus' tray. "Watching an old guy do exercise on TV."

"Yeah, well, so's your mom, Ing," Gus retorted. All the guys laughed at Gus' sorry attempt at a comeback.

"Hey, so what do you guys think this stuff really is that they're pumping us up with?" Sanchez asked as she chewed on a slice of roast beef.

"I dunno. Some sort of synthetic hormones or artificial steroid or something. I dunno if they know," TD answered.

"Hey! What's a hormone?" Gus asked. "Anything you pay her to!" he answered, trying again to get a laugh. All the guys groaned at the even sorrier attempt at a joke.

"Give it up, Gus. Some guys just can't tell a joke!" Ing told him.

"No, seriously, fellas," Sanchez continued. "Haven't you guys been wondering just what in the hell they've been putting in us?" She looked at each of her counterparts. "I mean, really. Look at how fast we are now. How quick our reaction times are." She looked at TD in particular. "Jimmy, look at how far you were jumping today. Tell me that ain't some kind of record breaker, right there!" She turned to Gus. "And Tracy. You're a big man. Tell me you ever ran that fast in your life?" Gus shook his head no. "I didn't think so."

Ronald took a moment to look each of the men in their faces. "No, she's right. Each of you tell me you haven't had some weird thoughts on this. Like maybe this is some alien genetics or something, yeah? I mean, where do they come up with this stuff?" He took another bite and continued, "And I hear that we still aren't even close to what our 'true potential' is before we're gonna be allowed to hit the muck."

All of the men were silent for a moment as the thoughts set in and they pondered Sanchez's question. Finally, Jacobs stated, "I feel sorry for the monster we run into first." And all the men laughed in unison.

After chow was over and the squad was allowed some down time for R&R, the surviving Monster Squad was brought in and introduced by the XO. Laura had the new members assemble in the break room for a formal introduction. Matt was afraid that the mixing of old and new members might cause some friction, but they had been informed beforehand that new members were already in place and their training had to be the number one priority. Surprisingly, all of the squad members agreed. Although they mourned the loss of their brothers in arms, they understood the mission and acted professionally when Matt spoke with them. They understood that, without the proper training, the new member's lives and their own could very well be forfeit on the battle field.

Laura waited until the squad members all filed in and it never failed to impress her just how large each man was up close. She could see how each sized up the other before approaching and introducing themselves. Laura started with a little speech she had prepared on how she hoped the two groups could come together and work as one, the new learning from the established and the established using their first-hand knowledge to train the new recruits in just what to expect in the field. She explained that at this moment in time, it was still unclear if the original squad members would remain as assigned or if they would, in fact, be creating two new squads with a mix of both established members and new recruits in order to have their strengths more evenly spread between the two squads.

Next, she introduced each of the existing squad members and had them give a brief history of themselves for the newer members to have a better understanding of who they'd be working with. First up was Donnie Donovan. Tall and with close cropped dark hair, he looked like a poster boy for spec op.

"Yeah, I'm Donnie Donovan. I guess my parents had a sense of humor. At least it's not David Davis, right?" Donnie smiled, setting the new people at ease. "I'm a Navy SEAL and all that implies. Of course, as the colonel will explain, if he hasn't already, the past is wiped once we sign on here. Rank and branch no longer apply, but...I *used* to be a SEAL. And yeah, I'm proud of that. Hardest job I ever loved," he said. "Well...until this one."

Next was the only black man of the group. Large and muscular, he stood a good head taller than the rest. He cleared his throat and tried to smile, but it looked a lot like a snarl. "My name is Apollo. Apollo Creed Williams. My pops was a huge fan of the old *Rocky* movies and loved Carl Weathers, and I was the first born son, so I got stuck with the name." He smiled, and this time it looked like a smile. The others smiled back and Sanchez even gave a little sigh. "Army Ranger, amateur body builder, now, full time monster killer." Apollo let loose with a beaming smile that made the others laugh.

A non-descript, but muscular man stood up and said, "I'm Spanky. Actually, it's Darren, Darren Spalding, but for some damned reason, these ass hats started calling me Spanky and I didn't beat them to death over it. It stuck." The new folks sort of looked at each other, trying to guess the meaning of the nick-name, but thought it best not to ask.

A darker-skinned fellow stood and introduced himself. "Pedro Gonzales. They call me Popo. Military police turned Army airborne." Then he sat back down.

A dark haired, good looking guy stood and smiled like a used car salesman. "Dominic DeGiacomo. Dom to my friends. Best looking of the group, as you can obviously see. Best shooter, too. Army Airborne. These fucks call me Guido, but what the fuck do they know, eh?" His self-depreciating manner brought a few chuckles from the new crowd.

The thickest of the group stood. He was blonde and blue eyed and looked of Nordic descent. "I am Neils Erikson. They call me Hammer. As in Thor's

Hammer. They think I'm Norwegian, but my family is Swiss. These dumbasses can't tell the difference. It's all Alps and chocolate to them," he said and sat back down. He quickly stood again and said, "Navy SEAL." And sat back down.

One man who had been standing in the rear of the room the whole time and remained silent through it all, continued to remain silent. Laura motioned to him, "Hank? Care to introduce yourself?"

He had a peaceful face, but everyone could tell he was wound tight as a drum, as if he were waiting for something evil to burst into the room at any given moment. His eyes were disconcerting to all of them, yet he made no overtly aggressive moves. Finally, he sighed and stepped forward.

Hank cleared his throat and said softly, "Hank Michaels. Marine Force Recon." Then stepped back to where he was.

Sanchez nodded. "Mm-hmm. A man of few words, I see." But her desired reaction wasn't reciprocated. There was no humor to be found.

Lamb nodded to Hank. "These guys got nicknames. They give you one, too?"

Spanky hooked a thumb toward Hank, "Just call him Padre." When that earned a few raised eyebrows, Spanky elaborated. "He's our resident warrior monk. He's also the only one of us to come search out this group to join it."

Jack awoke to find his arm feeling much better, but his head hurt. He leaned over for the water pitcher and was surprised that his back and ribs felt much better. Next to the pitcher was a platter of cooling mutton and sliced bread. Fresh sliced vegetables sat on the platter next to the mutton. He was starving and made a quick meal of the offering.

He sat up as best he could and made an assessment of his injuries again. His headache was fading, but his back ached as did his ribs. He could almost swear that they itched under his skin. His legs still throbbed, but not nearly as badly as they had when he first arrived. His arm ached, but was usable. Flexing his fingers and twisting his wrist, he felt only a slight pain in his arm. He could hear a sound approaching and knew from previous visits that Rufus was approaching the door. This time, though, no heavy bolt was thrown before the heavy oak door slid open slowly.

"Thank you for the lamb. It was delicious," Jack said, actually feeling grateful.

"You are most welcome, Mr. Thompson. I wanted to check to see if you had woken yet and I am glad that you found the meal satisfactory," Rufus replied as he entered the room. "Do you mind company?"

"Please. I actually have more questions for you, if you don't mind?" Jack asked.

"What knowledge I have is yours for the asking, Mr. Thompson." Rufus pulled the high-backed chair beside the bed where they had last spoke and settled in. "Please understand, though, I have only limited knowledge of what other tribes may or may not do behind closed doors."

Jack was more interested in what attacked his squad during broad daylight. Whatever it was had done so brutally fast and without warning. If the vampire would allow him to pick his brain for details, and if Jack ever did get the information out, then hopefully other squads could be warned to exactly what kind of monster is out there and be better prepared to face them. Jack felt it was time to test his hosts' generosity.

"How did I get here?" Jack asked.

"We had you brought here," Rufus answered.

Jack waited a moment for Rufus to expand on the answer, but he didn't. So Jack expanded the question. "By what?"

"By a werewolf," Rufus answered.

Jack gave Rufus a sidelong look. Werewolves transform at the full moon, and this op took place during the day. To the best of his knowledge, it was weeks away from a full moon. "Bull. What was it really?"

"It was truly a werewolf," Rufus answered.

"Ya know what, Rufus? Screw you. For a moment, I thought you were going to play ball with me here and answer some of the questions I had, but if you're gonna jerk my chain, then—"

"I am not jerking your chain, Mr. Thompson!" Rufus exclaimed. "*Dieu damn*! *Comment faire..*?" Rufus sighed and then sat back into his chair. He steepled his fingers together and rested his chin against them. Finally he raised his eyes to Jack and said, "Mr. Thompson, you have a lot to learn about a lot of things. I suggest you get comfortable."

Jack looked at Rufus suspiciously. He still wasn't sure if he trusted the vampire, but somehow he felt that he was about to get schooled on things that even the Monster Squad wasn't aware of. Cautiously, he leaned forward and shoved an extra pillow behind his back to support him better then pushed himself up on it and settled in. "Educate me, Rufus."

Rufus sat up straighter in his chair. His gaze drifted to the candle on the bedside table and he seemed to be lost in thought for a moment. His voice was barely above a whisper when he spoke, but Jack had no trouble hearing him. "Do you know the legends of our origins, Mr. Thompson?" Rufus inquired.

"No. We're only trained how to hunt down and kill the monsters that prey on humans," Jack answered, hoping his answer sounded cold and calculated. Rufus appeared unaffected, still staring at the candle.

"We, ourselves are unsure of our origins. We have only legends to go by," he stated. "But even legends have a grain of truth at their hearts, *oui*?" Finally he turned to look at Jack, a sad smile forming. Rufus sighed again and began his tale.

"Many centuries ago, it is said that one of the Disciples of Christ turned on him, *oui*? Judas." Jack was never really a religious man, but he remembered that much from his grandmother dragging him to Sunday School as a kid. "Judas' betrayal was the worst kind. A betrayal of a brother against another. However, this brother was the Son of God. So his punishment was everlasting. Judas indeed tried to hang himself out of guilt, but he never truly saw death. Rather, he became the undead. Never truly alive, never truly dead, never to die." Rufus, cleared his throat and turned again to the flickering flame of the candle and let his gaze stare into the glow. "Never to walk in the light of the sun again, forever cast into the darkness…this was his punishment. To be forever a creature of the night and to forever feed upon the very blood of mankind. A thirst more powerful than any mortal greed, and his only weakness, the same weakness that bought his treachery in the first place." Rufus turned again to Jack. "Silver."

"So you're saying that a disciple of Jesus was the *first* vampire?" Jack asked, somewhat disbelieving.

"So say the legends," Rufus answered. "And of those that he fed upon, if any lived, they too became vampire. Although few survived early on. Legend says that it took him many years to discover the pathway to truly create without destroying the mind."

"Sharing his blood with them."

"*Exactement*! Otherwise, they were mindless creatures, running rampant through the countryside without the sense to escape the burning sun when it rose, and were quickly disposed of," Rufus answered. "But once he discovered that sharing his own blood with others salvaged the mind of the victim, he chose wisely in who he turned. People of great wealth and power. And he ruled great lands with many wives, and sired many children. Natural born vampires, who's powers are very much like the stories you read in your novels and—"

"Whoa! Wait a minute, hold on a second!" Jack interrupted. "You mean to tell me that vampires can *breed*? We've been taught that once somebody is turned, they're basically sterile."

"*Oui*. For the most part, most *turned* vampires are sterile," Rufus explained. "But not all. This is why he took many wives, to increase the odds of siring offspring, and why the natural-born vampires rose to such prominence in the ranks of the families."

"This still doesn't explain the werewolves who operate during the day," Jack said.

"True. I am getting to that." Rufus shifted in his chair to face Jack better. "According to the legends, at the time that the first vampire came into being, the first werewolf was as well."

"One of Judas' first victims?" Jack asked.

"*Non*," Rufus answered. "The Roman centurion that he conspired with, the very centurion who pierced the side of Christ at the moment of death, whose spear became the 'spear of destiny'…*he* became the father of the wolves."

Jack was taken aback by this revelation. If what Rufus was telling him were true, if the vampire legends were true, it went a long way toward explaining the allergic reactions both had to silver, as the thirty silver coins were tied to both originators. Both had conspired to betray Christ and brought the wrath of God upon their heads. Both had personally wounded Christ, one with a kiss, the other with a spear. Still, it didn't explain how his team was attacked in broad daylight.

"So how did these wolves operate without it being a full moon?" Jack asked.

"They were natural born," Rufus answered. "Direct descendants of that Roman centurion. Claudius Maximus Veranus was the centurion. Many have tried to claim that Longinus was the centurion who pierced His holy side and then later converted to Christianity, but alas, that is not how it was. Longinus may have been present at the time, but he did not wield that spear."

Rufus stood and poured a glass of water for Jack then returned to his chair. Jack studied that glass as Rufus spoke further. "Like other shifters, natural-born werewolves can control their transition to the animal. They do not need a full moon. However, on the full moon, they cannot control it. The lunar cycle controls them. When a natural born wolf shifts during the full moon, the wolf has control of their mind. If they control the shift and do it on their own on any other day then they still retain their minds and have full cognizance of what they are doing."

"Other shifters? What do you mean, 'other' shifters?" Jack asked.

Rufus smiled slightly then responded. "There are shape shifters out there who can assume any animal shape they so desire. It could be something as large as a horse or as small as mice. Some prefer to take flight and will often take on predatory birds like owls or hawks."

"So the wolves who aren't natural born?" Jack asked.

"Survivors of an attack, usually." Jack could see that he was holding something back. What that something was, he wasn't sure, but what the vampire had shared so far was making sense. Too much sense to just be legend. As Rufus had said, didn't all legends have a grain of truth at their heart?

9

Mitchell had just sat at his desk and opened the day's summary reports when he heard a knock at his door. "Come," he said without looking up.

"Colonel? I think I have something disturbing to report from the squad attack in Texas." Mitchell looked up to see his lead lab technician at his door. The man was pale and holding a folder in shaking hands.

"Come in, Mike. What is it?" Mitchell only had a handful of civilians working for him and Mike Waters was one of them. One of the best pathologists and forensic investigators Mitchell could find.

"Matt, our clean-up crew scoured the area. We got every fiber, hair, scrap of clothing...hell, even trash that had blown in from off-scene." Mike finally met his eyes. "It is our best belief that one of the men is missing from the carnage."

Mitchell was unsure how to take the news. "Missing how? Like possibly still alive or dragged off and killed or eaten on site?" Matt's mind reeled at the thought.

"We looked at the depth of prints coming in and estimated weights of the incoming attackers. The sand was soft, so impressions were impossible, but we were able to discern that *one* set of prints that left, singularly away from all the others, were at least two hundred pounds heavier than any of the others simply by the depth of the impression in the sand and the spray off the prints. We think that these prints might indicate that one of the men was being carried away from the scene."

"Do you have any idea who it is yet?" Matt asked, hoping that at least one of his men was still alive.

"Thompson, sir." Mike handed him the file with the forensic data. "All the other men's uniforms have been more or less pieced together except for the Phoenix. We haven't found a single scrap of his uniform in any of the carnage." The Phoenix was Chief Petty Officer Jack Thompson's call sign that the squad members had given him after he walked out of a fireball of a building without a scratch on him.

Matt took the file and thumbed through the photos of the scene, the morgue photos where bodies were pieced back together like a puzzle, hair and blood analysis, soil analysis, photos of trash and shell casings, photos of boot and foot prints, blood splatters and sprays and a summary of evidential findings. "Anything else I need to know?"

"Not at this time, sir. This is the final report and the remains are being prepared for cremation," Mike responded.

"Very well," Matt said. "If anything else happens to come up, I want to know." Mike turned and left and Matt opened the blinds in his office looking down onto the training area. Squad members were gearing up for a live fire exercise in the CQB simulators. Laura had the drill instructors separate and mix them according to their strengths and while one squad went through the drill, the other prepared their gear. Matt watched the teams as they prepared for the exercise but his mind was on Chief Thompson and the possibility that he may be alive. *What could they want with him? Were they torturing him? Were they trying to get information from him? Would they try to attack the teams here at the base?* These thoughts and many others ran through his mind as he observed the squads perform flawlessly one after the other in different scenarios and with the DI's changing the layouts of the CQB platform between runs so that no two runs were the same.

Matt picked up the folder and headed for Laura's office. She needed to know that there was a possibility that Jack was alive. If the monsters had him, there was always the possibility that he could be compromised.

Senator Franklin walked through the lonely house, drink in hand, housecoat flapping behind him. His lambskin slippers didn't echo on the hardwood floors as he settled in to his favorite chair of his private study. He reached for his humidor, pulled out a Romeo and Juliet, and clipped the end. His true vice was illegal cigars…which he allowed himself to enjoy only at home.

As the flame licked the end and he pulled the smoke into his mouth to bring the end to full burn, he noticed movement in the shadows of his study and nearly dropped the lighter.

"How the hell did you get in here?!" he demanded.

"Hello to you, too, father," the shadowy figure answered, never quite stepping out of the darkness. "I would say that I've missed you, but we both know that would be a lie."

"Damien," Leslie Franklin stammered. "I didn't realize it was you." Franklin stood and approached his son. "Why are you hiding in the shadows, son? Come here and sit. Talk with me." But the shadow in the corner never moved. Franklin could almost feel the animosity radiating from his only son.

"I'd rather stand, thank you."

Franklin waivered a moment, then remembered his position. The power he held both in wealth and in title. He raised his chin slightly and went back to his chair. "Suit yourself, son."

"Son?" Damien responded. "Is that truly how you see me?"

"You've always been my son," Franklin stated flatly, without emotion. "What would you have me call you?"

"Truly?" Now the shadow moved, but not into the light. Staying at the periphery of the table lamp, Damien circled the desk to stand closer to the study window. "While mother was dying, and you were so busy screwing anything with a short skirt and a pulse, did you have the time for me then?"

"Do we have to go through this again?" Franklin sighed.

"No," Damien responded, "I suppose not. Nothing we say will change the past."

"No, it won't."

"What of the future, father?" Damien asked, an edge to his voice. "Have you taken care of Mitchell and our little problem?"

"I'm working on it, son. It hasn't been as easy as I thought it would be," Franklin replied, his voice wavering.

"Perhaps I should do it for you? Sometimes a politician isn't the best tool for the job. Sometimes—"

"It's taken care of," Franklin interrupted. "If you'll learn a little patience, you'll get what you want. All of you will. The Monster Squad will be irreparably embarrassed and there will be no possible way for them to continue doing what they've been doing."

"What wheels have you set in motion, father?" Damien asked, his voice dripping with accusation.

"You'll see, my son." Franklin was smiling now. "The Monster Squad will be outted to the public. The whole world will know exactly what they do, who they do it to, and it will appear to be an inside job." Franklin was actually proud of himself.

"You FOOL!" Damien snapped. "We can't risk the world finding out that monsters exist!" He stepped out of the shadows and approached the desk. His eyes were so pale, it was impossible to tell where the whites began. His skin so thin and translucent that the blue veins appeared ghastly and like that of a corpse. His incisors had grown out to attack

117

position and his nails extended. Franklin knew he was not long for this world.

"Damien!" Franklin exclaimed. "Don't you see? Monsters *don't* exist to the rest of the world! The squads will be made out as tax-dollar wasting idiots, jetting around, partying on the military's dime, all in the name of fighting off boogeymen that aren't *real!*" The good senator was almost hyperventilating now as Damien stood over him, hand pulled back to a strike position.

Damien considered his father's words for a moment. Slowly he lowered his hands and retracted his nails. Slowly his incisors drew back up and his skin darkened until he looked almost normal. And when Franklin looked into his son's face again, his eyes were sky blue...just as his mother's had been. "This had better work as you think it will."

"It will," Franklin stammered, breathing a sigh of relief.

"If it doesn't, and it is *we* who are outted...it will be open season on *all* humans," Damien said as he turned for the study window. Turning back to his father he added, "And you will be at the top of the list, father."

"So why would a werewolf carry me to you, Rufus?" Jack asked.

"This particular wolf works for my family, Mr. Thompson," Rufus answered. "We had to know what the Lamia Humanus clans were up to. They employ many natural-born wolves to secure them during the day. Many years ago, we urged one of our wolves to infiltrate and feed us information as she could."

"Wait a second, bub. One of *your* wolves?" Jack asked.

"*Oui*," Rufus responded as if Jack should simply accept what he was saying. When it became obvious that Jack expected Rufus to explain further, Rufus sighed and settled further into his chair. "Many centuries ago, an accord was met with a natural wolf family and my own. We both were of the same mind that human life was precious and should be protected." Jack nodded his head for Rufus to continue. "We came to an accord, an agreement. A *contract*, if you will, that our two families would bind ourselves together by blood oath and agree that no longer would either allow any in our clans to feed upon, prey upon, or hunt another human, so long as our lines continued."

"That's some pretty heavy stuff, Rufus."

"True. Very heavy when you consider that both wolf and vampire usually hunt humans to sustain themselves." Rufus took a deep breath and continued, "However, we both knew that we could satisfy ourselves with lesser animals. And so we *chose* to do so, and in doing so, we tied both our families together, forever."

"By blood?" Jack asked.

119

"*Oui,*" Rufus answered. "By blood, by sacred oath, and by honor. Three things that neither family would *ever* break."

"Okay, so the wolf that brought me here was one of your wolves that had infiltrated the group?"

"*Oui,*" Rufus said, "And by saving you and breaking away from the group, she cannot return or risk revealing herself as a traitor to their agenda." Rufus stood and replaced the chair along the wall. "We risked much to save you, Mr. Thompson."

"Why? Why risk your only spy to save my sorry ass?" Jack asked as Rufus opened the door.

"Because it is our sincerest hope that you will believe our tale and take the truth back to your people before it is too late. Before more *Lamia Beastia* are killed and the *Lamia Humanus* get everything that they desire…to rule the earth and subjugate humanity as their cattle."

"So if Jack's alive, what does that mean for the team?" Laura asked, studying the forensic data.

Matt toyed with the items on her shelf as she perused the file. He picked up a trophy from her college days. Tennis. Another trophy was for swimming. She earned it in high school. Another row of trophies were all softball. *A real athlete, this one.* He sat the trophy down and noticed there was no dust anywhere.

Not unlike his own office, but he had stewards that took care of such things.

"That's what I wanted to pick your brain over," Matt shook his head. "I'm not sure if we should consider him compromised or if we dare hope that he's holding his own." He turned his full attention back to Laura. "What does your gut tell you?"

Laura looked through the photos again and set the folder down gently on her desk, as if she were actually handling the remains of the men she once knew. She took a deep breath and looked Matt in the eye. "Sir, I don't think we can jump to any conclusions just yet. We both know that Thompson is a strong soldier. One of the best there is."

"True. But we have no idea what they could be doing to him right this moment, even *if* he's still alive."

"I understand, sir. And that is exactly why we need to keep this to ourselves." Matt nodded. He never intended to release the information to the squad or they would expect to tear through the countryside looking for the soldier, regardless of the lack of intel.

"Agreed. No sense in giving them false hope, and I definitely don't want them trying to man a rescue attempt when we have no idea where he may be."

"However, sir, should the time come that we *do* discover where he is, what then? Do we consider him persona non grata or do we attempt a rescue?"

"We'll cross that bridge when we get there, Laura." Matt sighed. "We simply don't have enough information to form a rational decision at this time.

Hell, at this point, we don't even know if he is still breathing. They could have taken him for a midnight snack!" Matt exclaimed, then immediately regretted it. Laura looked up at him with shock and confusion and Mitchell threw up his hands, "I'm sorry, Laura. That was totally uncalled for. I'm just at a loss right now."

"I understand, colonel," she said.

Matt reached across her desk and picked up the file. As he thumped it across his thigh a few times he noticed the small ice chest in the corner of her office. "Were you able to get more blood for Evan?"

"Yes, sir," she replied without looking at him.

"Have you two been talking much?"

"Some."

Matt avoided her eyes. "I've been thinking about his…'situation'. I may have a solution."

Laura looked up, more than hopeful. No matter how much she tried to hide her feelings for Evan, more people than she was aware of knew that she cared for him. Perhaps even as more than just a friend. Yet, she was the Executive Officer, so nobody was stupid enough to ask, nor ever say anything while anywhere close to being within earshot of her. "I'm all ears, sir."

"I want to talk to him first. You're more than welcome to join me if you wish," Matt said.

"Of course, colonel."

"And if everything goes well, we might have him out of that cage by sundown," Matt said.

10

Senator Franklin paced the floor of his office, his private cell phone pressed to his ear. His face was a nice shade of crimson to match the power tie he wore. He tried very hard not to yell as he whispered into his phone, "You promised me that you could deliver!"

"Well, that was before I actually got a chance to hack this system. You didn't tell me what I was getting into. They have a stand-alone setup. I can't actually hack them without *being there*. If they were connected to the internet, I could work my way in, but I can't. It's like they don't exist," the voice on the phone said.

"They have to have an internet connection somewhere. I can e-mail them for shits sake!" Franklin all but screamed.

"You still don't get it. You can have a network that is connected to the internet for day-to-day stuff like email and ordering parts and food and hammers and toilet paper and porn and Hulu and whatever. But if their operational stuff is on a totally different server and the two aren't connected…"

The little light bulb above Franklin's head was just starting to glow a bit. "If they aren't connected, then all of their operational data is unreachable…"

"Bingo! You win the stuffed teddy bear!" the voice said.

"Don't be a smart ass, you little…"

"Whoa, hold on there, senator. Let's not forget who the 'Distinguished Gentleman' is here," the voice laughed.

Franklin sighed and rubbed a hand down his face. He swore under his breath then put the phone back to his ear. "Fine! Tell me then…what exactly do you have to have in place for you to be able to access their data and do what I need done?"

He could hear breathing on the other end of the line so he knew the hacker was still there, but Franklin was just about to lose his patience. "I need to get one of their computers that are plugged into their main hi-security server online. *Or*, I need to get the server itself online. Either way, if I can get access to either one long enough to download the data and hack just one of their email addresses, I can do what you need done."

"So what you're saying is, I'm going to have to go there," Franklin said. "And I hate that fucking state. The most boring, backwoods state in the world next to Utah," he muttered.

"I don't care how it's done, senator, but that's what I need. The rest is easy-peasy, lemon-squeezy."

"Teenagers," Franklin muttered. "Fine. I'll call you back when it's done."

Franklin pressed the 'End Call' button so hard he almost wished that it had broken. He *hated* going to Oklahoma with a passion. They always made him fly a military transport to get there, and they were the most uncomfortable and odd smelling planes in the world. Plus, it never failed. As soon as he set foot on the tarmac to board the plane, some kiss-ass would call ahead and Mitchell would know that he was en route. No surprise there. So he couldn't even pull the old 'surprise inspection' routine. He wanted to scream at the very idea of having to shuffle his schedule, put off the meetings and the dinners. He'd much rather be rubbing elbows with the movers and shakers and doing what he did best. Moving money and making deals.

But, this had to be done. It was the best way he could think of to bring down the teams. All of them. In one fail swoop. Let them be undone by their own doings. Surely nobody in their right mind would believe that American troops were being used on American soil, spending taxpayer money chasing down creatures that go bump in the night?! Surely they would be laughed out of existence. Nobody could justify their existence once word was made public? It would be a PR nightmare for a short time, but like anything else that was a PR nightmare, it would make the rounds, promises of investigations would be made, heads would roll, people lower than him would be hung out to dry and the program would be shut down. No more Monster Squads. No more threat to his son…his only son. He *had* to protect him just as he had always done. Just as he always would.

Sanchez had found that co-ed living with over a dozen men wasn't the easiest thing in the world. There was no such thing as privacy. Luckily, for the most part, even though she didn't have the same plumbing, the boys pretty much treated her like one of the guys. Oh, there were the jokes. Like when Lamb found her bra and commented that he didn't know they made 'double-barreled slingshots'. Ha ha ha. Very funny. Not. Or when Mueller stumbled across her undies and asked if SWAT issued thongs. Again, not funny. But for the most part, it was all in fun. She would wait her turn, patiently, until the guys were done in the shower and then quietly go in and do what she needed to do. And though they could just as easily have walked back in and harassed her, none ever did.

One time, though she wasn't absolutely certain, she thought she saw the back of Apollo's head standing just outside the showers, standing guard while she was in there, but when she was done and stepped out, he was nowhere to be found. Another time, when she went to the bathroom, she heard voices outside. She could have sworn she heard Ing Jacobs, the Asian guy with the Jewish last name (seriously, what gives there?) say that he really needed to take a piss, but she could have sworn that Hammer told him 'No, Sanchez was in there.' Were the guys making accommodations for her because she was a female? She smiled to herself. At first, she thought it was sweet. But then, after a bit, she got a little angry. Who were they to treat her any differently? She was every bit as tough as they were. She earned the right to be there, didn't she?

The more she thought about it, the angrier she got. Her Latin blood started getting hotter and she hatched a plan. One that would either make her part of the team as an equal or drive a wedge between them that couldn't be pulled out.

The following day, both teams endured physical training, hand-to-hand combat training, live fire exercises and CQB drills until they were almost ready to drop. After they ate, they went on a twelve-kilometer run and then were allowed to shower. The men hurriedly stripped down and hit the showers. This time, Sanchez stripped down and followed them in. As she walked into the shower room, she could hear the guys all laughing and joking around, but as she turned the corner and they heard her shower shoes against the tile, they all clammed up and did an about face towards the walls. Suddenly they were silent automatons, going through the motions of taking a shower. Eyes front, slowly going through the motions, mouths closed.

Maybe this wasn't such a great idea, she thought as she approached an open shower head and turned on the water. She sighed as the hot water stung her skin and soaked her hair. She closed her eyes and tried to forget that thirteen naked men were in the room with her. Thirteen very well built, extremely muscular, very large, very strong *extremely naked* men were in the same shower with her. She sighed and reached for her soap box. When she snapped it open, she realized that in her haste to make her grand entrance, she forgot her soap.

"Damn!" she groaned, her voice echoing in the dead silence of the shower.

"Whatchu need?" Sanchez turned around to find Apollo standing there. Her first instinct was to look down, but she forced herself to keep her eyes UP at his face.

"I forgot my soap." Her voice sounded very small with all of the hissing of the shower.

"Hold on. You can use mine," Apollo said.

He went back to where he had been showering and pulled his soap on a rope off the shower head and brought it back to her. She found herself checking out his ass as he walked off but when he turned back, she forced herself to look back up again. But it was *so* difficult to not sneak a peek. She could almost swear that he didn't walk back, he swaggered. She averted her eyes, but she also made no effort to turn or cover herself either.

When he approached, he said, "Here. It may smell a little manly, but it will wash the grime off."

When she looked back at him, she was staring at his oh-so-wide chest. She took the soap from him by the rope. "Thank you."

"Just don't drop it. God knows, I don't trust none of these muthas in here, and I'm a guy!" he hollered over his shoulder. That comment was the ice breaker that brought a few snickers from the other guys.

TD finally turned around and with his best feminine imitation said, "Only cuz you got buns of steel, Apollo. Mm-mm, wanna get me some of *that*!"

Marshall lost it then and burst out laughing and Gus Tracy almost slipped from laughter when Apollo faked a swing at TD.

"You know I don't thwing that way, Jimmy!" Apollo said with a fake lisp.

Dom laughed so hard he got soap in his eyes then blamed Jacobs for flinging soap. The grab-assing started and it went back to business as usual in the shower. Just laughter, small talk and joking around.

Sanchez relaxed a bit as she glanced around. For the most part, the guys were ignoring her, but every once in a while, they'd make an offhand comment or tease her about leaving girly stuff in the showers. She caught one or two checking her out, but she also expected that. At least none of them left with raging erections. Not that she would have minded that either, she *did* work really hard to earn her body. And to be honest, she did more than her fair share of checking them out, and she didn't think she got caught.

At least, she hoped she didn't.

But she didn't drop the soap either.

Jack tested his legs again and found the pain had lessened greatly. He could put more weight on them than he had before and even though the sweat was forming on his forehead, he was able to take his full weight. He knew he shouldn't try to walk just yet. He didn't want to risk re-breaking the knitting bones and he gently sat back on the edge of the bed. He let out the breath he hadn't realized he had been holding and his stomach growled at him.

"You're getting stronger," Nadia said from his open door.

Jack didn't look up. He hadn't heard her approach his room this time, and he had been so focused on his pain and taking assessment of his injuries that he failed to notice her standing just inside the doorway. He had asked Rufus to leave the door open so that the breeze from the window could more easily flow through the room and carry the sea air through.

"I'm feeling stronger." He finally turned to look at her. "Thanks to you." He could almost swear that Nadia blushed slightly with his comment.

He noticed that her eyes looked different. She wore makeup this time. Subtle, but there. Just a slight eye shadow to accentuate the aquamarines of her eyes. A very light blush. She had pulled her hair back into a complex braid that allowed more of her face to be seen. His eyes traced the shape of her ear, how the lobe attached delicately to her jaw, the angle of her neck, and around her neck was a crucifix of gold.

"You wear a cross?" Jack asked.

"Rufus gave it to me as a gift, many years ago." She came in and sat with him.

"I thought vampires and holy articles didn't mix."

Nadia smiled almost bashfully. "A wives' tale," she said softly her eyes not meeting his. "Although, our legends say that a natural born vampire cannot be touched by such things lest they burn."

Jack simply nodded, still admiring the crucifix. "Well, either way, yours is lovely." He caught himself and felt the need to elaborate. "I mean, I'm not a re-ligious man, really. It's just that yours is perfect for you. It's not too froo-froo or too simple…it's perfect," he blurted out with a lopsided grin.

"Froo-froo?"

"Ehh, yeah. Well, froo-froo…you know? Like bling? Not too blingy?" Nadia shook her head at him. "Not too ornate? Too 'over the top'?" he said, using his fingers to make air quotes. "Like the Pope wears."

"Ah!" Nadia's eyes widen, "Now I understand froo-froo!"

Jack chuckled. "Yeah, stick with me, kid, and I'll teach you all kinds of useless words that will get you absolutely nowhere in life!"

Nadia smiled back at him and Jack felt this fa-miliar pain in his stomach. Like butterflies. He wasn't sure that it was an entirely unpleasant feeling, but he also wasn't sure that it was a welcome feeling either. After a few moments of awkward silence, he finally asked her, "Did you just drop by 'cuz you missed me, or was there a purpose to your visit?"

Nadia's hands were busy twisting at the corner of her skirt and it was obvious that she was nervous. She finally spread her skirt out and patted it flat with her hands then sat up straighter. "Jack, I must ask you a few questions, please."

"Okay, here we go…" Jack figured this time would come. Interrogation time. He knew the whole *'we are your hosts', 'you are free to go once you are healed'* thing was a load of crap. "If you people think I'm going to tell you anything about our operations or tactics, then you got another think coming.—"

"No, Jack!" Nadia pleaded. "Jack, please!"

"You sons-of-bitches think that because you help patch me up that I'm gonna just spill my guts to you out of what…a sense of gratitude?"

"No! Jack, please. You misunderstand me, Jack!"

"Bull! You think that I'm stupid? You think you can just walk in here and bat your vampire eyes at me and I'm gonna go stupid and just start spilling secrets to you and…"

"Jack! Stop it!" Nadia screamed. Rising to her feet, she took him by the shoulders and shook him. "Jack, it's about your blood!"

He finally stopped ranting and froze. He stared at her face, and she seemed frightened. That scared him more than anything else she could have said. Well, that and there were tears in her eyes. *Can vampires cry?* Or was this a trick? Many thoughts, half-thoughts, and blank thoughts ran through Jack's mind all at once, but he did calm down. Something innate told him he needed to know what she knew. Or at least, what she suspected.

"Okay, gal pal. You have my attention," he said. "Spill it."

"I must ask you some questions please," Nadia said, trying to calm herself as she sat back down. Her hands were shaking as she attempted to smooth her skirt again. A skirt that didn't need smoothing, Jack noticed.

"Okay, Nadia, ask your questions," Jack said slowly and softly, trying more to help calm her than himself.

"You told Rufus when you got here that your people had given you something that would prevent you from becoming vampire if you were bitten, yes?"

"Yeah."

"Do you know what this 'something' is?"

"Sorry, sugar, I'm no doc," he said honestly. He cracked a grin. "All I know is that it came in a needle along with a lot of other needles. Big needles. Some of them hurt, some didn't."

Nadia turned away, thinking. When she turned back to him, she looked him in the eyes and asked, "Is there anything else that they give to you, Jack? Something that you take regularly?"

"Yeah. All the time. We take supplements, vitamins, enhancement stuff. Things to make us stronger, faster, and keep our immune system beefed up."

He could see her eyes shifting as if reading a book or accessing parts of her memory. Then, her light bulb came on. Jack saw it and knew it as soon as she did. "The things they give you, was it bitter and dark in color?"

"Actually, it's in a capsule, but yes, it is dark." Her face fell when he didn't admit it was bitter. "But you know one time, I had a capsule stick to my tongue, you know, because it wasn't wet enough or something, and I guess it dissolved or melted before

133

I could pry it loose and wash it down. Anyway, it was the most gawdawful-tasting crap I ever had in my mouth." Her face lit up. "Seriously, it was horrible tasting. I thought maybe somebody took a dump in one of those little pill thingies, but then I was like, 'who could take such a tiny dump?' and then I was like, 'well maybe a leprechaun' or something 'cuz it really tasted like shit…"

"No, Jack! This is such wonderful news!" Nadia jumped up and hugged him. "Would you be sure of the flavor again if you tasted it?"

"The leprechaun shit?" Jack asked. "Just kidding." He smiled. "I mean, yeah. I'd know it. It's pretty hard to forget."

"Good!" She reached her hand into a bag tied to her belt and pulling out a pinch of some powder she had in there. "Open your mouth!"

"What?!" Jack started backing up on the bed. "What do you mean open my mou—" Nadia shoved her fingers into Jack's mouth and released the powder. What followed can best be described as a human imitation of a lawn sprinkler. Jack turning his head from side to side spitting as he went. Pft, pft, pft, pft, pft, pft, long turn, long spit, pft, pft, pft, pft, pft, pft! "What the heck did you do that for?!"

"I needed to know. Is this the same thing that your people are giving you?" Her eyes probed his, hoping.

"Water! Please, I gotta get this taste out of my mouth!" Jack reached for the pitcher beside the bed and bypassed the glass, drinking straight from the pitcher. "Oh my God. I think a leprechaun shit in my mouth again."

"So it is the same?" Nadia asked, obviously excited.

"Why would you do that?" He asked. "That wasn't even nice. I wouldn't shove powdered leprechaun shit into your mouth when you weren't expecting it."

"Oh, but you *were* expecting it!" Nadia got up and sat next to him, practically bouncing on the bed. She took the water pitcher from him and looked him in the eye. She took a deep breath and then sighed. "Jack. We need to have a very long talk."

"Hopefully about something better than leprechaun excrement?"

Her smile almost broke his heart. She almost seemed sad.

"Jack, we only have days until the next full moon. There is little time."

11

Matt and Laura approached the cell where Evan sat patiently in the darkness. He sat in a classic yoga lotus position, but far enough back in the darkness that any guards who may have happened by would not easily see him. Not that the guards ever really checked on him. He had been sent here to starve to death and his bars were coated in silver. The only time anybody ever came was if Laura came down to cry, or if Matt came down and stayed just out of what he thought was eyeshot and whispered, "I'm sorry." Or if, like the other day, when the squad got new recruits. But this day, both Matt and Laura came down, and it appeared official.

"Why aren't you dead?" Matt asked.

"Good day to you, too, Colonel Mitchell," Evan replied without opening his eyes. "You are looking well."

"I know why you are looking so well. Laura told me. But why didn't you die while you were down here?" he asked again.

"Colonel, need I remind you, I'm already dead?" Evan replied. This time he opened his eyes. "My body may shrivel, but it can't die any more than it already has."

"Wanna bet?" Matt asked dryly.

This time Evan looked up at him and raised his eyebrows. He cracked a smile. "*Touché*, colonel." Dr. Peters stood up and stretched his neck. It made the classic cracking noise and he sighed. "Did you come to finally let me out so I can get back to work, sir?"

"That's what I wanted to talk to you about," Matt crossed his arms and studied the vampire. Laura stayed in the background, standing at attention. She refused to show any emotion but her heart was pounding so hard, she knew that both men could hear it. "Evan, I don't know how anybody…" Matt paused, he just couldn't find words strong enough to convey the thoughts he was thinking, the thoughts he felt in his gut. "I don't know how anyone could endure what you've had to endure and not hold such a grudge that they wouldn't go on a killing spree." Matt was shaking his head. "If it were me, not only would I say anything, or do anything to get out from behind those bars, I would promise the moon and stars, then I would kill every last person that put me there."

Evan lowered his eyes a moment. He nodded his head as he considered the colonel's words. "I suppose I could see your point, sir, but you're not a vampire. You still think in terms of a 'lifetime' whereas I think in terms of 'eternity'. And eternity is a long time. What's a few years of hunger out of an eternity?" Evan stepped closer to the bars. "Besides, it wasn't you or your people who *really* put me in here, now was it?" He shook his head. "No. We both know that it was Leslie Franklin and his people who did it."

Matt nodded his agreement and started to say something, but Evan cut him off, "We don't know why. We don't know to what purpose, or to what design, but we do know he had a reason. The good Senator doesn't take a leak without a reason for it. Am I right?"

Matt cracked a smile. He knew what Evan wanted to say, but held back because Laura was standing next to him. "You are correct. He gives slimy politicians a bad name."

"Then I would suggest that whether you let me out or not, you find out what the senator is up to. Quickly. Because the time that was wasted with me down here turning into vampire jerky is time we won't get back."

Matt turned to Laura and nodded. She hit a button on the side of the wall and the door slid open. Evan didn't move. Matt and Laura walked in and opened a backpack. Laura pulled out a lab coat and a change of clothes for Evan and she handed Matt a bag. The bag held the cremated remains taken from a mortuary of unclaimed human ashes. "Let's get you out of here and back to doing what you do best," she said as she handed Evan the clothes.

"We have to make it look like you didn't survive being down here, though," Matt added.

Laura picked out a can of self-tanner from the bag and had Evan spread-eagle against the wall. "This is supposed to be the best there is on the market." She began to spray his skin. "Let's hope it works well with dead skin, too."

"Please, please, please, let it be copper and not orange," Evan muttered.

"Why, Doc, I never would have taken you for the egotistical type." Matt grinned.

"Not egotistical, colonel," he replied. "Survival-ist. Unfortunately, in my case, a bad tan job could be my undoing."

"Or if it's too dark, you might have to learn to talk with an Indian accent," Laura quipped.

"There's plenty of 7-11s that need night manag-ers," Matt tossed in.

"Oh, please. Let's just all have a hearty laugh at the vampire's expense!" Evan groaned.

"I really don't know why you're bitching. You're getting a spray tan from a pretty girl. I'm stuffing your years old underwear and prison garb with hu-man ashes to fake your death. I think you owe me a bottle of scotch."

"I think you owe me three years back pay, plus pain and suffering," Evan shot back.

"I think you boys need to stop griping and focus on the task at hand," Laura scolded both.

"Yes, mom," Matt deadpanned.

Laura finished applying the spray tan as evenly as she could. She picked the most realistic, light col-ored bronze she could find and even snuck into the morgue and tested it on the leg of a cadaver to see if it would work on dead flesh. It seemed to work well and she hoped there wasn't anything 'special' about vampire skin that would cause a reaction and so far, there wasn't one. She had picked a fast drying tanner because she feared time would be against them, but Evan assured her that nobody ever came down there. Still, when both the CO and the XO were missing at the same time, somebody was bound to come look-ing.

Once Evan was dressed and the death scene prepared, they left as quietly as they could. Laura took Evan back to her office and cut his hair in a military buzz cut. He showered and presented himself as Dr. Peter Evans. Not the most ingenious of aliases, but all agreed that when he was deeply focused on a project, it would be difficult for him to remember that his name was supposed to John Muckenfuch if somebody were to yell it from across the lab. However, if they yelled either his first or last name, he would pick up on it and his attention would be turned. The only people they really had to worry about were the Oversight Committee, namely Senator Franklin, and since they rarely if ever came to the base, it shouldn't be a problem. Evan was just happy to get his lab out of mothballs and back into operation and get back into his work. He had plenty of time to think while incarcerated, and he had many theories he wanted to put to the drawing board and then to prototype so the field agents could test them.

"It's still risky," Matt said, the ice in his glass tinkling in his hand.

"I'm willing to risk it," Laura said flatly. They both stood at the rail outside the administrative offices overlooking the lab and R&D areas. They could see Evan diligently setting his lab back up and pulling his research back out of the lockers, taking up right where he left off.

"I don't like the idea of you getting out of date blood from the clinic. Somebody will put two and two together," he said.

"If I'm caught, I'll explain that it's for his research."

"That much blood?" He gave her a look of disbelief.

Laura turned to him. She was going to argue, but she knew she didn't have one. She turned back to the rail and studied him. She knew she had to do *something*, but what could she do? "It's better than nothing. And we can't get animals anymore." She said. "I won't let him starve again."

"Neither will I," Matt said. "That's why I'm going to go in-house." He turned and walked into his office. Laura, confused, followed him.

"What do you mean, go in-house?"

"I mean, we're going to supply him ourselves. Fresh human blood."

Laura was dumbfounded. "How?"

"Volunteers."

Laura stood in Matt's office, her mouth open. She watched as he worked his computer for a bit. He sat back and studied it. "We have just under two hundred personnel with the team, correct?"

"Yes."

"Not counting the actual squad members, since we don't know what the augmented blood would do to him, that leaves a hundred and eighty-three actual people. So, let's say we can get a hundred volunteers. They can donate every eight weeks, so that will be close to two units per day. If we get more volunteers, that would be more blood. If we get fewer volunteers, it would be less, but either way, at least we'll be in-house and nobody is the wiser."

Laura was dumbfounded. "Do you think our people will do it?" she asked. "Will we tell them what it's for? Surely some of them will recognize him and…"

"Those who knew him, liked him. They all thought he got a raw deal," Matt sat back in his chair. "The new people either won't know or can think it's for researching new anti-vamp weapons. I don't give a shit what they think. I'm not going to twist anybody's arm to do this."

"Word of mouth or…"

"Post it on the break room doors, the rec room, the snack machines, the latrine doors, anywhere people frequent. Make it flyers. I don't want emails going out on this. Make it ambiguous, too. Let them think it's for the R&D department," Matt said. "If we can't order fresh human blood, then we'll use our own. Either way, make sure it's known that we gotta have it and we need a steady supply of it."

"Mission essential?"

"Eh, don't play it up that far. Not yet. If we don't get the participation I expect, then we can step it up."

Laura plopped herself into the chair opposite Matt and sighed. "We really did it, didn't we?"

"We stepped in it." Matt laughed.

"When you began this journey, did you ever think you'd be sitting here like this? I mean, not only did you have one of the 'enemy' working for you, but you just went against your orders to free a prisoner…one of the enemy…and put him *back* to work for you?"

Matt looked at her over his still untouched scotch. The ice had long ago melted. "Do *you* consider Evan an enemy, Laura?"

She didn't quite expect that question. She looked down at her hands and saw that she had been picking at her nails nervously. "No," she answered quietly. "But I've never blatantly went against so many orders before, either." She sighed and took a deep breath. "Honestly, I'm a bit scared."

Matt sat up and looked her square in the eye. "Well, don't be." This time he took a drink from his Scotch. "Those orders were bullshit and we both know it. Evan was no threat. Franklin had a hair up his ass, and Doc out there was a threat to his agenda." He hooked his thumb out the door to indicate the lab area. "Whatever the doc is learning out in his lab has Franklin running scared, and I want to know why."

12

"I don't care what the weather is going to be like, I need to be on a plane to Oklahoma City," Senator Franklin stated.

The voice on the phone said something back, and Franklin's face turned red. Why did people in the military always assume that because he was a politician, he must be stupid? Tornadoes meant nothing to him, he was a senator, for crying out loud!

"Then make it a civilian transport! In fact, I prefer civilian carriers, they're more comfortable."

The voice argued that the airports in and around Oklahoma City were closed due to the weather and would not be reopening until the weather passed. One of the largest storm cells in history was about to hit the metro area, and air traffic was grounded from Dallas to Kansas City in anticipation of it. Nothing was taking off or landing due to the extremely high winds and threat of tornadoes.

"My dear boy, you do realize you are talking to a United States senator, don't you?"

"Well, senator, your constituents must be proud that they elected someone who thinks he can control the weather, but the fact remains that the airports are *still* closed until further notice!" And then he hung up.

The Distinguished Gentleman from Illinois seethed at the insolence of the peon who dared hang up on him. *How dare he?!* Franklin screeched as he ripped the phone from the cradle and threw it against the wall. It shattered the framed photo of him standing with his wife before her illness and Damien when we was six (or was he seven?), before stretching the cord to its fullest and careening back across his desk and hitting him in the wrist, cracking the crystal of his Rolex.

Franklin rubbed at his wrist, nursing his wounded pride and his wounded wrist. His pride and joy, the watch that, he felt, helped to distinguish him as a mover and shaker amongst mere mortals had been damaged in his fit of rage. He was just about to blow up again when his secretary stepped into his office, "Senator? Are you okay?"

"I'm fine!" he snapped. "Did you clear my agenda?"

"Yes, sir," she answered. "I've got all of your appointments moved and your meetings are rescheduled."

Through clenched teeth he said, "Move them back another day. It seems Mother Nature has decided to toss a monkey wrench into my works." He grabbed his overcoat off the hanger and his briefcase from the side of his desk. "I'll be out of the office for the rest of the day." And he pushed his way past her leaving her staring at his back.

"What does a full moon have to do with any of this?" Jack asked.

Nadia sighed and took his hands into hers. She was surprisingly warm to the touch, and her hands were soft and gentle. Her thumb rubbed against the side of his hand and the butterflies returned to his stomach. Jack felt his face flush a little, but he tried not to show it. He squeezed her hand gently and looked at her face, the curve of her cheek, the shape of her eyes, the curve of her nose, the arch of her brows, and for a moment, he forgot that they were supposed to be talking.

"Jack, how long have you been taking the dark pills?"

"Huh?" His confusion at the question surprised himself. He had to think for a moment to remember how long he had been with the squad. "A few years, I suppose. Does it matter?"

"The length of time? Yes."

"Why?"

"Do you know how big the pills are that they give you?"

"Nadia, what's going on? What's with all the questions?" Jack asked, his hands still in hers.

She looked directly into his eyes and he saw sadness there. Genuine concern laced her face as she spoke. "We found a live virus in your blood, Jack. It is not what we thought we'd find, yet not exactly surprising." She shrugged slightly. "We do not have the equipment necessary to identify it, but we had our suspicions, so I came to you with these questions."

"A virus?" Jack knew that a virus usually meant a cold or flu, but he hadn't been sick since he joined the team. "What kind of virus?"

"There are many kinds of virus. Some make you ill, some can kill. All viruses cause mutations to the host's DNA through—"

"Whoa, hold on a second! Mutations?"

"Yes. They inject their own DNA material into the cells of the host," Nadia said. "The body usually fights off these foreign invaders through fever."

"But I haven't been sick a day since I joined the squads. In fact, other than getting busted up during the last op, I haven't felt better."

"I understand. And if you will allow me to explain—"

"What's to explain?" He pushed away from her. "Your tests are wrong. I'm not sick."

"Jack, you are most certainly *not* sick," Nadia stated. "You *have been* infected, though."

"Infected?!"

"Yes. And those black pills you take keep it from taking full effect. We need to get you taking it again to prevent unspeakable things from happening to you."

"What are you talking about, Nadia?"

"Jack," Nadia said calmly, "you were infected by your own people. The infection can be kept in check, but only with the black substance you have been taking regularly. Otherwise, very bad things can, and *will* happen to you. Bad things, that…once they are done, cannot be undone."

Jack's rapid breathing began to slow. He was forcibly calming himself. He had been pushing himself further from her as she spoke, but now he sat and calmly placed his hands back in his lap. Nadia tentatively reached for his hands and caressed them again. "Am I a vampire, Nadia?" Jack asked.

She smiled softly. "No, Jack, you are most certainly *not* a vampire."

Jack looked at her long and hard. Her soft smile broadened and slowly he started to grin. "Are you sure I'm not?" He smiled bigger.

"I am certain." Her smile grew larger.

"Oh, thank God," Jack let out a deep breath he hadn't realized he had held. "You were starting to scare the crap out of me."

Nadia laughed softly with him. "No, Jack, you are not a vampire." She laid her head against his shoulder and they sighed together. "You are a werewolf," she stated. Jack suddenly went stiff. "Like me."

With the weather outside growing nastier by the minute, the squads were forced to train indoors and underground. The majority of the Monster Squad's facilities were under the hangar; this included CQB training areas, indoor firing ranges, the gymnasium, basically everything that shouldn't be seen by the outside base or could possibly be stumbled upon. But whenever they possibly could, they squads would train off-base in real world scenarios. 'In the muck' as they put it. Without getting the sand in your teeth and the mud between your toes, it's hard to train for real-world situations. Popo argued that training during the storm would sharpen their senses, since they might one day be called to take down something in that exact situation, but the colonel shot down the request. The team was on stand-down. They basically had R&R if they wanted it, but each of the squad members were feeling restless. They wanted to get out from under the hangar and run in the rain. They wanted to feel the ozone charged air on their skin and howl at the thunder.

Lamb put it best when he said he felt like he was amped up on a dozen Red Bulls, even though he hated the taste of the stuff. TD said he felt like he could do a thousand pull-ups and still run a marathon. Spanky sat in a chair and stared at a crack in the wall as if he expected something evil to crawl out of it at any given second. Hammer, Donovan, and Dom all opted to hit the gym and take out their excess energies on the heavy bags and kickboxing dummies. Marshall, Tracy, and Mueller joined them rather than sit and let their energies build up like a pop bottle that had been shaken to the point of explosion.

Apollo slipped off to the showers. He snuck out of the locker room, straining his ears to listen for the footfalls of his teammates. When he was satisfied that they were on the other side of the facility, he slowly closed the door to the shower facility and opened the faucet to as hot as he could stand it. He let it blast across his neck and broad shoulders to try to release the built up tension. It seemed that at least once a month, tensions would build up in all of his team mates and they would all get antsy, as if their energy levels were amped so high they couldn't release enough. They couldn't work out hard enough to reach exhaustion, sleep was impossible to find, and sexual frustration was…well, now it was nearly impossible with that incredible little Latina SWAT girl and her sweet little ass that had started showering *with* them all. He wanted to just reach out and *squeeze* that ass of hers, to bite it, to pick her up and impale her on himself so many times…but she was a squad member now. A team mate. *His* team mate. He could no more make a move on her than he could make a move on the Padre. He lathered up as best as he could, but noticed that just the fleeting thought of Sanchez had his manhood standing at unwavering attention.

What the hell am I supposed to do with that? There was no way he was going to get caught dead spanking it in the shower. But he never had a chance to make any more decisions as a warm set of hands wrapped themselves around him from behind and he felt the distinct impression of soft breasts press into his lower back.

"I never thought I'd get you alone," Sanchez growled from behind him. Her searching hands ran down his soapy abs until they found what had moments before embarrassed him. "*Madre de Dios!*" she whispered. She grabbed him by the hips and spun him around to face him. This time, she didn't look up. Her eyes widened. And she smiled. When she did look up, she licked her lips and growled, "I've always loved a challenge." And her eyes grew darker as she tiptoed and raised her arms up to his neck. He bent down and grabbed a cheek of her ass in each hand and lifted her up to him and took her mouth with his. Apollo could feel her small muscular body sliding against his and it engorged him that much more. He could feel his need throbbing against her.

She let go of his neck and used her hand to guide him where he needed to be. She had to use her thighs against his hips and lift herself high enough to get him started. He helped by lifting her ass higher. When he was placed correctly, she relaxed her legs and he slowly lowered her. She gasped in his mouth and he covered her moans with his kiss. Slowly, so slowly he entered her tiny body until finally she placed her hands against his chest.

With stuttering words she said, "Wait." She shivered and her eyes glossed over. She shook there and he could feel her convulsing around him for quite some time. He was only halfway inside her. After what seemed an eternity, she relaxed and opened her eyes and stared at him. "Incredible," she whispered.

He smiled, his teeth seeming even whiter against his dark skin. "And we're only getting started." He kissed her again and slowly went deeper. Her breath caught in her throat as she kissed him back.

The shower door banged open and Ing Jacobs came walking in whistling a tune he heard from the radio. He tossed a towel up on a hook and turned to walk to a shower. He saw them in action and froze.

Apollo and Sanchez never missed a beat. Apollo was still holding Sanchez and slowly raising and lowering her on himself under the hot water of the shower. Ing couldn't move. He just stared at the two in action. He couldn't explain why, but he couldn't stop staring. If asked, it wasn't like watching a porn movie, it was something of beauty, and it took his breath away. A stupid thing to say, and he couldn't explain it, but it was what it was.

Sanchez pulled away from Apollo's kiss and looked over her shoulder to Ing. "Do you mind? Private party."

Ing was snapped out of his stupor. "Huh? Oh...uh, yeah. Umm, I was just...er...yeah. I just...like...wow. That was beautiful. I mean, that is beautiful. Ha! I mean...uhh...carry on! I'll just, um, stand out...you know. I'll just stand outside the door and umm. You know. Stand guard. You guys just...take all the time you want," Ing stammered as he stepped back out of the showers.

Apollo looked down into Sanchez's eyes. "Kids," he laughed.

Ing came back in quickly and grabbed his towel off the hook. Sheepishly he added, "Sorry. Felt stupid standing out there, naked," and he slipped back out the door.

Sanchez laughed and she and Apollo went back to what they were doing so well.

13

Mitchell stepped off the elevator and headed to the indoor range. He didn't often shoot, but when he did, he preferred his privacy. The one thing he did appreciate about his position was that he could take what time he did have and use it as proficiently as he saw fit. If that meant spending it in the gym, he could. If he wanted to go to the indoor range, he could do that as well. As he stepped behind the shooters table and attached a target to the clips, the motorized transom ran it out to distance. A life-sized target, he should be able to score easily with his eyesight. He began loading the magazines and setting them on the table for future use when some of the new recruits came in. The colonel glanced up for a moment then went back to loading his magazines.

The men looked down and noticed the colonel was loading 9MM rounds into one set of mags and .45s into another set. Lamb felt compelled to ask, "Colonel, you don't carry a FiveseveN like the rest of us?"

"No, son, I'm usually stuck in control and, to be honest, I still prefer the old classics." Matt rammed a magazine home and let the slide drop forward, chambering a round.

The men just nodded. They had grown fond of the new weapons, but some of them really wished they could trade out the carbine for the M4 they were so much more familiar with. They just didn't know how to breach the subject with the colonel. He seemed so adamant that they use the same caliber weapon for both their pistol and carbine that it seemed sacrilege to even broach the subject.

The colonel ran through a couple of magazines of 9MM and shot well. *Good enough for an officer*, Jacobs thought. "You ever shoot the FiveseveN, sir?"

Matt glanced at Ing over his glasses as he re-loaded his magazines. "Of course, Jacobs. I'm the one who approved the platform."

The men all just nodded. Finally, Matt set his ammunition and magazines down and turned toward the men. "Is there something you boys would like to discuss with me?"

Most of the men took half a step back, muttering, 'no' or 'no, sir' as they did, but Lamb stepped forward. "Sir, I'd like to request permission to transition back to the M4 battle rifle."

Matt raised an eyebrow. Of the two squads, none had ever requested anything like this before. They all seemed more than happy with the FN weaponry. They loved the cyclic rate, the power of the 5.7 round, the lethality of the low grain .224 bullet, the light weight of the weapon, the short barrel was perfect for CQB. He saw no flaws with it. "Is there a reason why, Ron?"

"Sir, with all due respect, it's just too small for me. I can't comfortably get a cheek weld on it and it feels like I'm trying to use a pistol as a rifle," Lamb shrugged. "You made an excellent decision in the round, sir, and the platform is more than sound, it's just too uncomfortable for me to get used to. My arms are too long and my neck simply doesn't bend right to get a proper cheek weld. I've tried using three different optics on it and I just can't get it." Lamb looked almost distraught over it.

Matt nodded his head. He looked around at the other new men and asked, "Any more of you having trouble adjusting to the new weaponry?" Robert Mueller and Gus Tracy both raised their hands. Matt nodded his head again and looked at the ground. "And all of you are wanting to switch to the M4?"

The two men exchanged glances. Tracy shrugged. "I might could make the SCAR work, sir, but the M4 is more comfortable. It was my go-to weapon."

"All right," Matt said. "First thing tomorrow go to Ms. Youngblood and put in a requisition for new M4s. Make sure we order enough hi-capacity magazines for you boys to both train with and for field use." Matt went back to loading his magazines for use on the range. "And make sure the armory knows that we'll have three squad members switching primary weapons. He's going to need to keep spare parts on hand, and probably spare weapons." Matt put his ear protection back on and took aim. "You boys are hell on weaponry in the field, and I damn sure don't want to end up short on equipment when the shit hits the fan."

He emptied his weapon into the target and dropped his magazine to the floor, sliding a new one in as the first one fell out and, releasing the slide forward, he was back on target in the blink of an eye and shooting the eyes out of his target. When that magazine was empty, he dropped it and blew the smoke from his Beretta. "I'm no squad member, but the old man can still hold his own."

Robert Mueller cracked a smile, "I'd let you cover my six, sir." With the nod of his head at the decimated target he added, "Any day."

Jack was still in shock from what Nadia had told him. She remained cuddled next to him and rubbing his hands, calming him. His world had been turned upside down in a matter of moments. He literally went from being relieved that he wasn't a vampire to finding out that he was a werewolf, and never had a clue.

"Are you sure?" he asked.

"Positive."

"How?" he stammered. "I mean, how can you be sure? And how are the little black pills the key?"

"The black pills are wolf's bane. They prevent you from making the shift if you take it regularly. This is why you need to start taking it again. The full moon is close, and we cannot take chances. You must start taking it again."

Jack's mind was reeling. Too large of a realization and too much information at one time, and to top it off, Nadia tells him that *she* is a werewolf as well? Or did he hear her wrong?? "And you're a wolf as well?"

"Yes, I too, am a wolf."

"And this is how you know so much?"

"No," she answered, smiling at him, cuddling closer. "Many of the things I've learned…I've only recently learned. I'm a natural wolf. My parents were natural born wolves as well. I've never known anything but being a wolf."

"So, you can shift at will like Rufus was telling me?"

"Yes. And as long as it is not the full moon, I control the wolf."

"But when the moon is full, you shift whether you want to or not, and then the wolf controls you."

"Yes."

"And this will happen to me?"

"No," she said sternly. "We will keep you taking the bane and you will not shift. You will not like the shift, Jack. The wolf will always have control of you, and never you having control of the wolf. You *must* keep taking the bane."

"What if I don't want to?" he asked, studying her face closely.

"Why would you say such a thing, Jack? Being the wolf is not an enjoyable thing. The wolf will always struggle with your humanity, struggling to dominate who you are. Its aggression will manifest in your daily life." She pulled away to look him directly in the eyes. "Slowly at first. But the more you shift, and the more the wolf becomes free, the more it will try to steal your life during the times it cannot be free."

"Okay, so I go back to taking the bane after—"

"No! It does not work that way, Jack." She was struggling to find the right words. She needed to make him understand that once you crossed the threshold, there was no going back. "Once you make the initial shift, you can never stop it again. No matter how much bane you take, no matter what you do, or whose help you seek, you will never be free of the wolf or the full moon's power. The shift *will* take you and you will take the wolf's form."

"Forever?"

"Forever," she said solemnly. "There will be no going back. Even if you lock yourself away as I do on the full moon, even in the darkest of dungeons, the deepest of caves, the moon's pull will transition you."

Jack thought about what she said. He pulled her closer to him and he felt her shiver against him. He nodded and wrapped his arms around her. "Okay," he patted her arm, "I'll start taking the bane again if it will make you happy."

She nodded and he could hear her sniffle. He didn't know why it was so important to her, but it was. He held her like that for a while and once in a while he could feel her shoulders tremble and he imagined she was trying not to cry.

"Nadia, I was just thinking about something."

"Yes, Jack?" she said, wiping her face.

"If you shift before the full moon, you keep control, right?"

"Yes."

"Is there a limit on how long you can keep that form?"

Nadia thought for a moment and then answered, "No. I suppose that if we chose, we could live our lives as a wolf and never shift back to human."

"So, if a natural born wolf shifted when it wasn't a full moon, and stayed that way…what happens *during* a full moon if they stay a wolf?" he asked, looking down at her.

Slowly she pulled away from him, thinking to herself. "I do not know, Jack. To my knowledge, nobody has ever tried what you suggest."

"So we don't know if a natural wolf would still keep control and have full control of their mind if they shifted prior to the full moon?"

"No. We do not."

"How long until the full moon?" he asked her, a grin spreading across his face.

Finally! Franklin thought as he took his seat on the commercial flight to Oklahoma City. The commercial flight gave him the opportunity to fly into that nasty state unannounced where he could rent a car and hit the base at the last minute. Mitchell wouldn't know what hit him. Franklin would call it an impromptu meeting. He'd claim that he had a layover in this god-forsaken state and thought he'd drop by and check in on his pet project. He'd paint on an unfelt smile and pretend that everything was hunky-freaking-dory and go about as if everything was just fine. But the whole time, he'd be looking for any and every opportunity to get access to a secure computer and plug in the little USB device the hacker had delivered to him. The little device looked harmless enough, but even Franklin knew that looks were deceiving. The little electronic doo-dad would be the Monster Squad's undoing.

As the plane lifted off and took to the skies, the fasten seat belt sign went off and the pilot announced that it was okay for them to get up and stretch their legs about the passenger compartment. First Class was much roomier and the seating more comfortable, so the need to get up wasn't really necessary. Franklin did unfasten his seat belt, though, and when the flight attendant came by, he lifted his arm.

"Stewardess, I'd like a Jack and Coke, please."

The flight attendant made an unkind face at the un-PC term, but she brought him the little bottle of Jack Daniels and a can of Coke with a plastic cup filled with ice. Franklin didn't bother with a 'thank you' or a 'kiss my ass', he simply popped the tops on both and began mixing. He smiled to himself when he thought of the chain of events that he hoped to unfold.

Plant the device, download the data, get it to the hacker, make the Monster Squad known to the rest of the world, and make it look like they released the information themselves. Paint them to be money wasting military show-offs and then disown them all. Ruin them, publicly, politically, and in the courts of the media.

Ah, it felt like a perfect plan. Nothing short of an act of god could stop him now.

The plane chose that exact moment to hit a small bit of turbulence, and Franklin spilled his drink in his lap. Despite the cold, the spilled drink made it look at as though he had wet himself. And it smelled of cheap alcohol. Just what he needed. He took the small cocktail napkin and dabbed at the spill on his trousers, then stood and headed to the restroom to try to clean the mess better. It was going to take more than a speed bump in the sky to deter Senator Leslie Franklin.

14

"Seriously?" Popo asked. "Apollo and Sanchez?"

"That's what I'm hearing, man," Dom said. "Heard it from one of the newbies. Said they was gettin' *bizzay* in the showers."

Donovan was leaning against his bunk listening to the gossip. "I don't buy it," He leaned down and picked up the latest copy of *Guns & Ammo*. "Apollo wouldn't go for another team mate."

"He might if it was you, bitch!" Dom said, punching Donnie in the arm, laughing.

Donovan smiled and shook his head. "Seriously, Dom. Listen to yourself."

"Up yours, man. Have you really *looked* at that little *mamasita*?" he said. "She's smokin' hot!"

"Yes, I've seen her. And yes, she is…very attractive," Donnie admitted. "But, this is Apollo. You know how strict he is about everything."

Popo spoke up, "And I've seen how protective he is about her, too." He hooked his chin toward the chow hall. "When she steps in the shower, his chest grows six inches. When she's in the room, he gets two inches taller."

"And when she's in the room, your nuts shrivel up!" Dom laughed, slapping at Popo's back.

"Okay, okay, give it a break," Donnie said. He thought a minute before adding, "I'll just ask him."

The other two simply stared at him. "You can't do that!" Popo said.

"No way, man, he'll kill you!" Dom said.

"Why?" Donnie asked. "We're grown men."

"Well…because," Dom replied.

"Watch me." Donnie walked toward the chow hall and entered through the barracks doors. He scanned the room and found Apollo and Sanchez eating together at a table, laughing at something that he couldn't hear. Donnie walked up and joined them. They both turned to him, smiles still on their faces.

"What's up, you two? Something funny?"

"Sanchez was telling me about the time she was on patrol and these two meth heads decided to—"

"Are you two a couple now?" Donnie interrupted.

"What?" Sanchez turned a shocked glare at him. Apollo just stared.

"Sorry, but there are rumors going around about you two, and rather than listen to grown men gossip like a bunch of blue haired old ladies, I thought I'd just ask you." Donnie said, straight faced.

"What business is it of yours?" Apollo asked.

"Officially? None. None whatsoever," Donnie shrugged. "Unofficially?" He glanced around the room, then turned to both of them, "I think it's cool as hell if the two of you are hooking up." That brought shocked looks from the both of them. "I like the hell out of both of you, consider you both my friends, and would be happier than a hungry hound in a bone factory if two of my friends found

163

something worth fighting for in a world as messed up as the one we live in."

Apollo and Maria looked at each other and burst out laughing. Apollo turned to Donnie, "A hound in a bone factory?"

He grinned back at them, "A perv in a porn shop?" His smile got wider. "Wait! A hungry baby in a strip club?"

Sanchez elbowed him in the ribs. "Okay, stop it! Good grief, your puns are horrible!" She and Apollo looked at each other for a moment then shrugged. Finally Apollo nodded. Sanchez turned to Donnie, "Yeah, we're 'seeing' each other. Sort of. Nothing really official, but yes."

Donnie nodded. "Okay. Cool. I can dig it."

Apollo smiled. "So we have your approval, *dad*?"

"I suppose, but if you're gonna drill the shit out of her, we have to find you a more private place than the showers." Donnie grinned. "I mean, for chrissakes, I *wash* myself in there!"

Apollo tried to stab his hand with a fork, but Donnie was quicker than he looked…even laughing. Sanchez grabbed his shirt, "Hey! Who ratted us out? Ing?"

"Oh, shoot…everybody knows," Donnie chuckled.

Sanchez and Apollo exchanged looks. "The colonel?"

Donnie shrugged. "I dunno about admin, but the rest of the squads know." He grinned again. "But I wouldn't worry about it. It gives them something new to talk about." He got up to leave again, then turned around, "Might make shower time a little more interesting, though."

Surprised that the airlines didn't lose his luggage, Franklin hurriedly rented a car and departed the airport. The girl at the rental counter did her best to sell him rental insurance, but Franklin wasn't born yesterday. He knew that rental insurance was a scam and he'd have no part of it.

He made his way up I-44 to I-40 and across the construction zones to the downtown area. Traffic was heavy, especially in the construction areas, and he was not surprised at the sheer number of pickup trucks and SUVs on the roads in Oklahoma. *Don't these people realize that they're destroying the planet with their greenhouse gas emissions? Couldn't they drive a Prius or an electric car? Hell, no faster than the traffic is moving, they could walk!* Franklin reached over and turned up the air conditioner on the Lincoln Town Car's dash. It was ungodly humid in this backwater state. He loosened his tie so that he could breathe a little easier.

He glanced at his watch, and missed his Rolex. He had dropped it at the jewelers for repairs and he had to wear a Patek Phillipe that his wife had given them on their 20th anniversary. It was a beautiful watch and was probably more expensive than the Rolex, but the Rolex was more well-known to even common people. He remembered the time difference between Oklahoma and D.C. and then looked at the clock on the dash. It was lunchtime. That helped explain some of the traffic. It also meant that there was a chance that Mitchell wouldn't be at the hangar. Franklin smiled to himself as he continued to force his way through the traffic.

He made his way through Oklahoma City proper, through Del City and to Midwest City, which, to Franklin, was just one big suburb of Oklahoma City. You couldn't tell where one ended and the other started. *Too many rednecks inbreeding in too small of an area.* When he reached the outlying fences of the Air Force base, he began to slow the car and watch for the gates. He debated on coming in the back way, but that would surely get a call to Mitchell. If he came in the front gate, he could use his Government ID and perhaps the gate guard would not know who or why he was there and simply allow him through. Weighing his options, Franklin decided to chance going through the front gates.

As he approached the main gate, he went into politician mode, plastering on his best fake smile and flashing his governmental identification. The gate guard waved him up to the guard shack and stopped him. Franklin rolled down the window of the car, "I'm Senator Franklin. Had a little layover here in your fine state and thought I'd do a little checking on some pet projects I oversee back in D.C." The guard looked at Franklin's identification and without expression or explanation, waved the senator's car off the side to the Pass & ID building.

"You'll have to get a visitor's pass, sir." Then the guard looked up for the next car.

"But son, I'm a United States Senator—" Franklin protested.

The guard looked down at Franklin and sternly stated, "Sir, I don't care if you are God, Himself, unless you have a valid military ID or other base commander approved form of identification, you will have to go to Pass & ID and get a visitor's pass. Thank you and have a nice day. Sir."

Franklin dropped his head in defeat. He knew better than to argue with a base cop. A 'rent a cop' gate guard at that. *I'm sure he'd like nothing more than to pull his weapon and shoot me right here for causing a scene, the gun-happy little bastard. Why else would anybody join a military organization? Probably get a medal for shooting a terrorist attempt at the gate if I argued with him,* Franklin argued in his mind as he pulled the vehicle over to the small building on the right of the gate.

Franklin went into the building to get his temporary visitor's pass only to find a bureaucratic nightmare. He had to show ID to get the visitor's pass, but in order to take the vehicle on base, he had to show registration, proof of insurance and that the tag was up to date. It didn't matter that it was a rental. After numerous trips back and forth to the vehicle to look for paperwork, he ended up calling the rental company and having them fax the rental agreement (he had forgotten to take his copy with him) to the Pass & ID building. Although the lady behind the counter wasn't hateful with him, Franklin could tell that she was not being particularly *helpful*. It took him over an hour and a half to get the single slip of paper to place on the dash with the date written on it giving him permission to enter the base and a temporary base pass.

Whenever he had his secretary set up his coming to the base, all of this was taken care of ahead of time. A car was waiting for them and they simply drove through a gate, but try to pull a surprise visit and…dammit!

Mitchell got the call as soon as Franklin entered the building and 'Debbie' the lady behind the counter at Pass & Id, made things as interesting as she could for the good senator. She informed Mitchell herself as soon as Franklin left. Matt did his best to appear surprised when Franklin came off the elevator and entered the underground facilities.

"Senator," Matt gave an award winning show of shock. "What brings you to Tinker?"

"Had a layover at Will Rogers and thought I'd drop by and see how things were going since the…'unfortunate incident' in Texas."

"Well, Senator, things are going splendidly," Matt said. He turned toward the hallway that led to the overlook on the indoor training range where both squads were training in the indoor CQB simulators. "If you care to join me, I can show you where we're at."

"That would be great, Matt." Franklin was in top form today, showing real concern and flashing smiles at all the right times. "I'd really appreciate it."

As they stepped out onto the overlook, Laura Youngblood was already there, observing the squads and taking notes onto her electronic pad. She pulled up a set of binoculars and observed the two snipers that had set up at a distance for a while then she made new notes. Mitchell and Franklin said nothing as the clearance drill finished up. When both teams yelled 'clear' at almost the same time, Laura hit her stopwatch and noted the times. She nodded and turned to Matt. She had a smirk on her face. Matt knew what it meant.

"I take it that everything is going well?" Franklin asked.

"Much better than expected, Sir," Laura answered.

"How are the new recruits doing in comparison to the other team?"

"The new squad members have been blended with the existing squad members to create two entirely new squads, sir," Matt answered. "Ms. Youngblood and I discussed this at length, and while we weighed the pros and cons of keeping the original squad together for continuity, we really felt that they had more to offer the newer squad members if we split them up and made two entirely new squads out of the group."

Franklin nodded his head as if agreeing and understanding. He wanted to give the impression that he was supporting the mission in every way. "Was there any…animosity among the original team members and the new people, Matt?" Franklin asked, trying to sound supportive and truly interested in the program at the same time. "Any friction due to the loss of their comrades?"

"Actually, Senator, they seem to be handling the loss as well as can be expected." Matt answered honestly. "As far as friction with any of the new people? No, I can honestly say that there hasn't been anything but support between both. They've come together and formed *one* team. True, it's two distinct squads, but they are truly one team now."

Franklin smiled and shook his head. "You know, Mitchell, I gave you a lot of grief when the team was hit down in Texas." He took a deep breath and let it out slowly, thinking about what he said next. "And, to be completely straight with you, I said some things that I immediately regretted as soon as we hung up the phone." Franklin was shaking his head and finally turned to look Matt in the eye. "I can't expect you to forgive a self-absorbed SOB like myself, but I would like to apologize to you…and to Ms. Youngblood."

Mitchell wasn't sure what Franklin was up to, but he could feel his skin crawling. He knew that Franklin was an excellent liar, but for just a moment, he almost thought the man was sincere. He simply gave him a slight smile and nodded his head. Franklin extended his hand to offer a handshake and Matt took it. If Franklin wanted to act like they were friends, Matt would play along. "Thank you, sir. I really do appreciate it," Matt said. "It takes a big man to say something like that, especially to someone that he doesn't have to."

"That's where you're wrong, colonel," Franklin went full speed into politician mode again. "There may be a pecking order, especially in government and the military. But this is still the United States where all men are created *equal*. As far as I'm concerned, I should have called you right back that night and *begged* your forgiveness." Franklin sighed. "But I am a proud man. And regardless of the personal problems and stresses I may have at work, I refused to do the right thing at the time."

"Thank you for doing it now, Senator."

"Long overdue, colonel." Franklin slapped his hands together to indicate the matter dropped. "Now, on to other business, since you have me as a captive audience." Franklin indicated the facility that Mitchell had built under the hangar at the far west side of Tinker. "I know we've seen this before, and you've taken all of us stuffed shirts on tours numerous times…" Franklin turned to Matt and lowered his voice, "but let's get real here a moment, Matt. What could we have done different in Texas to have prevented what happened to our boys?"

Our boys? Since when did he give two shits about these men? Matt thought a moment, then replied, "Proper support would have gone a long way, Senator." Matt began walking back toward his office and Franklin followed. "I don't know if you recall, but when we started this operation, we were promised all sorts of satellite support. We didn't get it, and it cost lives." Matt paused then added, "Those positions can obviously be replaced with other people, but the lives of those men can't. We spent millions training them, augmenting them, arming them, and deploying them all over this side of the world and then we left them hung out to dry because somebody wouldn't hand over a stupid satellite when we needed it?" Matt pointed his finger at Franklin and practically spat, "That's just bull!" He headed back down the hall towards his office and continued, "Our operation doesn't cost much in the way of black ops. You know that as much as anybody because you sit on our Oversight Committee. But if we could have had…even some unmanned drones. They don't have to be armed drones, but that would be nice if we

171

happen upon a group of trolls or, God forbid, some leprechauns end up on our shore. Or hell, if we got a dragon over here somehow." Matt opened the door and allowed the Senator into his office. He went in and continued. "I know that there are contractors out there that are making some pretty cheap these days, but our budget is tight. And it gets tighter each year."

Franklin was nodding his head. "Yes, it has been. And it doesn't help that Canada and Mexico haven't been paying their portion of the bills, either. It's pretty much just us picking up the tab." He scratched at his chin and thought a moment. "If I can push for a ten percent increase in your budget, will that help?"

Matt was shocked at first that Franklin was even willing to increase his budget. Something was definitely amiss here. He was always the first the try to cut the legs out from under the Monster Squad, but now he seemed to be…well, at last *acting* supportive. "Ten percent would help, but with fifteen I could purchase two drones. One armed. It wouldn't get me much in the way of armaments, but I might could procure those from here through regular non-black op channels," Mitchell stated. "It still won't be easy."

"Perhaps the hangar above could be converted to something useful?" Franklin added. "Drone re-manufacturing?" Mitchell could read between the lines on Franklin's face. He meant more than he was saying.

"Use my people to 'remanufacture' drones?" Matt asked.

"Maybe a few are too damaged for repair? A few extra spare parts are relocated to our use?" he added.

"Just thinking out loud," Franklin stated with a smile. *One more nail in your coffin once everything goes public.*

Matt rolled the idea around. "It would mean more than just my people might have access to the hangar."

"Only in limited numbers, and for limited amounts of time," Franklin stated. "And, since many drones are very classified, you could definitely have a reason to post guards outside the hangar."

Mitchell was liking the idea less and less. Possibly, just possibly, Franklin was coming around to their way of thinking, but now he was condoning illegal activities. "I'll bounce the idea off Laura and see what she thinks. If there's any holes in it, she'll find them and we can plug them before we try to implement it," Matt said. "But you're pretty sure you can get me the increase in funding?"

Franklin chuckled. "Matt, as much as I hate to admit it, I was the reason you didn't get your funding increase last time." Franklin stood and stepped to Matt's private bar. He nodded toward it and Matt simply nodded, giving permission. Franklin poured two fingers of scotch. "If I go back to the OC and tell them you need an increase in funding…*me?* Do you really think they'll try to shoot it down?"

"I suppose not."

"No. You would suppose correctly." Franklin swallowed the drink and sighed. "As I said, I know I've been a real son-of-a-bitch where you and your people are concerned. I've been struggling with that ever since the Texas incident." Franklin stared out of Matt's window and noticed the lab was back in operation. He could see a young man in a lab coat working diligently on something.

Franklin nodded with his chin. "You have the lab back up?"

Matt tried to appear nonchalant about it. "Hmm? Oh. Yes. Laura found this guy and brought him in a while back," Matt said. He stood and went to the window where he could just make out Evan below. "Sort of a quiet fellow, but he does good work according to Laura."

"Is he following up on that…what was his name…the vampire? Is he following up on his work?"

"I don't know," Matt lied. "Laura receives his reports and follows up on his work. Too sciencey for me."

Franklin stood there and watched the man for a moment. If he recognized him, he made no mention and his face didn't show it. After a few moments he turned and set his glass down. "Show me the new men."

15

"Nadia has told me what you would like to do, Mr. Thompson," Rufus said, his voice solemn. "I do not think this is a very wise decision."

"What could go wrong?" Jack asked. "Nadia said she usually locks herself in the dungeon to shift on the full moon, right?"

"Yes, but there is no way to know if she will have control of her mind or if she will be wolf."

"Sure there is," Jack said. "She'll tell us."

"Monsieur Thompson, she cannot speak while wolf!"

Jack laughed. "She doesn't have to, Rufus. You still don't get it. If she has her own mind, she could choose to just tap on the wall or knock three times or…we could come up with a pre-determined signal beforehand."

Rufus sighed. "I think this is very dangerous, Mr. Thompson." Rufus stood from the chair and walked to the door. Nadia appeared just as he was leaving. "Please, Nadia, if the two of you insist on trying this, prepare him first. Show him your wolf. Let him know the dangers involved." He kissed her hand and stepped away and down the hall.

"Why is he so concerned about this, Nadia? I thought if you had control, then everything would be okay?"

Nadia came and settled in next to Jack on the bed. She held a long walking stick in her hands and held it out to him. "A gift. So that you may move around easier and explore the castle."

"Yeah...about that," Jack said. "Last I remembered, I was in Texas, and now I'm in a castle? I didn't know there were castles in Texas."

Nadia giggled. "We are on a small island in the Gulf," she explained. "Rufus purchased the island many years ago and had one of his father's castles moved here stone by stone and reconstructed. He wanted a piece of his past brought to the new world."

Jack gave a low whistle. "I bet that cost a pretty penny."

"Yes. Rufus' family had much money at one time. He was forced to sell off most of his holdings to support himself and his family as he got older." She looked up at Jack. "Not all things are worth more as they get older though." She spread her hands to indicate the castle. "Although they are beautiful and easy to defend from foreign invaders, few people can afford to buy up old castles, and fewer still can afford to heat them!" she smiled.

"So, the Gulf of Mexico seemed more appropriate?"

"Actually, vampires do not care about heating their homes. But their visitors do tend to catch a chill," she said. "Come. I must show you something."

Nadia took Jack by the hand and led him slowly down the hallway. They reached a set of large double doors and she opened them wide to reveal a large dining hall. She walked Jack to the end, past standing suits of armor and many sets of crossed swords with shields of coats of arms. When they reached the fireplace, she turned and helped Jack to seat himself at the head of the table, then slowly removed her dress. Jack was riveted. He couldn't take his eyes off her. She was curvy, yet athletic, soft, yet firm, his eyes devoured her and he felt an urging grow inside him as his eyes studied every inch of her body. When he finally got to her face, her eyes had turned amber and he knew…she was about to shift. He could almost feel an electrical energy about her. She stood nearly ten feet away from him and he wanted so desperately for her to come to him to wrap her arms around him. She stepped out of her dress and the way she moved was like liquid silk. He could feel his arousal growing and then he heard a guttural growl. Feral in nature and frightening as hell, yet even though it made the hair on his neck stand on end, it made his loins even tighter.

Nadia took a step back from her spilled clothes and he felt his pulse quicken. His breathing increased and he could smell a musty smell in the air. She lowered herself to the ground and she sprung herself at him. Time slowed down as she sailed through the air toward him. Her lithe body took on an ethereal glow and he watched as she transformed from the woman of his dreams to a large gray timber wolf and land directly in front of him. She shook herself as if she were wet and raised her eyes to meet his and he was lost forever in those golden amber eyes.

Jack sat in the chair and looked down at Nadia, speechless. He was awed by her transformation. Slowly a smile spread across his face, and he reached down to gently grab the sides of her head and lift her face up to meet his. She placed her paws on the seat of the chair between his legs and raised herself up. She was now a full head taller than Jack and looked down on him.

"You are so beautiful," he whispered. Nadia whimpered and licked him about the face and neck. Jack rubbed his face against the side of her face and felt the coarse and soft hairs of her fur against his skin. "I wish I could do what you do. Be what you are with you. Like you." He felt his eyes begin to water and she licked his face again. She kept licking his face and he closed his eyes, fighting away the tears. He could feel the electricity in the air, and this time, a cooling effect; then, just as suddenly, he felt her lips on his as she kissed him. She pulled herself into his lap and he held her. Softly at first, then more firmly and he kissed her back.

"You don't want this, Jack," she whispered in his ear. "You just think you do. It's not a gift. It's a curse, and I would break it this day, right now, if I could."

"You don't understand," he said. "You can control it. You make the decision when and if…"

"But not when the moon dictates." She stared deeply into his eyes. "Then, the moon lets the wolf loose." She turned away. "And the wolf can do terrible things if it's allowed to. That is why I lock myself away."

"And that is why we need to know if this will work," Jack whispered to her. "I still don't understand why Rufus is so concerned, though."

"Did you not see my size? My teeth? My claws?" she asked.

"No. I saw a wolf," Jack answered. "A timber wolf. Not a werewolf, but a timber wolf. Hell, if not for the eyes, I would have thought you were like any other wolf in nature."

Nadia sat back and stared hard at Jack. "This cannot be." She appeared to be shocked. "I should have been in werewolf form...half wolf and half human!" she exclaimed.

"No, Nadia, you appeared as a normal wolf. Only with amber eyes that seemed to...glow." He shrugged.

"But you have never shifted," she stammered. "And you are not natural born."

"So?"

"So?!" Nadia exclaimed. "Do you not understand?" She rose from his lap and began pacing the dining hall. Jack found it extremely difficult to concentrate on what she was trying to say while her naked form pranced liquidly back and forth in front of him. His eyes kept devouring her form, and he kept wishing that her long blonde hair would move out of his way so he could see her flesh better. "The only way I should shift entirely to wolf and not the Halfling is if...but that is not possible because you are not...yet it seems that it is possible because you say that you saw...but shouldn't I know?"

"What is wrong, Nadia?"

"You are her mate, young man," a woman's voice stated from the other side of the dining hall.

Jack turned his head as best he could to see who was speaking, but the voice was out of eyesight. Nadia stopped her pacing and turned toward the voice. "Mother?" She ran to the voice, and Jack used the walking stick to stand and turn to see a woman with Nadia's facial features, but light brown hair. She appeared too young to be her mother. At best, an older sister. Nadia ran and embraced her mother, her nakedness in the presence of a strange man, apparently a non-issue. She appeared to be sobbing in her mother's arms.

Jack tilted his head toward the woman. "Jack Thompson, ma'am."

"I am aware of who you are, Mr. Thompson." She stroked her daughter's back and held her head to her shoulder.

"I'm afraid I have no clue what's going on right at the moment, though."

"I do, Mr. Thompson." Nadia's mother guided her back to the table near Jack and seated her next to where Jack was. "There, there, dear. If what we think is true, it's nothing to be sad about," her mother soothed. "It's something to celebrate."

Yet her mother's face was stoic, devoid of any emotion. Jack thought seriously, with a mother like that, he'd have needed years of therapy. There's no telling what effect it would have on a young girl, especially one that would grow up and find out she was a werewolf.

When Nadia's mother took a seat next to Nadia, she motioned for Jack to sit as well. He repositioned his chair at the table, and though Nadia was still stifling her sobs, her mother ignored her emotional state. "Mr. Thompson, when a natural born wolf first encounters their mate and they attempt to shift, they bypass the Halfling state and shift into the form of the full wolf," Nadia's mother stated rather plainly.

"Okay. And this means what exactly?"

"Under normal circumstances, natural born wolves are mated only to other natural born wolves," her mother said with what could only be described as a distaste in her mouth. "However, it would appear that somehow the Fates decided to throw my daughter a certain… 'twist' when choosing her mate."

"Again, I guess I'm not quite following—"

"*You* are her mate, Mr. Thompson," her mother declared. "I don't know why, or how, but somehow, the natural order of the universe was upended and my daughter was mated to you." Jack could almost detect a snarl forming in the corner of her mouth.

"Now, hold on a minute," Jack said, throwing his hands up in his own defense, "Yeah, I kissed her. I mean, who wouldn't? She's freakin' gorgeous. And she was naked and sitting in my lap…"

"Not *that* kind of mating, Mr. Thompson!" her mother practically shouted. Nadia cringed when her mother raised her voice. Her mother cleared her throat and gathered herself. "Wolves… mate for life, Mr. Thompson. Since you are not a natural born wolf, you do not *have* to follow this precept. You could choose to abandon any call of nature and simply walk away and no harm would come to you."

Jack nodded his head. "Okay. So, what's the downside?"

"Nadia is not so fortunate." She pulled her daughter to her roughly, yet in an embrace. "She is a natural born wolf. She is bound by the laws of the wolf. Once she is mated, it is for life. Her heart will love no other and her body will be surrendered to no other willingly." Then her mother glared at Jack, "And should she ever be taken physically by force, it would kill her."

Jack's eyes nearly bugged out of his head. "You gotta be kidding me."

"No, I am not. I am deadly serious," her mother growled. "For a real wolf, the mating is literally a life or death situation."

Nadia sat up and sniffled. She cleared her throat and looked at Jack. "There are other things involved with the mating that you should know, Jack. I couldn't expect anybody who is not familiar with our ways to simply accept it or to…"

"Tell me what I'm getting into," he said.

Nadia was shaking her head. "You don't understand what it entails. It means a bond that is stronger than life itself. It is more than a human marriage or even the sharing of—"

"Tell me, Nadia." He used the walking stick and stood from the chair. As he worked his way around the table to Nadia, he pulled the chair next to her out and sat so that he could hold her hand. He peered deeply into her eyes and then held her face. "Tell me everything. I need to know it all."

Nadia's mother stood up and lifted her chin high. "Perhaps once you are fully informed, you'll reconsider your position, Mr. Thompson."

182

Without looking at the bitch, Jack said, "Some-how, I doubt it."

Both squads had been pushed to their limits, and before their day was done, they checked in with the team doc for one last checkup. They drew blood and ran scans and checked heart rates and reflexes. It was getting to be routine, but it had to be done to make sure their augmentation regimen didn't need tweak-ing.

When the doc let them go, they all went to the locker room then hit the showers. The hot water went a long way towards washing away the dirt, grime, sweat, and stress of a long day of training.

"Yo, Spanky," Lamb shouted over the sounds of the others cracking wise.

"Yo, yourself."

"Hey, when you guys were new, did you train as long and hard as this or did they ramp it up because of what happened to the other squad?" Lamb asked.

"Honestly?" Spanky responded. "I think it's a lit-tle of both."

Popo added, "Yeah, I think maybe we trained as hard, but not so much on the tactics. It was more physical training."

"So, you guys went for twelve solid from the get-go?" TD asked.

Dom thought a minute. "Maybe not at the very first. But it wasn't long after the augmentation kicked in that the trainers kicked it up to that. I'd say maybe a week?" The others nodded.

"I think they started you guys out full bore because we need two squads ready ASAP." Spanky added.

Gus asked, "Had the squads ever lost a member before this? I mean…like a single person or something?"

Apollo answered, "This was our first fatality. And to lose a whole squad like that…man, it was tough." They were all quiet for a moment as the original squad members reflected on their fallen comrades and the new members realized the possibilities. "It's worse than losing a brother. It was like losing half your family."

They all nodded and the Padre offered up a silent prayer then crossed himself.

"Well, you got me now to watch your back," Sanchez told Apollo with a wink. Apollo cracked a toothy grin and winked back.

"Oh, for the love of Pete…" Marshall muttered. "Get a room!" he laughed.

Dom laughed and asked, "Yo, Apollo, I gotta know something, man. How in the world can you fit that monster into such a little—"

"Hey!" Sanchez barked, pointing a finger at Dom. "Privileged information, *pendejo!*" The other members all laughed and ribbed Dom for pissing off their resident Latina hothead.

"Well, heck, I was just curious!" Dom laughed. "I mean, Christ, we could cut his cock off, stuff it into a uniform and stick a helmet on its head and people would think it was standing guard!" he laughed.

"And it would still be smarter than *you!*" she added.

"Ooh, burn!" Jacobs shouted tossing his soap at Dom. The others joined in with catcalls and insults at Dom and ribbing him for his stupid comment.

"Apollo, you gonna let your woman cut me to ribbons like that, man?" Dom asked.

Before he knew what happened, Sanchez swept his leg and laid him out on the shower floor. She stood over him holding a bar of soap in her hands threateningly and glared down at Dom. "I'm *nobody's* woman!" she shouted. "I'm my own person, and I belong to nobody!" She was shaking and she was pissed.

Dom's eyes were big and his arms were raised to show he was disarmed. Slowly he brought his hand over to the bar of soap and with one finger, he placed it against the soap and slowly pushed it away from his face. "Please, Sanchez. Be careful where you point that thing." His face was deadly serious. "We wouldn't want it to go off, now would we?"

Her face went blank and she stared at him sprawled on the floor, looking scared shitless. The rest of the members in the shower were dead silent. Slowly a smile cracked on her face. It spread to Dom's face and they both broke into laughter. She lowered her hand to him and helped him off the shower floor.

She leaned into him and gave him a slap on the back. "Sorry about that," he muttered.

"Yeah. I'll get over it."

"Just so I got this straight...Apollo's *your* bitch...right?" And they both started laughing again.

Franklin insisted that Matt show him the operations center again. If they were going to be including high altitude air support in the form of drones, Franklin wanted to be sure that the command center would be able to support it. At least, that was what he told Mitchell. Mitchell assured Franklin that the Operations Control Center was as state of the art as he could make it within the confines of the military supply chains, but Franklin asked that he indulge him.

When they entered the command center, Mitchell flipped on the lights and the computer screens booted up. Hard drives whirred to life and flat screens dropped down from recesses in the ceiling. Mitchell stepped up to the platform and motioned for Senator Franklin to follow him. "From here, we can follow our squad's actions, maintain communications, triangulate the combat grids, transition from satellite to helicopter based video feeds...and hopefully soon, we'll be able to add the drones to the mix. This is the nerve center of the operation when our troops are on the ground."

Franklin nodded, a smile spreading across his face. "Excellent." He walked across the control center, running his hand across the different keyboards and looking at the different screens. He looked back at Mitchell. "And all of this equipment is up to date? You aren't in need of anything newer?"

Mitchell reflected back to the attack. He knew exactly what they needed, but he also felt that it would never be approved. "We could sure use a dedicated satellite."

Franklin's brows rose slightly. "Satellite?"

Matt sat in the command chair and hit a series of buttons. "Senator, we've had to make do with borrowed satellites from other agencies, and even then, at their discretion, and those were so out of date that they failed us in the field." While Matt's attention was directed to his keypad, Franklin slipped the USB from his pocket and inserted it into the side of the computer station where he leaned. He did his best to keep his body in front of his actions so that it would be hidden from the colonel's view. He waited to feel it vibrate, indicating that the preloaded software had done its job and could safely be removed. It felt like it was taking forever.

Matt looked up at the overhead screen and indicated toward it with his chin. "If you'll notice the video feed here. This was taken when Second Squad was in Texas. We borrowed a piece of sh...a much older satellite that did not have microwave capabilities. We felt fortunate that it had IR capabilities." Matt fast forwarded to where the heat signatures faded in and out of view. "As you can see, we couldn't keep a track on our squad members because their body temperatures were nearly identical to the outside temperatures."

Franklin tried to pay enough attention to at least interact in the conversation. "Could it not at least show them in...what is it called? A bird's eye view?"

"IRL. Real life, no. That camera wasn't strong enough. We had to stretch the bird to its maximum to get this pixilated infra-red view," he said. "If we had an updated satellite...hell, even an old Cold War spy satellite...and get it repositioned into a synchronous orbit over North America we could make do. Surely there is *one* satellite that could be spared from one agency for this mission?"

Franklin continued to stare at the screen and observed as the bright red, fast moving tangos came into the scene and attacked and shredded the commandos. He hadn't realized he held his breath during the attack until it was over. The vibrating USB in his hand almost made him jump. He slowly pulled the small device from the side of the computer and slipped his hand into his pocket. "I can't imagine what it must have been like to watch that happen and feel so...helpless," he said softly.

Matt watched Franklin stare at the screen, and for a moment thought the man may actually have a heart. "It was the hardest thing I've done since assuming command."

"Matt, I will do everything in my power to see to it you get your drones and a dedicated satellite," Franklin said, coming to his full height. "If I have to shake down every federal agency that has one, we'll find one that fits your needs and get it put into service for your use only."

"We would truly appreciate it, sir."

"I think I've seen enough, Colonel." Franklin stood and turned for the door. "I'll do everything I can. Of that, you have my word."

Before either of them could make a move for the door, the lights in the command center shifted to red and began flashing. Franklin froze. "What is that?"

"Security breach." Matt answered. "Wait here, Senator. It may not be safe." He went for the door and shut it behind him. Stalking down the hall, he pulled his two-way from his belt and called for Laura. "Sitrep."

"Security breach, sir." Laura answered.

"I'm aware of that. What do we know?"

"Unauthorized computer access," Laura sounded out of breath. "Geeks are on it."

"Location?"

"OPCOM," she responded. Matt spun to a stop. *Fucking Franklin! I knew that bastard was up to something!*

"Security to OPCOM. If they encounter Senator Franklin along the way, detain him!"

"Yes, sir!"

Matt made it back to the operations center and kicked open the door. Franklin was nowhere to be found. Matt turned back out the door and encountered a security team coming up from the way he had just come. "Find Senator Franklin. Do *not* let him leave!"

"Sir, yes, sir!" they shouted and took off at a dead run.

Matt went into the operations room and accessed the internal security cameras. It didn't take him long to find Franklin. He was making his way past the elevators and towards a stairwell. The elevators would have automatically shut down when the security breach happened. Mitchell picked up the phone and dialed topside security. He notified them that the good Senator was heading up through the south stairwell. Meet him at the top and then escort him back down and to Mitchell's office. Let the son-of-a-bitch get winded taking five floors worth of stairs trying to make his escape.

Mitchell picked up his two-way again. "Laura, get Evan and meet me in my office. Topside security should have Franklin any moment now and will be escorting him back down."

"On our way, sir."

Mitchell made his way to his office, thinking the entire way. Franklin may be a United States Senator, but he broke the cardinal rule. Any breach of security here, and his ass was toast. Mitchell was authorized to use any force necessary to determine exactly what occurred and to what extent the damage was. And, if he deemed necessary, he could make Franklin disappear. But considering he was a Senator and sat on the Oversight Committee, he had damned sure better be able to prove that the damage was irreparable.

Mitchell approached his office to find Laura and Evan standing outside his door. Both looked very nervous as Matt opened the door and ushered them in. "Did he discover Evan?" Laura asked.

"He's the one who breached the computers," Matt answered. "I don't know why, I don't know how, and I have no clue if he had help. But I do know that he will not be a cooperative witness against himself." Matt turned to Evan. "Do you have anything in that lab of yours that will get this son-of-a-bitch to talk and tell the truth?"

Evan thought for a moment then smiled. "I think I have just the ticket."

"Will it hurt him?" Laura asked.

"If you mean, will it turn him into a vampire, then no. Will it turn him into a drooling mass of political crap…well…only for a little while." Evan smiled. "In fact, while he's under, he'll be *extremely* susceptible to suggestion." Evan wiggled his eyebrows.

"What do you mean?" Matt asked.

"I mean, that as long as you don't go crazy with the suggestions, you can come damned close to brainwashing him while he's under."

"And he won't remember a thing?"

"Nope. He'll totally forget the last twenty to twenty-four hours," Evan stated. "Just, please, if you do make suggestions, try not to get too crazy. If the suggestions are too far from the norm for him, it acts like a short in the wiring and causes them to get…wonky."

"Wonky," Matt repeated. He looked at Laura. "Must be one of those big-time science type words."

"Exactly!" Evan exclaimed.

"Go get it ready. He'll be here shortly and I have a feeling we're going to have to dose him up pretty good with that stuff."

"On it, boss. Back in two shakes."

Matt paced his office while Laura watched Evan from Matt's window. Matt caught movement from the window on the other side of his office and watched the security detail drag a kicking and screaming Franklin back towards his office. "Here the bastard comes now." Franklin tripped and did a face plant. The security patrol had handcuffed him. Matt chuckled. *The sanctimonious bastard has it coming.*

Shortly there was a knock at the Colonel's door. "Come!" The guards entered with a very disgruntled looking Senator Franklin in tow.

"I demand to know the meaning of this!" he screeched.

"You know exactly the meaning of this, Franklin."

"That's SENATOR Franklin to you!"

"How about *traitor*?" Laura said through gritted teeth.

"I *never*—"

"Enough!" Matt yelled. The anger was seething from him and for just a moment, Franklin almost wet himself. "Have a seat, Senator."

"I was just leaving. Before your apes tackled me!"

"Before you committed espionage, you mean," Laura added.

"Laura. I'll take care of this."

Evan approached the door with the hypodermic in his hand. "Ready, colonel."

"Franklin, you have one chance to tell me what you did before I *make* you tell me."

"I did nothing. I have no idea what you're talking about. I demand that you allow me to leave. I am a United States Senator and…"

"Do it," Matt said.

Evan took the senator by the arm and plunged the needle deep into his tricep.

"What the hell was *that*?" Franklin screeched.

"A little something to help you tell the truth," Matt stated.

"You can't do that! You can't...you can't...you...wow. I feel... I...I feel..." Franklin shook his head slowly. "The room...is fuzzy."

"Put him in the chair before he falls and hurts himself. Again," Matt ordered. The guards half dragged the Senator and placed him in the chair. They uncuffed one of his hands and ran the chain through the back of the chair and reconnected his wrist.

Matt walked over to face Franklin. He slapped him gently across the face to get his attention. "Hey! Are you still with me?"

Franklin looked up and smiled at him. "I know you." He squinted at Matt. "I really hate you, you know that?"

Matt smiled. He looked at Evan. "This is some pretty good stuff, eh?" Evan smiled and nodded back. Matt turned back to Franklin. "What did you do to our computers?" Franklin's head was bobbing up and down and a wee bit of drool was forming in the corner of his mouth. "Hey, shithead, what did you do to our computers?"

Franklin looked up at Matt again and smiled. "I stuck a bug in them." Then he chuckled and the drool slipped from his lips. "Yup. Stuck a bug in it so a hacker can steal all your little secrets."

Matt's jaw clenched. "Why?" Franklin's head started bobbing again. He slapped him again...harder this time. "Why did you do it, Franklin?"

"Why?" He acted like he really had to think why he did it. "Why? Because. I need to destroy you. You and the Monster Squad. Need to take you all down at one time," he said, his voice trailing.

Now Matt was pissed. "Why are you trying to take down the Monster Squad?"

"Because. If you keep going, you'll kill my Damien. And I have to protect him. I have to protect him. He's all I got left. All I got."

"How were you going to bring us down, Franklin?" Matt yelled at him.

Franklin jumped a little. "How? Ummm. Expose you. All your secrets. Inside job. Emails from your accounts to the outside and make you look like fools. Nobody believes in monsters. It's the real world. Silly rabbit, there's no monsters. Go back to sleep, it's just the wind…then bang! You're all gobbled up! Heeheeheehee…"

"Expose us and you expose yourself, Franklin. You'd go down with us," Matt said through clenched teeth.

"Plausible deniability. I don't know you, and you crash and burn because you are wasting tax payer dollars, you know that, don't you? Yes you are! Yes you are!" Franklin sounded like he was talking to a puppy.

Laura turned to Evan. "How much of that stuff did you give him?"

Evan nodded. "Mm, that's about the right dose. He's just an idiot."

Matt turned to Evan. "So how do we do this suggestion thing and make it right?"

"What do you want him to do?" Evan asked.

Matt thought for a moment, then grabbed a pen and pad. He scribbled some notes then handed the pad to Evan. Evan scanned it and then looked up at Matt. "Seriously?"

"Yes."

Evan smiled. "I think he's just twisted enough that this is doable. Just give me about ten minutes."

16

After Nadia had redressed and Jack helped her to calm down, they walked the grounds a bit. The gardens outside the dining hall were beautiful and Jack couldn't help but notice how Nadia seemed to fit perfectly here, but he couldn't seem to get her to open up to him. She always stayed one step away from him, just out of reach. She had led him out past the rock walls, beyond the ramparts surrounding the castle and toward the small natural woods that surrounded the island. When Jack looked back at the castle, he could see how, if the castle were shrouded in fog, one could almost imagine it floating above the earth on a cloud like a child's fairy tale.

He started to feel an ache in his legs and slowed himself. He found a fallen log and took a break. Sitting on the log, he rubbed his legs to try and stimulate the blood flow again. Nadia, who had barely spoken to him since they stepped outside the stone walls of the castle, slowly worked her way back towards him. She took a seat next to him and slowly inched her way closer to him. He stopped rubbing his legs and finally looked at her. "I don't bite, ya know." He gave her a cheesy grin.

The sadness in her eyes was heartbreaking. She laid her head on his shoulders and closed her eyes.

Jack sighed and patted her shoulder. He couldn't blame her for being upset. Who'd want to be stuck with him as a mate? She was a natural born wolf. He wasn't even a 'made' wolf. No, instead, his own government had stuck him with a needle and forced him to swallow pills to keep from changing. That was the source of his strength. His speed. His highly attuned hearing and eyesight. They hadn't created super*men*, but rather, low-powered werewolves. Wolves that never finished what nature…or would that be, the supernatural, intended.

"Look, you don't have to be stuck with me," he said. "We can find a way to break whatever this is so you can live your life the way you want it to be."

She lifted her head and gave him a quizzical stare.

"I mean it," he said. "You don't have to be mated to me. I'm sure there's a plant or herb or talisman or spell or magic bullet or some damn thing out there that can rid you of me. You can find yourself a nice natural born wolf and…and…well. Do whatever it was you pictured yourself doing."

Nadia slowly shook her head. She was shaking and Jack was ready to kick himself. Well, he would if his legs were healed better. Then he heard her giggling. So. She wasn't crying this time. Who could tell with women? Christ, he thought human women were complicated, he was never going to figure out female wolves.

"You are thick in the head, aren't you, Jack Thompson?" she said, tapping him on top of his head.

"Well, I've been accused of that a time or two," he said. "But I don't underst—"

"I do not want another," Nadia said flatly. "The mating is not just random."

"Huh?" Jack was thoroughly confused now. "But I thought your mom said…"

"No, Jack. The mating may seem to *strike* at random, but it is not random. We were pre-selected, even before we were born." She was smiling again.

"Wait a minute. I couldn't have known I was going to be a werewolf before I was born. Hell, I didn't even know until you told me just a little while…"

"No, Jack. We were selected to be mates long ago. Fate turned the wheels to make it happen," she said, caressing the side of his face.

Jack just nodded. He knew better than to argue with fate. "So then, why were you crying? Why be so upset?"

"Because the mating is not like a marriage, Jack. It binds us together at the soul. We will feel the same things, become one, not just in the flesh, but in our life force," she said, her face suddenly very serious. Still, she could see that Jack didn't understand. "If you get hurt, I will feel it. If I am in danger, you will know it. If one of us dies…"

Suddenly Jack figured it out. "The other dies, too."

She smiled sadly and nodded her head.

"So, when a wolf mates for life…"

"It is quite literal."

Jack sat quietly while it all digested in his mind. He slid down the log and sat in the green grass. He let it cushion him as she curled up next to him. He played with her hair as he contemplated the entire enchilada.

"Were you the one who plucked me out of the attack?" he asked her.

"No," she said. "It was my mother."

Somehow, this answer struck Jack as more than just odd, but downright strange. The woman seemed so...off to him. Emotionless, almost hateful, even where her own daughter was concerned. "Why would she do that?" he asked.

"Rufus asked her to," she said flatly.

"Is she always so 'warm and fuzzy'?"

Nadia lifted her head and looked at Jack strangely. "I would not think you would describe her in such a way."

"I was being sarcastic, actually," Jack said.

"Oh." Nadia nodded. "Then yes. She has always been so warm."

"And fuzzy?" Jack added.

"Only when she is turned. Then she is *very* fuzzy." Nadia laughed.

Jack groaned. "Okay. I guess I had that one coming."

They sat in silence for some time longer. Jack kept bouncing a hundred different thoughts through his head. Finally he asked Nadia, "If we mate, will you only be able to shift to the true wolf, or will you still be a werewolf?"

"Once my mate has accepted me, I will begin shifting to the Halfling form again."

"And if your mate doesn't accept you?" he asked.

"It will take time, but once my chosen one is gone from me, I will eventually change to the Halfling again."

"And how does your mate 'choose' you, once he does?"

Nadia spoke very carefully, "He must be absolutely sure of what he does. For there is no going back."

"He knows."

She simply nodded.

"So how does he do it?"

"He will take me," she said. "Either in human or wolf form."

Jack sat quietly for some time. Nadia was very still beside him. "You do realize I'll have to 'take you' in human form, right? You're making me take the little black pills again."

She smiled at his comment and nodded. "If I decide to *let* you, you mean," she said playfully.

"You couldn't stop me," Jack said. "I'm your mate. You'd die without me."

Nadia turned very serious when she turned to him, "And you could die with me, Jack."

"I think you would be worth it," he said as he lowered his mouth to hers.

Apollo had the squads separated into two equal groups. Colonel Mitchell had him work with the trainers to assess each person's strengths and weaknesses and formulate a working plan to fill each squads needs based on each person's abilities. He was torn as he thumbed through the grades and assessments made by Ms. Youngblood and the trainers. Each squad member was assigned different scores based on marksmanship, leadership abilities, sniper abilities, CQB ratings and each squad had certain needs. Apollo wanted to keep Sanchez with him, but at the same time, he worried that working with her might impede his judgment.

It was time to come clean about him and Maria's relationship and let the brass know that it was affecting his ability to do his job. At least, to this point. Part of him knew that she could work equally well on either squad, and part of him wanted her on his squad so that he could help keep her safe in a shit-hit-the-fan situation, but at the same time, he knew that she could hold her own with the best of them. He put the folders back into the pile and went to Laura's office. He stood outside her door for a moment and tried to think of a way to professionally tell his boss that he'd been screwing his teammate, but he just couldn't find the words. He almost turned around when Laura opened the door and nearly ran into him.

"Apollo! Sorry. I didn't expect to find you here. Can I help you?"

He cleared his throat and tried to find the words. "Ma'am, I…umm. I need to speak with you about a…umm...personal issue."

Laura paled. "Oh lord, you're not pregnant, are you?"

Apollo stepped back. "What?!"

Laura laughed, "Nothing, just trying to make you feel more at ease." She opened her door and ushered him in. "See, if you're not pregnant, then it's all gravy, right?"

"If you say so, ma'am," Apollo said as he walked into her office. Even though the chairs were oversized, his large frame barely fit them. And to top it off, he still felt like a little kid at the principal's office. He was just waiting for her to yell at him and call his mommy in to spank him, or stick his nose in the corner.

"So, what seems to be the problem?"

"Well, ma'am, I've been going over everybody's records. Trying to fit each member into which squad?"

"Yes, I remember the trainers said that you'd be best suited for the job."

"Well, ma'am...I, umm..."

"Spit it out, Apollo."

"Well, ma'am, I feel I may have a conflict of interest." There! Those were *good* words! Professional sounding words. Please, God, let them be enough for her!

"Because of your relationship with Sanchez?" Laura asked flatly.

Apollo didn't realize his mouth had fallen open, but he distinctly remembered having to close it. "You knew about that, ma'am?"

Laura actually laughed. "Who doesn't?" She stood up from behind her desk and walked around to Apollo's side. She was almost looking him square in the eye. "She's not exactly 'quiet' in the shower, Mr. Williams, if you catch my drift," Laura patted Apollo on the arm and signaled for him to get up. "Now, I suggest you go back to the files and just...do the best that you can." As Apollo stepped out of the door, Laura added, "We've always trusted your judgment in the past, and I'm sure that you can make the best decision *for the squads* now."

Apollo found himself standing back outside her door almost as confused as before he went into her office. Only now he knew that the brass was aware of his and Sanchez extracurricular activities. He sighed and headed back to the stack of folders. If Ms. Youngblood trusted he could do it without letting his personal feelings get involved, then he knew he could do it. He just had to detach himself from what he felt for Maria and place her based on what was best for the squads.

Senator Franklin woke up in a hotel suite and his head was killing him. It tasted like someone had washed his mouth out with battery acid and his eyes were blurry. Yet, something told him that he had to get out of there and back to D.C. He had to do something, but...he couldn't remember. It was just outside of his memories.

He sat on the edge of the bed and his hand rested on another person's butt. He allowed his eyes to focus and he realized it was a female butt. A very *nice* female butt. He had no idea who she was or how she got there, but she was in his bed and she had no clothes on. He smiled to himself. *Still got it.*

He stumbled out of the bed and to the bathroom. The plastic placard said, 'Welcome to the Ritz-Carlton, New Orleans'. *New Orleans?* Franklin ran the water in the sink and took the glass from the edge and rinsed his mouth out. He carried the glass out to the room and found the ice bucket. Most of the ice was melted but there was still some in it. He shoved the glass down into the bucket and scooped up some of the ice. It felt good in the back of his throat and he drank down the melted water. He walked over to the window and cracked open the heavy curtains. The sun was either just coming up or just going down. He had no idea which. The heavenly body in the bed let out a tiny little moan and rolled over. He could just see a glimpse of the side of her breast and decided that he must have had one hell of a nice time. He ran his hand along his manhood and it came back sticky. He chuckled to himself. *I may not remember a lot, but at least I got lucky.*

His head was muddled, but he had this nagging feeling in the back of his mind that he needed to do something. Desperately do something…important. It was on the edge of his mind, if he could only remember what it was. Franklin rested his head against the window pane and closed his eyes; if he could only remember why he was here in New Orleans. What could have brought him here? Did he have personal business here, or was it government business? Too many questions racing through his mind. His ears picked up the sound of a helicopter in the distance and the ghost of a memory flashed in his mind. Something about airplanes or air travel. He knew he would have flown here, but this tickle meant more. He needed to do something about an airplane or…air support. Yes. He needed to make sure somebody had air support. He stepped away from the window and got another glass of the melting ice. It soothed his aching head and wet his throat.

This air thing was important. He knew it. He glanced around the room. The telephone, the radio, the television, the placard for the fire exit, the placard advertising the best in satellite television…satellite. Satellite? Floods of fuzzy memories came rushing into his head. He *had to get air support and satellite coverage for the Monster Squad!* He didn't know why it was so important, but he knew it was. It was life or death…but whose? His? He was about to hyperventilate, but he felt like he had to get this done. He didn't know why…it made no sense. He hated Mitchell and his fucking monster hunters. They threatened Damien's very existence…well, in a roundabout way. But this air support, this was important. It couldn't wait.

He glanced at his watch. Patek Phillipe? Where was his Rolex? What the fuck was going on? No…it had to wait. He stepped to his pants and fished out his phone. He scrolled through his Blackberry and found the head of the Oversight Committee. It was either late or early, but this was important.

Franklin waited until the man picked up the other end and began babbling about how the Monster Squad had to have their own satellite and drones. Predator drones if we could swing it. "Budget be damned, we have to make it happen!"

He argued until he was blue in the face, although the lead on the OC didn't need convincing, he just wasn't sure that it was actually Franklin on the other line. He assured Franklin they'd get it done, though he wasn't sure what caused the change of heart in Franklin. Even Franklin couldn't explain it; he just knew it had to be done, that it was life and death. Life or death, dammit!

When he hung up the phone, he finally breathed a sigh of relief. He tossed the phone down onto the pile of clothes and went back to the window. Ah. The sun was coming up. Good. The start of a new day. A wonderful day. He heard his bedmate shift under the covers on the bed and he stole a glance at her curvaceous form. He walked over to the bed and ran his hand along the firm round cheek of his bedmate's ass. He licked his lips then leaned down and bit down on the succulent cheek. It bought him a giggle from under the covers. He couldn't see her face still, but who cared at this point. He wanted something to remember from this trip. He began kissing his way up her back and along the side of her ribs, working his way to her breasts.

She giggled and play-swatted at him. "That tickles," she murmured.

"I got something for you," he said and placed her hand on his stiffening manhood. She giggled again and squeezed it in her delicate hand. He moaned when she did.

"Are you wanting to play again already?" she asked. "I barely got any sleep."

"Who wouldn't want to play again?" he teased, pulling the pillows away from her. He finally saw her face and was captivated by her beauty. Deep auburn hair, emerald green eyes, curvy hips and full breasts.

"Okay," she said, and rolled over again.

She started licking her way up his leg and took him with her oh-so-talented mouth. Franklin gasped at just what she was capable of. For the slightest moment, he actually thought, *this is marriage material*, before he came back to his right mind. She pushed him back on the bed further and lifted herself over him, suckling him like he had never been in his life. When she leaned over him, he reached down and cupped her heavy breasts in his hands and played with them. Lifting their heft and kneading them between his fingers. She moved around further on the bed and he worked his other hand around to squeeze her beautiful ass. He cupped each cheek and squeezed and worshiped her glorious body with his hands as her wonderful mouth milked him. He reached further between her legs to slip his finger into her and felt…balls?

Wait? Were these…actually…testicles? Large, dangling *NUTS?!* Franklin froze, but she kept working away on him. His mind was racing a mile a minute and she never missed a beat. The full force of what was occurring hit him, just as his own testicles betrayed him and fired his own Senatorial semen down her…er, …*his* throat. She continued until he went completely limp and Franklin was still frozen to the sheets. She sat up and Franklin's eyes betrayed him…although he begged them not to look, they did. From the waist up, she was ALL woman. Beautiful, curvaceous, bountiful woman. From the waist down, she was built like a porn star and had the largest nuts he had ever seen. She leaned over him and kissed him deeply on the mouth, his own froth still on her lips. When she was done she slid off the bed and said, "I got to pee. Don't worry, sweetie. You don't have to do me this time. Last night was enough."

Franklin thought he was going to be sick. He lay on the bed and felt his stomach turn. He looked at the table and saw an empty bottle of Jack Daniels and a two-liter bottle of Coke. Those were definitely his favorite drinks. And he did like redheads. And man, what an ass that one had…but she had much more. He felt his stomach start to turn again when he heard her peeing in the toilet…obviously standing up.

He got up and looked for his clothes. They were scattered everywhere. Intermixed with women's clothes and an emerald green dress and high heels. He kept shaking his head. This can't be real, this can't be real, this can't be real…she came walking back out with her flag waving in the wind. *Oh my God, it's real.* She flopped down on the bed and pulled the sheet back over her.

He went into the bathroom and stepped into the shower. He turned the water full blast on hot and let it scald him. He rinsed his mouth and spit it into the shower. *Damage control…think damage control. Nobody knows. And what was the harm, really? I thought she was a woman. She performed oral sex. No harm there, right? A mouth is a mouth, right? It's not like I'm going to catch AIDS from a blowjob, right?* He shampooed his hair and then started lathering his body. But when he ran the washrag across his rear end, he felt a soreness that he really thought should *not* be there.

Franklin sat down in the shower and began to cry. "Oh, no…"

17

Nadia and Jack worked their way back to the castle proper just as the sun fell behind the horizon. Rufus was waiting for them when they entered the great room. He was sitting in front of a fire with a book and drinking from a Brandy glass. "I trust you had an enlightening day."

"You have no idea," Jack said as they entered, hand in hand. Rufus took notice and raised an eyebrow.

"I see that what Natashia has told me is true then?"

"Natashia?"

"My mother," Nadia answered.

"If you mean that Nadia and I are mates, then yes," Jack said.

Rufus merely nodded. "This is…unfortunate."

"Why is that?" Jack asked. "From what I understand, some wolves can go their entire lives and never find a mate."

Rufus set down his drink. "Jack, what do you intend to do once your wounds are healed?"

"Go back to my team."

"And Nadia?" Rufus asked. "She would go with you?"

Jack looked at Nadia who suddenly had fear in her eyes. "I hadn't thought of…"

"No. You hadn't. Your kind *hunt* and *kill* her kind, Jack. Is this the future you would bring to our Nadia?"

"No, of course not."

"Then what?" Rufus went on. "Stay here with us?"

"I don't know. I guess I could. I hadn't really thought that far…"

"Jack, we brought you here…we *saved* you from slaughter at the hands of the *Lamia Humanus* and their forces for one thing and one thing only. To take word of our struggles to your people in order to put an end to the wholesale slaughter of innocent lives." Rufus stood and faced Jack. "You would throw away everything we put at stake for…what? Puppy love?"

Nadia gasped, "This is not fair! You know that the mating is much more than—"

"Silence! Know your place!" Rufus ordered.

"Now hold on just a goddamned minute," Jack struggled to keep on his feet, as his legs were killing him but he worked his way between them. The walk through the castle and out to the woods recharged his batteries, but took a real toll on his still-healing legs. "What happened to the 'peaceful vampire host', huh? What's with the orders and barking at her like she's a slave?"

Rufus glared at Nadia then gave Jack a solemn look. "She *is* a slave, Mr. Thompson. Her entire family are my slaves. A gift from the *lupus prosapia* to me. To do with as I wish."

Jack was aghast. "And here I thought you were just being a nice guy and all, but you're just a modern day slaver." Jack's face twisted in disgust. "I should have known better than to trust a damned blood-sucker!" He raised his walking stick to knock Rufus' head from his shoulders, but Nadia stopped him.

"Jack! No." She held his hand back. "It's not like you think."

"It's exactly as he thinks."

"Rufus," Nadia pleaded. "Why do you antagonize him?" Jack pushed against her to get to Rufus, but she held him easily at bay. "He can still do what you need done as my mate."

"How?" they both asked at the same time.

"True, my family was gifted to Rufus to serve him, but he does not treat us as slaves." Jack eased up and Rufus sighed, falling back to his chair. "Be honest with him, Rufus. He needs honesty now more than ever. His own people have manipulated him enough for three lifetimes." Rufus looked at the two of them then ceded her point.

"Rufus treats us as his own family," she began. "Remember when I told you that he sold off most of his holdings to help support his family?" Jack nodded at her, "That was to support us and to keep us safe and away from those who might hurt us. To prepare safe places for us to shift during the full moon, and to provide this island with safe places for us to shift and run and hunt during other times." She waved her hand toward Rufus. "He is as much like a father to us as any of our own fathers. He is no slave owner."

She now turned to Rufus, "And you…how could you say such things? I know you want him to

212

take our plight to his people, but do not try to manipulate him like this. He deserves better!" She reached out and pulled Jack in tight to her. "He *is* my mate."

"Or, will be soon if I have my way," Jack added.

Rufus nodded and gave her a wave of his hand. "Go on. Please, explain to me how you two can be mated and he can go back to his people?"

Nadia paused. "He can either mate with me and then return to his people to deliver the message…and maybe return one day…"

"Or…" Jack asked.

"Or I can go with you and we do not tell them that I am wolf."

"No!" Jack and Rufus both interjected at the same time.

"At least we can agree on something," Jack said. He turned to Nadia and held her face in his hands. "Look, Nadia, I'll be the first to admit that this is all going really, really fast, okay? I mean, I feel things for you that…I can't explain. Maybe it is this fate thing you've been talking about, or maybe it's just plain magic. I really don't know. I don't care! But I do know that I won't do anything that puts you in any kind of danger, alright? It just ain't going to happen." Jack turned to Rufus. "Look, if she really is some kind of slave or indentured servant or…whatever, I'll make a deal with you."

Rufus looked up at Jack. "Go on."

"I'll take your plea to my people and I'll give it my absolute best shot to explain to them what's going on. Hell, I'll even try to get my CO to agree to a sit down with you so you can explain to him what's going on. But either way…win, lose or draw, she's free to leave if she wants to." Rufus started to argue, but Jack stopped him. "That's the only way. I'll do what you want, and I'll give my word that I'll give it my best shot, but I get Nadia. Free and clear. If we both want to leave afterwards, then we are free to do so. Or if she talks me into coming back here and we live happily ever after making puppies or...whatever the hell it is werewolves do, then...so be it." Jack stuck his hand out to Rufus to shake. "Deal?"

Rufus contemplated Jack's proposal. "How do I know that you simply won't return to your people for a short time, ignore our plight and then tell me that you tried your best?"

"Because I'm a man of honor. I stand by my word. It's all I have."

Rufus stood and took Jack's hand. "Agreed."

Colonel Mitchell pulled the Humvee into the hangar and met Laura at the topside guard shack. "Everything go as planned?"

Laura rubbed her temples. "Yes, sir. I definitely need some sleep, though," she responded. "We got Franklin set up in the Ritz in New Orleans, the IT Geeks did their thing, everything went smooth as warm butter," she said. "Just, one thing, Matt. Please, if we ever need to do something like this again, let me stay behind and have somebody else supervise. I feel like I need a week's worth of a hot shower after that one."

"I thought you CIA types did this sort of thing all the time?"

"I haven't been with the company in a long time, Colonel. I think I've grown a bit since then."

Matt smiled at her. "Does somebody have a conscience now?"

"Just have one of the guys do it next time, okay?"

"I owe you, Laura. Next time, I'll send one of the guys," Mitchell said, unloading his gear from the back door of the truck. "How long did it take the Geek Squad to crack the encryption?"

"They finally smashed through it on the plane," she replied. "His hacker name is f3rr3747ru7h, or 'ferret for truth', AKA Eugene Sanders. Apparently he was a minor player in the wikileaks fiasco and then went underground. How Franklin tracked this guy down, I have no clue, but it was his signature all over the algorithm."

"Geek squad is positive?"

"Oh yeah. They used the routers on the plane and tracked an ISP embedded in the algorithm back to a series of user accounts tied to him. Most are still active, so he's definitely our guy."

Matt set his stuff on the hand cart and headed to the elevators. "So, if Franklin suddenly wakes up one day and remembers everything and tries to go back to Plan A?"

"He'll call on Sanders and the whole thing gets released to the media."

"What are the odds Franklin will check the data prior to release?" Matt asked as he entered the elevator and pushed the down button. Laura entered with him, still rubbing her eyes.

She stifled a yawn. "Honestly, sir? Knowing Franklin, he'll be so manic that he'll probably run with what he has, but should he actually be smart enough to *check* it first...well, then he'll know that we'll have something on him to go public with should he decide to screw with us again. Either way, we should be good to go."

"Excellent work, XO." He gave her a light punch in the arm. "You did good."

"For a girl," she said with a grin.

"For anybody, Laura." Matt grinned back. "Unfortunately, you only have until tomorrow to catch up on your beauty rest."

"Sir?"

"First thing tomorrow I need you putting together a team that can handle our new predator drones."

Laura raised an eyebrow at him. She was barely off the plane and Matt already assumed they were getting them? "Are you sure, sir?"

"Head of the OC called me first thing this morning and said that Franklin called him at sunrise blathering on about how they *had* to get us our own satellite and predator drones. The satellite is in the works, and the drones are on the way. Everything is approved. Apparently Franklin was the only thing standing in the way the whole time." Matt smiled.

"Sunrise? Jesus, Matt, we were barely out of his room..."

"Don't look a gift horse in the mouth, Laura. You did good." The doors opened and he stepped out. He turned to her as she exited. "Get some rest. You deserve it."

Laura walked back to her office and plopped down on her couch. She lay there for a moment and thought, *I really should go back to my place and get a good night's rest. I really should just go home, crawl into a soft, flannel sheeted bed and hope to sleep through my alarm clock. I should, but I can't get up. So maybe a catnap and then I'll do it.* She rested her eyes for a moment, and fell dead asleep.

Jack stood at the window and stared out at the open sea. He was lost in thought when Nadia came into his room and wrapped her arms around him. He could smell her scent. He knew the full moon was close because his senses were so heightened. Nadia had been teaching him about how, as the full moon approached, his senses would sharpen and his energy levels would skyrocket. How his desires would increase and his temper could shorten. He felt so protective of her.

"I remember when I first saw you, I thought maybe you were a vampire," he said softly.

"Really?"

"Yeah. Your skin is so pale and your hair so light. And your eyes…I've never seen eyes that color before."

"Hmm. Well, you should see me as a Halfling." She nuzzled his neck.

"I've been meaning to ask you...once we mate, will you then be able to control your shift and be a Halfling?"

"Shortly thereafter." He could feel her rubbing her face against his neck and inhaling his scent.

"So...no werewolf can shift all the way to the wolf? I mean, unless they've found their mate? Right?" he asked.

"True."

"So, if I wasn't taking the bane, I would shift into a wolf instead of a Halfling?"

"No, sweetheart," she explained. "Created wolves can only shift into the Halfling. Even in the presence of their mate. Only the natural born can shift to the wolf."

Jack only nodded, yet Nadia sensed a sadness to him. "What is wrong, Jack?"

He sighed and leaned his head against hers. "I feel a loss." He shook his head, the words escaping him. "I really can't explain it, but...I *want* to be a wolf. Not a Halfling like you describe, but a wolf. Like I saw you shift into." He turned and faced her, staring into her eyes. "I want to shift *with you* and run through the forests together, free and unhindered. I want to be wolf with you. I can feel it inside me. It's something I want more than I've wanted anything in my life."

"Oh, Jack." She pulled him to her and kissed him. "I wish I could give this to you, but it isn't within my power."

"Could anybody give this to me?" he asked.

"No," she said softly. "It is impossible."

Jack slowly nodded his head and pulled Nadia close to him. She rocked slowly in his arms as he held her. "If something happened to me before we were mated, is it possible you could ever find another mate? Maybe a natural born wolf?" he asked.

She shook her head. "No. There is only one mate for each wolf. Some wolves go their entire lifetime and never find their mate."

"So I guess your mom was lucky she found hers."

"Very true."

"Didn't sweeten her disposition any, though, did it?" he muttered.

"Mother wasn't always so bitter." Nadia said. "It wasn't until we were gifted to Rufus from the pack that she…changed." Nadia turned toward the open door to hear if anybody was within earshot. "The pack has its own hierarchy, and our family was very well respected, very high within the ranks."

"Okay. Go on," Jack urged her, hoping to gain some understanding to her mother's behavior.

"When our old pack master left and the challenge was laid out for the new pack leaders to lay claim to the head of the pack, my father was away. He was the strongest and was expected to take the reins of leadership. It was his right and he was the heir. The full moon was upon them before he could return and the rules of the pack are clear. A claim to leadership must be made and those who stake their claim must fight for the role of pack master on the eve of the full moon." Her face was so full of sadness that Jack's heart broke for her. "Three laid claim and the victor who became the new leader of our pack

219

had borne a grudge against my father for many, many years. He also knew that my father would most likely kill him to take back the pack…so, he banished my family, more or less."

"How can he banish you if you were part of the pack?" Jack asked. "It doesn't make sense. What little I know of werewolves tells me that they protect the pack no matter what."

"Usually, this is true, but sometimes, politics come into play," Nadia explained. "The new pack master was acting as a surrogate for a female wolf…a blood-thirsty and ruthless woman who would stop at nothing to continue ruling the pack, even through a surrogate. She knew that father would take his right-ful place and things would change, so she engineered the takeover very carefully." Nadia turned her face to hide her eyes from him. "It nearly destroyed my father."

"Why didn't your father challenge the new pack master when he returned?"

Nadia sighed and shook her head. "The wheels had been set into motion before his return. For many years, we had a blood covenant with Rufus. We were *familia* with the vampire coven. The new pack master used the security clause to banish us, to bond us for-ever to Rufus."

"What if Rufus wanted to set your family free?" Jack asked. "Could your father then challenge the pack master?"

"It would break the covenant," she whispered. "Neither my father nor Rufus would allow the dis-grace of breaking the blood covenant."

"Where is your father now?"

"He is doing business for Rufus on the mainland, but he will return soon. The moon will force him to return."

"All of you lock yourself in the dungeon?"

"It's not really a dungeon," she said. "It's really more of a basement. But this is a castle and dungeon sounds more appropriate considering its use every month."

"Still, it doesn't sound very fun."

"The entire experience isn't much fun."

Jack pondered a moment then asked her, "How many wolves are here on the island?"

"Twelve. Most are my family, including aunts, uncles, cousins...but there are a few who were already here as a security detail. They're true security."

"And all of you lock yourself in the basement for that one night?"

"Yes. It's the one night that Rufus is truly vulnerable."

"But it's at night, so, he's not really vulnerable, right? I mean, he really only needs the security during the daylight hours." Nadia nodded. "How many vampires does Rufus have here with him?"

Nadia gave Jack a puzzling stare. "Are you milking me for information? Assessing the strengths of the castle, soldier?" she said playfully.

Jack laughed. "No. Not really. I'm just curious. You don't have to tell me. I was just wondering..."

"There are a little over two dozen vampires here, but most are women."

"Oh, that's right. More women to increase the chances of having kids..."

Nadia laughed again. "Perhaps if Rufus were a natural born vampire. He was created, just as you were. "But he was sort of... 'adopted' into a natural born family. He is considered an heir, but he'll never truly be accepted as a natural born. Nor will he ever bear fruit."

"Oh yeah," Jack said. "I remember now him telling me how he got made." Jack pointed at his head. "Not the brightest bulb and all that."

"Rufus will forever be in a young man's body, with a young man's appetites. He prefers to be surrounded with many female lovers," she said. "But enough speak of other people's lovers. Come. Let us get you fed and get your strength up."

"Get my strength up?"

"You *did* intend to mate with me, yes?" she said with a sly smile. "You will need your strength."

The squads were in the common room listening to the cleanup crews give their spiel. For all intents and purpose, the initial training for the new members was complete, but there were still a few procedural processes that they needed to be aware of. For the veterans of the group, this was old news. Apollo and Spanky sat and drew doodles on their notepads. Donnie did his best to stay awake, but was failing miserably. Drool was threatening to escape the corner of his mouth. Hammer sat ramrod straight, eyes wide open, staring straight ahead. Dom and Popo debated that he slept with his eyes open. Finally, Dom reached over and waved a hand in front of his face and when he failed to respond, they both snickered and debated ways to screw with him. Meanwhile, the cleanup crews droned on with their procedures and the new members gave them the courtesy of trying to appear to listen, albeit with glazed looks on their faces.

After approximately thirty minutes of their monotonous droning, Tracy muttered to Lamb, "Do we really have to listen to this crap?" Lamb shrugged and yawned. Before the yawn was completed, both found themselves falling to the floor in a tumble, their chairs having been pulled from under them.

Hank Michaels stood behind them, holding the legs to their chairs in his hands, his face twisted in disgust. He dropped the chairs and walked to the front of the room.

"What's your problem, man?" Gus asked, getting up from the floor.

"No shit, dude. Uncool, brother..." Lamb began.

"I've watched you newbies blow off just about everything that didn't involve shooting or blowing something up," Hank said through gritted teeth.

"Padre..." Apollo began.

"Don't!" Hank warned. "This needs to be said." Hank turned toward the cleanup crews with a wave of his hand. "These guys do ten times the work we *ever* do and never get one single 'thank you' or an iota of recognition. They are the ones who *truly* keep the people safe once we eliminate the threat. But you wouldn't know that because you haven't heard a word they've said, would you? Do any of you even have a clue what they actually do?"

The new squad members all looked at each other and gave shrugs or shook their heads. A few muttered to the negative.

"They've been addressing you for the past half hour trying to give you the details of their job in order to drill home the importance of *how* you do your job in order to keep people safe, and you're all falling asleep or worse, totally ignoring them." Hank stared them down. "You should all be ashamed of yourself."

Hank turned and stalked away muttering to himself. Sanchez could have sworn she heard him say something about 'romper room' and 'fucking toddlers'. "What's got up his ass?" she asked.

Apollo leaned in toward her and the others, "I'll fill you in later. For now, let's let these guys finish up."

The cleanup crew guys milled about for a few moments, unsure how to carry on. One glanced at his watch and then at the crowd of operators. "Umm, we're about out of time. I, uh…well. Here it is in a nutshell. You guys are the rock stars, okay? You get to go out and blow stuff up, right? You go in the field and kill the bad guys, okay? Well, we're the poor schmucks who have to go in behind you in the bio-suits and clean up after you." He nudged one of the fellows next to him who held up one of the bulky suits with the re-breather attached. "These things are hot, heavy, bulky and just generally a pain in the ass to work in, especially in hot weather. But we do the stuff that has to be done." Another cleanup crew held up some of the tools of the trade, shovels, industrial drum liners and with his foot pushed a wheeled vacuum in front of them. "When you guys splatter a monster, we have to make sure there are *no* biologicals left behind."

The tech stepped forward and used his hands to emphasize his point. "Imagine vampire blood left behind where a child might accidentally be exposed? Or you splatter a zombie and the body fluids get into somebody's well? Depending on the type of zombie, an entire family, or even a group of families could be exposed, spreading the disease exponentially." Slowly the new squad members began to pay attention. "That's why you train to take the head shot with the zombie infestation. Yes…it is the only way to truly stop one, but you could also throw one into a wood chipper. It's just a whole lot messier. And the chance of spreading the disease increases a thousand fold. A field mouse gets hold of a tiny piece of tissue and *voila*! New infection, and a short time later, we start all over…just with a new vector."

The tech looked at his watch again. His time was up. He sighed. Somehow he felt he failed to drive the point home. "The point is, boys and girls, don't make a mess if you don't have to. Don't use a canon to swat the mosquito, okay? The less mess you make means the easier our job is and the less time we have to be exposed to the rest of the world who always asks, 'why are there spacemen washing the Johnson's house out?' It's a thankless job, but it has to be done." With that he stepped back and simply said, "Thank you for your time." The cleanup crews began re-crating their gear for mobilization.

The squad members were about to break up when Sanchez cornered Apollo. "Nice speech there, but what gives with Michaels? What was his little outburst about? I mean, the guy hardly says two words the whole time we train with him, then BAM! He goes off on us for nothing." The other new members had gathered around her. They, too, were curious what his problem was.

Apollo sighed. "Yeah, I told you I'd fill you in." He scratched at his jaw and contemplated how best to breach another man's story. "You all know the rest of our history pretty much...I mean, what there is to know. But, the Padre? He's sort of tough to describe. I really wish it were him telling y'all this, 'cuz it's his story, ya know? But, he ain't opening up, so...I guess it's really up to me.

"He used to be this total operator with the Jarheads. Volunteered for all these suicide missions, but always came back. He was the best of the best. Used to train operators, too. They said that you could drop his ass in the Antarctic in his skivvies with nothing but a compass and a pocket knife and two weeks later you'd find out he overthrew the dictator of some backwater third world country, and he'd be sitting on the beach drinking a mojito. If you looked in the dictionary under the word 'badass' his picture was right next to it."

"Okay, we gotcha. He was the real deal," Jacobs said, waving his hand on for Apollo to continue. "So what happened to him?"

"That's just it, bro. Nobody knows. One day he's volunteering to jump in the muck, he's trained himself to be one of the world's foremost knife and sword fighters, he's like a one-man army…then he just comes back from a mission and tells his CO that he's done. He can't do it anymore. He wants to 'conscientious objector' out."

"What?!" Tracy exclaimed. "Nobody goes from badass to pussy in a heartbeat."

"Nobody said he was a pussy." Apollo shot Gus a stern look. "Something happened. I dunno what. Maybe one too many innocents on his last mission? Too much collateral damage? Who knows? But that's what I'm told.

"Anyway, his CO didn't know what to do with him. He still had about sixteen months left on his last hitch, so they did the only thing they knew *to* do with him. They assigned him to the God Squad. He worked with a Catholic priest and a Lutheran minister for the last of his hitch and…I dunno, I guess it stuck, 'cuz when he got out, he left and never looked back.

"Word was, he put on a robe, slapped on some sandals and a cross and went to some little border town in like Arizona or New Mexico or some shit and found an abandoned church. He just moved in and started rebuilding it with what little money he had. The locals started coming to his church, and word is he started an orphanage. Anyway, here's where shit gets real.

"One night about four years ago, a pack of baby vamps hit this small town of his and they slaughter *everybody*. The Padre didn't know that they even existed, but he knew that this gang was killing his people and he went nuts. Said that 'God spoke to him.' Told him to 'Protect my flock.' And Hank went off on the vamps. He had no weapons, but he pulled a wooden cross from the graveyard and went Mickey Mantle on them. One survivor actually said that the Padre there literally ripped the arm off of one of the vamps and *beat him to death* with it!"

"Oh my God…" someone muttered.

"Then he hears the orphans screaming and he knew some of them got past him and got into his church," Apollo's face turned solemn. "There were three of them. And they feasted on those kids before Hank could get back in to stop them. It damn near killed him losing those kids."

"No doubt," Mueller said, thinking of his own son back home.

"Anyway, the worst part was, one of the dead vamps fell into the town well," Apollo said, his eyes searching the others and seeing the horror spread across their faces. "By the time the squad and the cleanup crew got there, it was too late. Hank and seven other people were all that survived from the entire town. Nearly a hundred and thirty people all gone from start to finish."

"No wonder he snapped during the presentation," Marshall said softly. "He lived through a nightmare."

"When the squads arrived and the cleanup crews were trying to do their thing, Hank shows up and tells the squad leader that he's coming back with us. The squad leader tells Hank politely to go back to his church and do whatever it is that preachers do and Hank laid him out on his ass." Apollo smiled, rubbing his chin. "Even with all of the training, augmentation and strength enhancements, he not only held his own, but got the upper hand. When the squad leader got his feet back under him and tried to retaliate, Hank disarmed him, took his knife and put him back on his ass. Then he told him, 'if you people hunt these monsters, then I'm coming with you.' The other squad members were about to drop him but the squad leader ordered them to stand down. He saw the pain in his eyes…how broken he was from the attack. So we had a chat with the Colonel. They pulled his service jacket from back in the day and Hank got a ride back with us. The rest is history."

"That must have been some squad leader," Lamb said. "I think if it had been me, I would have painted the wall with his brains."

"Yeah, well, when the weather changes, my jaw still hurts," Apollo said, cracking a toothy smile. "But I don't regret it one bit. The man is a walking Cuisinart with a blade. Give him his machete and his *katana* in a fight and he's more deadly than any three people with carbines." The others shot him shocked glances. "I once watched him slice open a vampire from nutsack to forehead with one motion. *That* shit is impressive."

"Super warrior or not, I have a newfound respect for the man," Ing said.

18

Franklin walked the halls toward his office, feeling the eyes of his peers on him. Somehow, he felt, they knew his dirty little secret, but they couldn't. Nobody knew but himself and the redhead at the hotel, and she kept calling him Stewart. Thankfully, she...he...it? What should he call her? Regardless, she didn't recognize him, or know his name. His secret was safe.

Sex scandals were not uncommon on the Hill, but a homosexual sex scandal for a heterosexual Senator from the Bible-belt would ruin him both politically and financially. He slipped past the front and into his office, ignoring his secretary. She tried to catch up with him, but he wanted nothing to do with her. He shut the door on her and locked it as she continued to attempt to talk to him through the door. He'd deal with her later. He could feel himself trying to panic and he needed to calm himself.

It was barely 9AM, but he desperately needed a drink. His hands shook as he poured the Jack into the crystal. When he reached for the Coke, memories of the Ritz Carlton room and the redhead flooded back to him. Flashes of her splayed across his bed, her auburn hair spilled across the pillow, her round hip slipping from the sheets, the flash of breast just showing in the crack of light through the curtains. He felt a growing twinge of excitement in his loin and he practically dropped the soda at his own surprise at himself. He shouldn't feel want for a person like that. She wasn't a *she* for shit's sake! She had more... Not just a more, but a *huge*, swinging one that dwarfed his own. That just wasn't right...on so many levels. It was bad enough that such a seductive and gorgeous creature should even *have* a penis, but even more wrong that she should have one so large!

Franklin forced himself to calm his hands and pour the soda into his glass. He gulped the drink down and made another. He went to his desk and sat down hard. Resting his head in his hands, he couldn't shake the image of the redhead. What she had done to him...that he could remember...and how much he enjoyed it. He kept seeing her eyes, the curve of her jaw, the lines of her face. The shape of her ass haunted him, taunting his memories. She was so...damned *perfect*...except, she wasn't. He reached for his drink and slammed it back hard.

He reclined in his chair and swiveled back and forth. *Maybe with enough whiskey I could convince myself it was just a huge clit?* He joked with himself and chuckled, then shook his head to clear it. What the hell was he thinking?! Why was he allowing himself to be so enamored with this...person?

His intercom buzzed. Franklin jumped at the noise then sighed to himself. He wouldn't be able to put off his secretary forever. "What is it, Ellen?"

"The jeweler called, sir. Your Rolex is repaired and ready," she replied.

Franklin glanced at his wrist. The Patek Phillipe was still strapped to it. His Rolex hadn't been on his dresser so he put the Patek back on this morning. He knew it was 'wrong' but…he couldn't put his finger on 'why'. "Which jeweler was it?"

"Sir?"

"Which jeweler called, Ellen? I don't know where my damned watch is!" he yelled at the box.

"Huguley's, sir. In Annapolis." Ellen sounded as if she were about to cry. Surely she thought her boss was losing his mind.

"Thank you, Ellen."

Franklin looked up the number and called the repair shop. After a brief conversation, he discovered that he had the crystal repaired and the watch cleaned and serviced. They had to 'remind' the good senator that the crystal must have taken a pretty good blow to be cracked that badly. When Franklin hung up, his head was throbbing. Why did he have no memory of his watch going to the jeweler? He had even paid extra for them to expedite the repairs. He felt wrong without the Rolex on his wrist, and he couldn't remember any part of it. He stood from his desk and felt lightheaded. Surely it was the whiskey at such an early hour and on an empty stomach. He looked around the office, but everything seemed in its place. Perhaps it occurred at home? But when he finally looked completely behind him, he saw it. The family photo was broken. The last family photo taken before his wife announced she was ill…Damien was so little…and the glass was broken.

But how?

His head was killing him, but Franklin had to have answers. The watch. Maybe having it back would stir a memory? He left his briefcase and his overcoat. Taking only his suit jacket, he stepped out-side into the outer office. "Ellen, I'm going to pick up my watch. I'll be back later."

"Your schedule is still cleared until tomorrow, sir, so you should be okay," she said.

Franklin paused at the outer door. "Tomor-row?"

"Yes, sir. You had me clear your schedule? Until tomorrow…"

Franklin nodded. "Yes. Of course I did." Then he headed out of the door.

A tech knocked rapidly on Colonel Mitchell's door. "Come!" Matt bellowed and the tech nearly tripped over himself coming into the office. Mitchell looked up from the stack of reports on his desk. "What is it?"

"Troll, sir," the tech said, his face pale. "Double verified, and close to a populated area." He sounded out of breath. He must have run all the way to the colonel's office.

Matt stood from his desk. "Location?"

"Kansas, sir!" the tech sounded surprised. "Usu-ally they'll show up somewhere near a coastal area, sir. Wash up onshore or something, but *this* far inland? It's unheard of, colonel."

Mitchell grabbed his two-way and keyed it. "Alert. Ready Squad One. All hands to Operations."

Almost immediately, red lights along the wall began flashing and a claxon began blaring through all levels of the facility. Mitchell took the report and began scanning it as he and the tech headed to the Operations Command Center where Laura met him in the hallway. "Colonel?"

"Trolls in Kansas. I've got First Squad gearing up. Prep us a fast runner so the boys can chute in on this thing and drop it before it gets into a population center."

"Kansas is pretty close, sir. We could use helicopters and be able to transport…"

"Negative. This thing is headed for a town, XO, and I want it dropped before it gets in front of too many sets of eyes. It's going to be hard enough to explain as it is," he said. "How we got a stinking troll this far inland without being noticed beats the hell out of me, but the son-of-a-bitch is here and I don't intend to let it get any further than we have to. I want eyes on the subject ASAP and I want it fed to Op-Com so we can see what the hell we're dealing with."

"Yes, sir."

First Squad was quickly gearing up in the locker room and about to head out on their first mission since the new members were added to the ranks. Apollo had chosen Lamb, Jacobs, and Tracy to join himself, Donovan, Gonzalez, and the Padre to form First Squad. It had been a tough decision not to include Sanchez, but Second Squad needed her abilities both as a sniper and as an entry team member a lot more than he needed to satisfy the desire to keep her safe. And when it came down to it, he knew that she could take care of herself and having her on his team would only distract him from the mission.

With the men all geared up, they headed to the armory to receive their weapon assignments. As Apollo followed his team out the door, Sanchez grabbed him by his tactical vest and pulled him aside. She had to practically climb him like a tree to plant a kiss on him. "You come back in one piece, you hear me, soldier?!"

Apollo smiled down at her. "Yes, ma'am." He gave her a mock salute. Then, with one more quick kiss, he jogged to catch up with his team.

Most of the men were loading P90 magazines into their vest and BDU pockets, pistol magazines into side magazine pockets and flash-bang and concussion grenades into satchels. Fragmentation grenades went into a separate satchel to prevent getting mixed up in the heat of battle. Lamb looked up and noticed that the Padre only loaded up on phosphorus grenades and frags. Lamb, Mueller, and Tracy were loading up their fifty-round M4 magazines, and Tracy actually sighed when he hefted the M4 in his hands. Training is one thing, but knowing

235

you are about to go into battle with a weapon platform you knew like the back of your hand, it just set his mind at ease. Lamb nudged him and nodded at Hank who was scratching a cross onto each of his grenades before placing them into his satchel. Gus shrugged, "Whatever works for him, brother."

"Amen to that," Lamb said as he loaded a magazine and slapped the bottom to ensure it was seated.

First Squad double timed out to a freight elevator and began the ride up to the hangar. Along the way, Laura briefed them of the threat in Kansas. Apollo groaned, "The only thing worse than a damned troll is a stinking hydra."

"Why's that?" Jacobs asked.

Popo answered for him. "Their skin is like armor and they're too stupid to realize they're being attacked. Once they *do* realize it, they get mad as hell and destroy everything. Then they're even harder to kill."

"Head shot with AP ammo?" Lamb asked.

"Brain is too small," Apollo said. "Like shooting through a tank to hit a matchbook, and you have to hit it *dead-on* to truly kill it."

"And they're freaking huge," Donovan added.

"Wait. How big is 'freaking huge'?" Tracy asked.

Apollo was double-checking his gear and never looked up. "Anywhere from three to five stories tall, depending on the type. They've been known to eat entire cows in one bite as a snack." Finally he looked up and smiled. "Let's just hope it isn't a rock troll."

"Do I want to know?" Tracy asked.

"Thicker skin, uglier, smellier, thicker skulls, smaller brains. Basically, everything that makes a troll hard to kill, they have in spades," Apollo said. "Oh…and they can go through the ground faster than a duck through water. Leaves a helluva mess."

"Great." Tracy sighed. "Anybody want to lay odds on the type of troll we're about to see?"

"Twenty bucks says it's a rock troll," Lamb said, his face like stone.

"I'll take that action," Apollo challenged just as the freight elevator opened.

Laura stepped out waved the loaded out crew ahead of the squad. "Good luck, and remember to keep your coms open. The Colonel will have visual set up for us ASAP and I'll get a feed to you en route." She got a thumbs-up from Apollo as they loaded into the short bus and began rolling to the runway.

Laura went to the other end of the large hangar and entered the secured area. Techs were prepping the computers and workstations for the new drones as she entered. "Are they ready?"

"Ma'am, we literally *just* took them off the truck. I'm not even sure if they're flight worthy."

"These were detoured from a shipment headed to Iraq, they should be ready to go," she said.

"Yes, ma'am, I understand that, but even then, they have to go through a prep period, a shakedown run…I don't know if we can just throw them into action." The tech said in exasperation.

"Make it happen." She glared.

"We're giving It our best, ma'am. Honestly."

Laura went to the far wall and picked up the internal phones. She keyed OpCom. "Get me the colonel." She waited until Mitchell picked up. "Colonel, we may not have air support from the drones. We may need to send the Apaches."

Matt really wanted to keep the Apaches out of this one, but made the call best suited to keep his squad safe. "Get 'em up and over there Laura. Make sure they're armed to the teeth, too. Send 'em both."

"Yes, sir."

Laura stepped out of the secured area and pointed at the Monster Squad's pilots. She spun her fingers in the air and both men gave a single nod. Both pilots turned to gather their co-pilots who were still gearing up and all four men took the team's Humvee to the helipad and their waiting Apache attack helicopters. First Squad would have air support, even if it was a few minutes later than Mitchell wanted. Although the Apaches were fast and would be leaving before the plane took off, the plane would pass the helicopters in little time to get to northern Kansas in record time. The plane would then reduce air speed, fly lower in the atmosphere, and First Squad would parachute into the area and engage the troll. The last troll that the squads faced was along the western coast of Mexico. The team fought the beast for nearly an hour, expending most of their ammunition to turn the beast's attention from a nearby village before the Apaches flew in and shoved a rocket up its ass. Literally. As the rocket was fired, the troll happened to turn and bend down to pick up a squad member. The rocket hit the troll right in the butt and blew it's intestines out through its belly. Needless to say, the cleanup crew was not happy that day. They used bulldozers commandeered from a nearby construction site to assist in the cleanup.

19

Nadia lay curled next to Jack in his bed and he swore that he could feel the heat from her radiating off in waves. She had a fine sheen of perspiration across her forehead and in the waning light, she never looked more beautiful. He remembered being shocked that she had been a virgin, yet had no inhibitions with him. It was as if she had mentally given herself to him long before she ever gave herself to him physically. He glanced further down and saw the faint hint of a smile on her face. It made him smile and he wrapped his arm tighter around her. She was his now. And he was hers. They were mated.

For all intent and purpose, she was his wife. As far as the wolves and vampires were concerned, they were married. They were bonded by something far stronger than any piece of paper or legally binding government recognized agreement could ever make them. He sighed as he realized, his life was hers. They were forever bound…and as he stared at her lying against him, he knew without doubt, that he wouldn't have it any other way.

He thought he would feel…different, somehow. That the bonding process would do something to him magical that he could detect. But, in all honesty, it was *just* world class, toe curling, fantastic, lovemaking with the woman of his dreams. If you had to debase it, that is.

He couldn't express the mix of emotions he felt, because he did feel very strongly for Nadia, but he expected something spectacularly magical to occur as soon as they did it. And honestly, he was somewhat disappointed when it didn't. But she didn't seem to be. She came back for more, and more, and more until they were both exhausted.

He ran his finger across her shoulder and watched as goose bumps appeared across her arm. He smiled as she groaned and rolled closer to him. "Stop. It tickles."

"I can't stop staring at you."

"Sleep," she said. "The moon will call us soon."

"I thought the pills would prevent that?"

"It does, but the moon still calls." She looked up into his eyes. "Have you not felt the restlessness of late? The unease?"

Jack chuckled. "I thought it was sexual tension from seeing your perfect form naked!"

She smiled at him and cuddled closer to him. "The moon still calls, even if we prevent you from answering."

"So, if we pull this off and you can control the wolf during the moon's call…could you control me if I shifted?" Jack asked carefully.

Nadia stiffened perceptively under Jack's arm. "Why would you ask such a thing?"

"I want to change with you…"

"And I want you to remain you, Jack."

Jack sighed. "I feel like I'm missing out on the biggest part of being a wolf."

"Perhaps if you were natural born, then you would be. But there is a reason why all created were-wolf call it a curse."

Jack simply nodded but Nadia could tell that he didn't agree. Perhaps it was because he had failed to take the bane for so many days and now he could feel the pull of the coming moon so much more intensely. Or perhaps it was because they had found each other, but for whatever reason, his wolf was calling him. Strongly. Perhaps if she could show him, just how bad the Halfling truly was? Maybe then he would not desire it so deeply. In her heart, she knew that what she planned was wrong, but if it saved Jack from trying to experience the shift and becoming the Halfling, it would be worth the betrayal.

Senator Franklin stared at his Rolex. It looked exactly as he remembered. So why did he have it re-paired? This was driving him crazy. He felt like he was missing parts of his life and he still felt like there was something he needed to do, but, for the life of him, he couldn't figure out what it was. It tickled his brain like an itch he couldn't reach, and it drove him nearly insane.

Franklin decided not to return to the office. The time it had taken him to navigate to the jeweler and then back, fighting the D.C. traffic and having to stop to clear his head twice, he felt as though his mind was splitting. Home. He would go home. Perhaps the answers he was seeking lay there.

Franklin made the drive as the sun was setting, and he remembered looking out the window of the Ritz Carlton in his fog and not knowing if the sun was coming up or going down. The redhead's curves flashed through his mind and his arousal angered him once more. He pictured her walking back from the bathroom and became even more aroused and even more angered. He yelled and beat the steering wheel of his car. He refused to accept what had happened, dammit!

To a passing vehicle, he may have seemed crazy or simply upset at a sports team score, but Franklin didn't care what he looked like to other people. He was losing his mind and he couldn't take it anymore. He screamed until his voice was a screech and his throat was sore. He thrashed his head until his perfectly coifed hair was tossed. He beat the steering wheel until his hands throbbed, the whole time his car swerved dangerously from his lane to the next and back.

Somehow, he made it to his home safely and pulled into his oyster shell drive. He pulled the car around to the back of the house and parked outside the garage. He didn't even wait to put the vehicle away, he simply shut off the engine and darted into the house, escaping to something familiar, to something warm and inviting and safe.

Franklin shut the door behind him and locked it. The gloom of the old house engulfed him and the silence was deafening. No children echoing in the hallways, no wife to prepare dinner. Not even a housekeeper anymore. He had a Mexican woman who came in twice a week to clean and do laundry while he was at his office. He didn't mind paying her for her duties, but he never wanted to actually *see* her.

He shuffled off to his office and collapsed behind his desk. With his head in his hands, he began to sob. *Of all the things I've lost, I miss my mind the most,* he thought. He knew he had heard that somewhere before, but he couldn't remember where. Perhaps on television. A t-shirt at the beach? A poster? He sobbed harder. He couldn't tell what was going on now that his once great mind was failing him. Between his sobs he had a horrible thought...*what if this is what Alzheimer's is like?* If this were the beginnings of the dreaded disease, would he even know it?

"Bad day at the office, Senator?"

Franklin nearly jumped out of his skin at the voice. It took him a moment to recognize Damien's voice as his son slowly stepped from the shadows of the hallway. The sun had set while Franklin had his pity party. "Son. I didn't hear you."

"Obviously," Damien deadpanned.

"What brings you by so early?" Franklin asked, trying to wipe away the evidence of his breakdown.

"Seriously?" Damien asked, sitting across from his father. "Well, I just thought I'd stop by and we could catch up on things, *dad.*"

"Oh," Franklin replied, trying to straighten himself up somewhat. "Isn't that nice? I'm so happy to see you, son. Would you care for a drink?" He stood and prepared himself a Jack and Coke.

"Got any O-positive?" Damien asked with raised brows.

Franklin startled, then paused. "You know that I don't, son. But I do have a nice cognac."

"Cut the chit chat already, will you? Did you get what you needed from Mitchell?"

Franklin froze. Mitchell? His mind began racing...Mitchell needs...he needs...he...needs drones. And a satellite to...be able to perform his mission. "Mitchell?" Franklin asked. "Mitchell? Mitchell needs...he needs...Mitchell needs drones, son." Franklin turned around, his eyes desperate, "He *has* to have the drones or his mission will *fail!*" He slammed his drink down on the table.

Damien stared at him and then slowly raised an eyebrow. "You have got to be shitting me."

"No. He does. He has to..."

"He got to you."

"What?"

"Mitchell got to you," Damien said, coming around the desk to stand directly in front of his father. He grabbed him by the face and stared into his eyes. "For shit's sake. He brainwashed you, you weak-minded idiot."

"What?!" Franklin was aghast. "You can't speak to me that way, I am still your father!"

"Shut up and sit down!" Damien commanded. Franklin immediately sat, looking up expectantly. Damien chuckled. "I have no idea what they used, but apparently, you're still under the influence." Damien pulled out a cell phone. "Don't move!" he commanded, pointing a finger directly in his father's face.

He dialed a number and waited. "I need help. Mitchell got to him." After a moment, "Yeah, brainwashed him. Cooked him. Probably chemical. I doubt he's got a born vamp working for him." Damien nodded, then turned and looked down at his father who was still staring straight forward. He shook his head in disgust. "Okay, I can do that. Be there in an hour. Thanks."

Damien sighed and stuffed the phone back in his pocket. "Time for you and me to have a little quality father-son time, pop." He picked up Franklin and laid him over his shoulder. Damien opened the second floor window and jumped down to the yard, gently touching down. He walked to the backyard fence and cleared it with a quick jump. Behind the house and waiting for Damien was a black SUV with dark tinted windows. He opened the back door and shoved Franklin in the back, then slipped in behind the wheel.

"No worries, old man. I know somebody who can get you back to your old self in no time. You'll be back to your back-stabbing ways and kissing hands and shaking babies before you know it. Then we can get you back to bringing Mitchell to his knees."

"Team Leader, this is OpCom actual."

"Go for Team Leader."

"We have eyes on the target. We're uploading visuals to your portables. You're not going to like this, Apollo."

"Let me guess, Colonel. Rock troll?"

"Negative. We've got no record of anything like this one, Team Leader. I hate to say this, but you are on your own this time."

Apollo turned to Lamb. "Looks like you're out twenty bucks, Ron!" he yelled into the coms over the roar of the transport.

"Not a rock troll?" Lamb asked.

"Unknown type. They're uploading visuals from the sat feeds."

The squads all turned their wrists and tapped their uplinks. Pictures of the beast started downloading to their ruggedized PDA's. It was approximately thirty-five to forty feet tall, naked and had three digits on each hand. It appeared to be covered in growths that looked similar to giant warts.

"If that don't look like something from a B-movie," Jacobs breathed.

"No shit," Donovan added. "Check out that cranial ridge. Sumbitch is gonna have an armor-plated skull. I don't know if depleted uranium could pierce that forehead!"

"DU rounds shoot *through* tanks, Donnie. You don't think it will go through this guy's noggin'?" Tracy asked.

"Maybe through an orbital socket, but look at how small those eyes are. They don't stand still long enough for that kind of shot," Donnie answered.

"Wonder how thick his skin is?" Popo pondered.

The yellow light came on indicating it was time to prepare to jump and the jumpmaster started getting them prepped and ready to exit.

"I'll find out for you, Popo," Padre said. "I brought my pig-sticker." He patted his *katana*. "Never leave home without it."

The jumpmaster had the jump doors open and their static lines attached. When the light switched to green, he started shouting to the squad, "Go! Go! Go!" and they streamed out of the plane and into the fading light.

As their chutes opened, each man scanned the night sky for his squad mates, then, when he was sure that all were accounted for, began scanning the ground for the monster in question. Each began negotiating his chute to bring him closer to the target, but Hank had a different plan. Trolls being stupid and slow to react, Hank intended to land *on* the monster. "Team Leader, Sierra 3, I need a distraction."

Apollo wasn't expecting anything this soon. The game plan was simply to distract the monster until the Apaches arrived and bomb the bastard into oblivion. "What's your plan, Three?"

"I'm going to find out how thick this thing's skin is. But I need you to draw its attention low with fire. Preferably while you're still in the air and the moment you hit the ground."

Apollo mulled it over a moment. It usually takes both hands to steer these chutes, but one could possibly handle the P90 and still maneuver for landing. "We're on it. Team Leader to all squad members, concentrate fire low on the tango. Let's give Three the distraction he needs."

Apollo received numerous 'Roger that', 'Copy Team Leader' and 'Affirmative' replies. The moment they were within any kind of effective range, they opened fire. Hank had maneuvered his chute to descend slower than the rest in the hopes that he could come in high and then try to land on the monster's shoulder. Instead, he landed square on the beast's head, his chute collapsing over its face. Hank disconnected his chute while the beast was still trying to figure out why it couldn't see and used his survival knife to bite into the side of its head and slide down to the shoulder. He popped a phosphorus grenade and shoved it as deep into its ear as he could, hearing a sickening sucking and pop when he pulled his arm free. It was covered in something disgusting that could only be described as centuries old wax, oil, and filth, and it smelled of dead flesh. Just as the first pop and hiss of the grenade going off was heard and the flash of light shone, lighting up the side of its head, Hank jumped, *katana* in hand.

He hit the sternum of the chest and sunk his blade as deeply as he could, then rode it down, but only a few inches. The beast's skin was thick and tougher than saddle leather. Hank hung there a moment debating what to do. The beast had just plucked the parachute from its face when it realized that its ear was on fire. It had stopped stomping through the countryside and the squad was shooting up its lower legs…but as thick as its skin was, it was nothing more than a minor nuisance.

Suddenly the beast let out a roar and shook its huge head, trying to figure out what was biting its ear. It swung a slow, but mighty hand up and slapped the ear with a thundering clap that *had* to have ruptured an ear drum, and seemed to knock the beast silly. It also shook Hank and caused the blade to cut down and through another foot or so of flesh. Hank renewed his grip and began to bounce on the handle of the razor sharp sword. With each downward bounce, the blade cut downward a little more.

The beast slowly recovered from slapping itself silly and shoved a mighty finger as deep into its ear as it could in an attempt to dig out whatever was stinging it. Its tiny eyes were squinted shut as it dug in earnest to dislodge the stinging nuisance from its ear.

Apollo directed his squad to spread out in a semi-circle around the front of the troll, concentrating their fire about the ankles and knees. Even the heavier M-4s with their heavier round were having no effect on the troll. The hide was just too damned thick. It was like shooting BBs at a bull. It might feel it, and it might make it mad, but you aren't going to hunt down and kill anything with a Daisy air rifle.

"We have to keep this thing distracted or Hank is toast. Look for a tender spot and concentrate your fire!" Apollo barked.

Hank continued to bounce on his blade, and each bounce brought him closer to the ground, but he was still near the top of the beast's great belly. Cutting through the chest was taking forever, and Hank was beginning to think that soon the effects of the grenade would wear off on the monster and it would notice another pest stinging it on its chest and use a mighty paw to swat him like a fly. He continued to bounce, faster and faster, the cuts coming quicker, but with less length. Soon he found himself at the roundest part of its pot belly and Hank feared that he wouldn't be able to make the underside of the cut.

He continued to bounce, his hands and arms beginning to feel the burn of holding his weight on the thin handle.

He dared to break his grip on the blade and keyed the coms. "Team Leader, target the cut! Target the cut!" He grabbed the handle of his katana again and continued his bouncing in earnest.

"You heard him, redirect! Redirect! I want a line of fire on that incision!" Apollo ordered, instantly, all the weapons fire was redirected with precision. The cut was barely an inch wide at this point, but their training and superior eyesight and reflexes had the grand majority of the shots hitting the mark.

Almost immediately he heard bullets ricocheting off the beasts hide near him. He closed his eyes and continued his bouncing until he heard a great ripping sound and he was suddenly free-falling through the air. When he hit the ground, he rolled as fast and hard as he could and rolled against the troll's foot. Hank scrambled like made to get over the foot and away from the spillage that he knew must be coming.

He ran and jumped behind a natural berm, trying to catch his breath. When he finally turned and looked back, the beast was simply standing there, its intestines hanging almost to the ground; but very little blood below it.

"Son of a..." he muttered.

Over the coms he heard Apollo order, "Switch to frags."

The squad members began lobbing fragmentation grenades into the hanging innards of the troll. As each grenade exploded, pieces of troll innards blew out, and then the fluids came. Soon there was a puddle under the monster. The troll, in its simple-mindedness, had no idea what was going on. It kept looking below it, wondering what this stuff was coming from its belly. When it tried to take a step, it literally got hung up on its own intestines and tripped, slipping in the gore.

When the troll toppled, the ground shook and trembled from the impact. Dust blew out in all directions and many of the squad members almost lost their footing. The troll wasn't dead though, and tried to push itself up out of the gore. Tracy ran up with the M-4 and emptied two full magazines into the closest eye. He barely dodged a great hand that swatted at him, but he rolled out of the way in time. As the hand withdrew and settled back to try to push the troll back up, he ran back to the troll's face, pulled the pin on a fragmentation grenade and shoved it as far into the destroyed eye socket as he could, then was lifted off the ground as the troll rose. He dangled momentarily before falling to the ground and rolling away. A moment later the grenade detonated and the troll staggered in mid-rise.

Smoke rose from the destroyed eye socket and the troll seemed badly disoriented. At first it tried to continue to lift itself, then one arm gave out and it tilted. Then the other arm gave out and it collapsed on its face, breaking a tooth and biting off a portion of its thick and meaty tongue upon impact.

The squad surrounded it, barrels trained on its head, carefully watching it. Looking to see if it was breathing still, but it appeared to be stopped. Donovan climbed up on its back and pulled a stethoscope out. He listened to the beast for a moment then shook his head.

"OpCom, Team Leader. Tango neutralized."

"We see that, Apollo. Good job, son. Apaches are inbound and cleanup crews are en route." He could almost hear the colonel smiling over the coms. "We'll have transport ready for you boys inside the hour."

"Copy that, sir."

Apollo turned to his squad and gave them a thumbs-up. "Another Atta boy from the boss. Ride home is on the way. Smoke 'em if you got 'em!"

"Right. Smoking isn't good for your health, Apollo," Hank said, wiping the troll blood from his katana.

"Neither is riding a troll without an approved saddle, Padre, but that didn't stop you." He gave him a wink and a smile.

"That has got to be a record, Colonel." Laura turned from her console.

"Makes you wish we kept records of response reactions, doesn't it?" Matt smiled.

"We never got a chance to use the drones, sir," she observed.

"True, but there will be other times," Mitchell responded. Looking about the room and the numerous techs making their notes and doing their related

253

tasks, he nodded, "There will be plenty more oppor-
tunities."

"Ahem, Colonel?" Evan had stuck his head in
the door of the command center, "If the operation is
concluded, sir, could I borrow you and Ms.
Youngblood for a few moments?"

"Of course, Dr. Evans," Mitchell stated almost
too loudly. Even to Laura, it sounded 'off'. She didn't
think they were fooling anybody who actually
worked there, but if Matt insisted that they continue
the charade, she would go along with it.

As they stepped into the hallway, Evan directed
them back toward his lab. "I've found something that
I think you might be interested in seeing."

"Care to clue us in while we walk, doc? You
know the whole science talk is over my head," Matt
admitted.

"Certainly, Colonel," Evan began, "as you
know, we have numerous samples of blood from different…umm…'donors' that have been collected
over the years."

"Correct. This is what you were working on before you…well, before?" Matt asked.

"Yes. It is." Evan smiled slightly. He found it odd
that the Colonel found his incarceration more difficult to speak of than he did. "Anyway, sir, I may have
found something that we can weaponize."

Matt stopped in midstride. "A vamp-specific
weapon?"

Evan smiled. "Not *just* a vampire specific
weapon. A *natural born* specific weapon."

Matt thought a moment. "So we're talking one kind of vampire? That might not be so helpful, Evan—"

"No, sir. Not just vampires, but natural born vampire or natural born werewolf." He sounded almost giddy. "And I'm not positive, sir, but it might also work on other creatures that can transfer their disease vectors, if there is a 'natural born' monotype, then there is a distinct possibility that the weaponization complex can work on the homogenous..."

"Okay, you're losing me," Matt said, shaking his head.

"Right. Okay. Like an eighth grader...gotcha." Matt frowned at him as he continued. "If I'm right and we can get this developed into a working prototype and it actually works as expected, then it should work for natural born 'anything'...vampire or werewolf. And if there are other monsters out there that have the same...umm...'virus' in them like the vamps and wolfs, then there is a good possibility that it will work on them as well." Evan was practically jumping up and down.

Matt was nodding his head. "Okay, Evan, I can see you're really excited about this. But I thought that the whole 'natural born' thing was really rare?"

"Yes, but if you go by the legends, and let's face it, so far the legends have been pretty darned spot-on, if the natural born *creator* dies, then all of their progeny dies along with them." Evan was nodding his head, waiting for Matt to catch on. Slowly the light flickered to life. Laura's mouth stood agape.

"Do you *really* think it possible?" Matt asked, incredulous.

"Very." He was smiling from ear to ear.

"That's great news, Evan. Keep us abreast of what you find." Laura said quickly, then grabbed Matt's arm and pulled him away, "What about the squads, Matt?"

"What about them?" he said.

"What do you mean, 'what about them'? You can't be that callous!"

Matt was honestly confused by her anger. "Explain yourself."

"Matt, let's say this thing works and we go off killing all the natural borns?"

"Then hooya, let's do it!"

"And if we happen to accidentally kill the natural born that we extracted the virus from for the 'augmentation' for our squads?"

"So?" He shrugged. "Laura, they've never been allowed to transition. Technically, they aren't 'wolves', therefore, no harm, no foul!"

"Bullshit!" she whispered. "That is complete bullshit and you know it. We prevented their shifting, but that doesn't stop them from being what they *are*!"

"Remember your place, XO," Matt warned. Laura stiffened and narrowed her gaze. "First off, if he's right and this is all based on 'legend' then let's just take a good goddamned look at these legends, shall we?"

"Fine, let's do that." She crossed her arms defensively over her chest.

"Where exactly did we learn about the wolf's bane in the first place? The legends. And it worked. Do you remember the story? The woodsman that was attacked and took the wolf's bane for two years

256

to prevent the shift so that he could *hunt down* and *kill* the wolf that attacked him so he could break the curse?" Matt was red in the face. "Ringing any bells now?"

Laura considered his words. "But what if that one is just a story? What if it's wrong?"

"What if Evan is wrong and all the legends are bullshit? Then all his weapon will do is kill a few natural borns and it's still no harm, no foul."

Laura calmed considerably. "I still don't like gambling with the squad's lives…"

"We aren't." Matt said. "For all we know, his drawing board idea won't go anywhere."

"It still scares me."

"You're tougher than this," Matt said, turning away. "You need to start acting it."

20

Damien pulled the black SUV into the underground parking garage and began the slow descent into the lower levels. Deeper and deeper he drove until he reached the lowest level. He slowly pulled the SUV to the furthest wall and turned off the lights. He checked his mirrors to ensure nobody had followed him then tapped his horn twice.

Rolling down the driver's window, he looked up at the digital camera mounted in the corner and waved. Slowly the back wall of the parking garage parted and allowed him to pull the SUV into the hidden parking level on the other side. He drove another 50 yards and parked the truck. He stepped out into the cool air of the lower level and his eyes instantly adjusted the blackness. He saw three figures approaching him and he opened the back door of the SUV and pulled his father's prone body out and tossed him over his shoulder.

"Why isn't his head covered?" one of the guards asked.

"His mind is toast, man. He couldn't tell you where he was if he had to," Damien explained, turning slightly to show the blank expression on Franklin's face. "Now, take me to Paul."

The guards looked at each other as if debating whether or not to trust Damien. The larger of the two touched the earpiece in his ear then said, "Let them through. Foster's orders."

"See? I wouldn't shit you guys." Damien smirked. *You're my favorite turds.*

They led Damien with his package across the parking area and to a set of ornate double doors. The largest guard reached up and grabbed the oversized knocker and struck once, echoing through the room before opening the doors.

The room was lit entirely by candles. Large and small candelabras stood throughout the room. Heavy tapestries hung from the walls and rich Persian rugs lay upon the floor. Across from the doors stood a large four-post bed with colorful fabrics draped from it. Antique furniture was set about the room and a grand piano sat to one side. Large pillows were strewn about and women lay upon them or draped themselves from the furniture like decorations. Paul stood from the edge of the bed and slowly walked across the room toward Damien. Damien kneeled, his father still across his shoulder.

Paul walked slowly toward Damien and observed that he kept his head bowed, his eyes never left the floor. He knew that Damien not only feared him, but respected him, and he appreciated greatly the life that Paul had bestowed to him. As Paul approached, Damien realized that Paul wore no clothing. He must have been feeding, and he interrupted it. "Forgive me, father, I did not mean to interrupt your meal."

"No need, my son. I was fucking, not eating." Paul smiled and extended his ring hand for Damien to kiss. "I never mix the two pleasures." Paul laughed slightly. "Aww, hell, who am I kidding? I mix them all the time." He took Damien by the chin and pulled him to his feet so that he could look him in the eye. "So tell me, my child, how bad is it?"

"They did something to his mind. If I didn't know better, I'd think a natural had gotten to him. Most likely chemical brainwashing."

"Why could it not be a natural born?" Foster inquired.

"Mitchell, sire. He detests our kind."

"*Our* kind?" Foster turned to Damien, his inquiry clear. Did Damien dare to compare himself to his sire, a nearly three hundred-year-old natural born vampire?

"I meant only…our kind…in…that we are both vampire, sire." Damien's eyes were lowered.

"I know what you meant," Foster said softly, his voice like music to Damien's ears. "You want so desperately to be like me. The power, the nobility, the money, the *abilities*."

Damien was smart enough to hold his tongue. Nothing he could say at this point would be the right answer. If he disagreed, that would be telling his master that he was wrong. If he agreed, his master may well kill him for coveting what he had. Damien could only bow and scrape to him and hope that he would soon tire of toying with him. Luckily for Damien, Paul Foster simply enjoyed messing with the minds of his minions.

He reached down and grasped a handful of Franklin's hair and lifted his head so that he could look into his face. "What's with the stupid look on his face?"

"He's still highly suggestible. I told him to sit down and shut up and he did," Damien responded.

"Very well." Foster turned and retrieved a robe from a nearby chair. Wrapping the heavy garment around himself, he somehow looked smaller. Foster was barely six foot tall, but he seemed much larger to those who witnessed him. Damien assumed it was a trick of the mind from the power he exuded due to his age. He appeared to be maybe forty years old, but at nearly three hundred years old, Paul was in incredible physical shape. "Set him here so he doesn't fall over."

Damien sat his father in one of the high back chairs and held his shoulders steady. Foster pulled another chair over and stared into his eyes. "Tell me."

"Tell you what?" Franklin said drunkenly.

Foster smiled coldly. "Tell me what they did to you."

"Who?" Franklin asked, his face a blank slate.

"Mitchell's people...tell me what they did to you. From the beginning."

"Mitchell?" Franklin struggled against Damien's hands. "Mitchell? Mitchell needs...he needs...he needs.."

"What did Mitchell do to you?" Paul Foster's stare intensified.

"Mitchell needs…" Franklin tried to break eye contact, but Damien held his face. "He needs…he needs…needs…"

"What did Mitchell *do to you*?!" Foster practically shouted.

"He needs…needs…needs…*needles*! Needles! They stuck a needle in me," Franklin gasped. He was gulping air, like he was trying not to drown. He kept trying to pull his head up and away from Damien's grasp but he held his head still, their gazes locked. "They stuck a needle in my arm, and I told them my plan."

Foster never broke eye contact, but he contemplated ending Franklin's life there and then. He needed to know how much Franklin told them. Their survival may depend on it and Franklin's most certainly did. "What exactly did you tell them?"

"That I was trying to save Damien. I had to save Damien. He was all I had left."

"Save him from what?"

"From Mitchell." Franklin was sobbing. "From his damned Monster Squads."

"What else did you tell them?"

"Nothing."

"Did you tell them about me?"

"I don't know who you are," Franklin admitted. "Who are you?" he asked almost hypnotically.

Foster smiled. "Did you tell him of your plan to expose him and his squad?"

"Yes," Franklin admitted.

"How did they catch you?"

Franklin's brows knitted together. "I don't know. I stuck the USB bug into the computer and all went well. I was leaving and a guard tackled me. Treated me like a common criminal. The twit."

Foster smiled at the thought. "And then?"

"Then they cuffed me," Franklin said with apparent disbelief. "When I wouldn't cooperate, they stuck me with a needle and everything got fuzzy. I felt woozy. And they made me talk to them," Franklin pleaded. "I didn't want to, but I *had* to," he whined.

"Yes, of course you did," Foster cooed. "What happened next?"

"I woke up next to the most beautiful redhead I'd ever seen. She sucked my dick and I really liked it," Franklin smiled.

Foster's face went blank. "You what?"

"I was in New Orleans and there was this beautiful redhead with the most enchanting green eyes…" Franklin was smiling. "She had the biggest penis I'd ever seen."

Damien let go of his father's head, "What the hell?" Foster hissed and Damien's shocked eyes met his. He reluctantly reached back down and held his father's head in place. Foster continued staring into his eyes.

"What then?"

"I went back to Washington. But I couldn't stop thinking about her," Franklin admitted.

"Let's not discuss the transsexual for the moment. How did you get to New Orleans?"

"I don't know. I can't remember. I just woke up there. Maybe she brought me there. She had the most beautiful green eyes." Franklin smiled. "I think she put her penis in my butt because it was really sore..."

"Gah! Focus! What transpired between Oklahoma City and you waking up in New Orleans?" Foster asked.

Franklin's brows knitted together in thought. "I can't remember. There's nothing there..."

Foster sighed. "He's useless. There's nothing useful in there." He waved him away with his hand.

Damien was torn. On one hand he was totally disgusted by his father's sex life, but at the same time, he still felt that his connections in Washington were their best shot at getting the Monster Squad shut down without either exposing themselves or losing any of their own numbers.

"Sire, I still think he can be of use to us," Damien said. "If you can clear his mind of this...blockage, he will remember his rage toward Mitchell. He will have back his old desires of destroying them. He will stop at nothing. And he may still have usefulness in Washington."

"We never needed a politician before, and the one time that we tried to use one, the attempt failed us," Foster said, obviously ready to give up entirely on the idea.

"It never hurts to have friends in high places," Damien whispered. "A United States Senator, whose only son is a vampire in *your* service?"

Foster debated on simply feeding on the old man. Still, the boy had a point.

"And I think that if you could clear his mind of what Mitchell did to him, give him back his true focus, he could be a powerful ally, and he could very well take up more of Mitchell's time in battle than we ever could." Damien pointed to the withered man in the chair. "If he were given back his direction, he may still be able to see this through."

Foster weighed the options and decided that even if Damien was wrong and he still allowed Franklin to live, and somehow Franklin failed at every attempt at Mitchell perhaps the boy had a point. Franklin's attempts to engage Mitchell and bring him down could keep his focus redirected...at least long enough that when they did structure a strike against the Monster Squad, they could coordinate it so that it did enough damage to truly cripple them.

"Very well," Paul said. "I will give him another chance and hope that he proves useful. Hold his head and I will clear his mind of what Mitchell has done to him." Foster smiled. "Then we shall see if your father has any real teeth and knows how to use them."

When morning rolled around, Jack found the bed empty next to him. He slipped some clothes on and grabbed the walking stick that Nadia had brought him and strolled down to the kitchen. He didn't feel the need to use the walking stick, but it was a gift from his beloved and it felt good in his hand.

Jack entered the kitchen and Nadia wasn't there. He found some coffee and filled a mug, added some sugar and cream into it and walked out into the garden. Nadia wasn't there either. He went past the stone walls and climbed the ramparts. He checked the tree line, but couldn't see any movement there either. Coming back into the dining hall, he ran into Natashia.

"It is done?"

"By 'it' I take it you mean my mating with Nadia?"

Natashia's eyes narrowed but she said nothing.

"Yes, it is done," he said. "And I'd do it again in a heartbeat."

"Stupid human!" she spat and spun around.

"Don't you mean, 'stupid *wolf*?'" he demanded.

Natashia spun on him, her eyes glowing amber, her voice a growl, "No. I meant what I said. *Human.* You are not worthy of my daughter."

"It wasn't just my choice, *mom*. It was your daughter's as well. *And* the Fates," he goaded.

"Insolent fool!" she yelled and advanced. Jack kicked his walking stick up into his hands and spun it like a bo stick. He assumed a defensive posture and prepared to knock out his mother-in-law's teeth. She paused and laughed at him. "Seriously? You think you could stand against *me*?"

"Any day, any time, *mom*."

She dropped her robe and although Jack's impression was not 'mom', but 'hot older sister', she did nothing for him. It was probably the really high bitch-factor. Before he could think much more, she shifted and Jack faced her Halfling form. She nearly tripled in mass, standing close to seven foot tall and, if Jack's assessment was right, close to four hundred pounds of rippling muscle, teeth, and claws, her reach would be unreal. Jack assessed the damage she could do and realized, even with his augmentation and nearly healed body, he was in deep shit.

He lowered his stance and took a half step back, assuming a forty-five degree angle, keeping the stick extended slightly to his front so that he could extend his reach. He knew it wouldn't be enough.

He heard a noise behind him but didn't dare divert his attention or he'd risk losing his head to his bitch in law.

"Mother!" Nadia screamed.

The bitch-in-law roared back, and every hair on Jack's neck stood on end. Hell, even the hair on his arms and legs stood on end. He really thought that if they could, they'd jump off his body and run like hell. They'd seen what these damned things could do once before and no part of him wanted another encounter. The last time, they were armed with silver bullets and automatic weapons, but the wolves got the drop on them. Now, he stood here with little more than his dick in his hand. He was poorly outgunned.

"Come on, you foamy-faced bitch. If you're gonna eat me, let's do it now and get it over with. At least I'll get the satisfaction of knocking a few of your teeth out before you do. And I hope to God I give you the worst case of indigestion you've ever had."

Natashia paused and looked at him sideways. She actually stood sideways and...was she laughing at him? Seriously? Was he being laughed at by a seven foot tall she-bitch? Oh, hell no. Jack advanced and swung the walking stick as fast and hard as he could, aiming straight for her snarling mouth. But as fast as he was, she was faster. Her paw came up and caught the end of the walking stick and stopped him from connecting his blow. She gripped the walking stick and pulled it from his hands with one smooth motion, pulling him in closer to her at the same time.

Jack's mind was racing as he was pulled in to his attacker. With her ginormous arms, the only chance he had to inflict any pain before his death would be to move in close and try to work her from the inside. As she pulled him in, rather than try to withdraw, he dove for her middle and tried to get inside her arms and land a blow...but before he could complete a thought, much less an action, she held him by both of his arms, just below the shoulders in her massive paws and lifted him from the ground.

"Mother, that's enough," Nadia said. "Obviously, he isn't going to back down." There was no panic in her voice. "I think he's passed your test."

Jack was struggling to get free but could barely breathe he was being held so tight. She had him held perfectly. He couldn't get enough momentum to get a good kick, he couldn't move left or right. All he could do was lift his forearms. So he did. He lifted both forearms into the furry chest of his attacker and grabbed...boobs? There were boobs under that hair?

The Halfling's eyes widened momentarily and she looked down at the tiny man in her arms who now held her breasts in his hands and a low growl escaped her throat. His eyes narrowed and he stared right back at his bitch-in-law. He set his jaw and told her point blank, "Surrender now, or suffer the worst purple nurple to ever be laid upon man or beast!"

Natashia froze in surprise, then as best as Jack could tell, the wolf laughed so hard she dropped him.

In the blink of an eye, his bitch-in-law was human again and holding her sides. "My dear," she gasped for breath, "I'll give your man this much...he *does* have spunk."

"I tried to tell you, mother. He is worthy," Nadia said as she approached Jack and wrapped her arms around him.

"Would somebody mind telling me just what the hell is going on here?"

"Mother needed to be able to confirm to father that you would stand for me...no matter what," Nadia explained.

"And you performed exemplary, my boy," Natashia said embracing him.

"Umm...thanks. I think," Jack said. "But this would be so much less awkward if you'd put your clothes back on."

Natashia looked up at Jack and smiled. "But, Jack, just a moment ago you held my breasts in both of your hands..."

Jack was shocked! "Yeah...but...in self-defense!" Jack pleaded. "And if we are being totally honest, you *were* about to face the 'titty-twister of death'..."

Natashia and Nadia both laughed as Jack sputtered.

Laura came out of the Base Exchange with the few things she needed. Her mind was still preoccupied with Matt's behavior lately. He seemed to be hell-bent on destroying anything and everything no matter what the cost. It used to be, protect the squad first, take out the monsters after. But since the loss of Second Squad and the replacements blending so smoothly, she felt that he was taking chances. Or was he? Was it just her reaction to his desire to use whatever Evan could come up with? Or was he changing? What he did to set up Franklin seemed over the top and Evan went right along with it, happily.

Could she blame him? If somebody had locked her away and starved her for three years, she might be surprised what she would be willing to go along with. Still, she expected more from Evan.

And she expected more from Matt.

Maybe it wasn't them that were changing, maybe it was her? She left the company because she couldn't go along with a lot of the things that they pulled to 'get the job done' and she felt that Matt was a cut above. Had she deluded herself? Or maybe she just wasn't cut out to make the 'hard decisions' as Matt would put it.

She jumped into her Jeep and sat staring out the windshield, holding the key, but not hitting the ignition yet.

What was wrong with her? Why was she second guessing herself? She had devoted her life to this job. She had no private life to speak of. The closest thing to a relationship she'd had was with Evan over three years ago. And nobody else had stepped into that roll since then. Since his release, neither one of them had the time or had put forth the effort to pick up where it had left off.

She wanted to cry. But instead, she twisted the key in the ignition and headed back to the hangar. She had some soul searching to do and she wasn't going to be able to do it sitting in the parking lot of the BX.

21

The HH-60 Pave Hawk approached Tinker Air Base in Oklahoma City and Apollo breathed a sigh of relief. It had been a long night and an eventless morning as the squad set a deep perimeter around the battle scene allowing the cleanup crews to do their job. The story, as far as he knew, was that a military transport train had derailed and the military was cleaning up a fuel spill and some chemicals that, when mixed, could result in a deadly gas. It kept a lot of the civilians away and the Apaches kept any nosy reporting aircraft away.

Satellite imagery found the tunnel that the newly termed 'gopher troll' had emerged from. The squad followed the road graders dragging the carcass back to the entrance and then searched the interior for any evidence of secondary invaders. The risk was very low as trolls are usually solitary creatures, but not all trolls act alike. Once they were assured that the creature was alone, the cleanup crews sprayed it down with aqueous film forming foam used to fight fuel fires to slick it's skin, then pushed it back into its hole and buried it. The foam and high pressure water was used to wash away blood and gore from the battle scene into a pit and buried in the middle of a wheat field.

The real question of the day was, 'how did a troll end up in Kansas of all places?' Trolls are indigenous to the European continent, although sometimes the smaller ones were known to hitch a ride on transport ships or wander close to the coast and fall off a pier and wash out to sea where they bob and float across the waters to another continent. That was how trolls were established in Nordic countries thousands of years ago and evolved to survive the colder climates. But on those rare occasions that a troll ended up in 'the new world' it was almost always along the coast. Perhaps this one had washed up on a shore and being so happy to have land under its feet again, it began to dig and didn't come up until it hit Kansas? He had no idea, but it was taken care of and people were safe again.

The Pave Hawk made its approach for Tinker, and rather than heading for the normal helipads, received clearance to land at the reserved helipad closest to the MS hangar. Apollo hit the coms to his squad mates. "Ready your gear. We're about to land."

The HH-60 touched down and the door slid open. Apollo and his team stepped out, gear in hand and walked into the hangar. Taking the freight elevator down into the bowels of the facility, Apollo really expected Sanchez to be waiting for him when the elevator doors opened. She wasn't.

The squad headed to the armory and checked in their weaponry, then to the locker room and stowed their gear. As the rest of the team headed to the showers, Apollo went in search of Sanchez. She was propped on the couch in front of some cable news show cleaning her nails with a survival knife. "Hi home, I'm honey!" Apollo joked, his arms spread wide.

"Meh." Sanchez waved him off. "News says there was some military train derailed in Kansas. You wouldn't know anything about that, would you?" her voice nonchalant.

Apollo plopped down on the couch beside her and raised his arms up, locking his hands behind his neck, "Who, me? No idea. I don't do trains." He grinned.

"*Santa mierda*, what is that smell?" She held her nose. "Is that you?"

"What? I don't smell nothing?"

"Did you fart on me? *Cabron*, we aren't married, you can't do that!" She began hitting him.

Apollo was smiling and grabbed her hands and pulled her in for a kiss, but she struggled away from him. "Kiss me, I missed you." He smiled.

"You smell like shit!"

"I smell like *troll*," he corrected.

"Ugh! You got it on me!" she said disgustedly. "I'm going to need a shower!"

Apollo pulled her in close to him and held her, this time she gave up and allowed him to hold her. "You can scrub my back and I'll wash your hair," he whispered into her ear.

"You're lucky you have a nice ass," she mumbled. "I'm going to enjoy kicking it when we're done." She wasn't smiling.

"Aw, come on. You love me and you know it."

"You wish, big boy." She elbowed him in the ribs. "You make me smell like troll poop just to get me naked in the shower? That is bad, *cabron*. Very bad for your health."

"I care about you too much to…"

"What?" she asked, turning to him. "Wait. No, Apollo." Maria shook her head. "Apollo, no."

Apollo was confused. He loosened his hold around her waist and she pulled away slightly. She turned to face him, and he could tell, this wasn't going to be good. "What's wrong?"

She shook her head. "Apollo, I really enjoy what he have." She nodded. "Yeah, the sex is good. I mean, it's world-rocking fantastic, okay?" He smiled. "But, we have to be careful just how far we… 'invest' ourselves into this. Okay?"

Apollo's eyes narrowed. "I don't think I'm following you, Maria. I care about you a great deal. I'm falling in love with…" she put her fingers over his mouth.

"No. Don't say it. Please? If you say it, you'll jinx us." She sighed. "We have very dangerous jobs. Either one of us could be taken out at any given time. So, I think it's best if we don't get any more emotionally involved than we absolutely have to."

"Are you breaking up with me?" he asked, his mind racing. His heart was thumping so loudly in his chest that he didn't know how she couldn't hear it.

"No! Not at all. I'm just saying, we shouldn't get so involved that we…let ourselves fall into the L-O-V-E trap, that's all."

"Are you afraid of a commitment?"

"What?!" Sanchez pushed off him. "Do you have any idea how much of a commitment it takes to make it through SWAT? How much dedication you have to have to hang with the men?"

"You can have commitment to a job, but not to another person, Maria," he explained. "You're afraid to get too close to someone who cares about you."

"You're insane," she muttered and started to get up. Apollo pulled her back down into his lap and held her.

"Let me up, *puto!*" She struggled against his massive arms and began to kick at him.

"No. This is loco, Maria." He held her tighter.

"Let me up or I'll bust your balls."

"I'd rather you bust my balls than break my heart, dammit!" She struggled a moment more, then stilled.

"Why you say that?"

"Because you're killing me here," he said so softly that she could barely hear. "I thought we had something special, and you're wanting to play it like we're just fuck buddies." Apollo sighed and released her from his grip, but left his arms around her. "I don't think I can do that." She turned to look at him. Her face was still angry, but her eyes were softening. He lowered his head and pressed his face into her neck. "Maybe once I could have been happy with that, but you deserve more. I *need* more than that.

"Look, I'm sorry if somebody hurt you or if you're just not ready for somebody to love you. But I can't help it. I do love you. And I'm gonna tell you that I love you. I'm gonna show you that I love you…because I do. And unless you tell me to hit the bricks, I say that you're absolutely right. Life is too short *not* to love somebody every moment of every day when you got the chance to. Just because there's a chance that one of us might die? Hell, what if we live to be a hundred? Think of all the time we would have lost not loving each other? I don't want to lose a minute of it."

He felt her hand against his cheek, and he raised his face to meet hers. She had a silly smirk across her face. "You should be writing cards for Hallmark or some shit, you know that?"

He grinned. "I can't rhyme."

"What? A brother who can't rhyme? So you can't rap?" she joked.

"Nope. Can't dance either if you can believe that," he said, flashing a toothy grin.

"Tell me that you can't play basketball and I'm going to start thinking that you're white with a really dark tan!" she laughed.

He raised his eyebrows at her. "With a 'unit' like this and you gonna call me white?"

She smirked at him. "Pft. I've seen bigger, *cabron*."

Suddenly jealous he asked, "You have? When?"

"On my uncle's ranch. On a horse he had. Big white stallion." She smiled.

"I should have known…" He kissed her. After just a moment, she pushed him back.

"You really stink, you know."

"I know." He motioned toward the showers. "Care to join me?"

"I knew you got me stinky just to see me wet and naked."

Franklin awoke in his own bed. He lay there and blinked his eyes. His head still ached, but nothing like it had. His memory fell together like pieces to a puzzle. It was almost like remembering a dream, but rather than visions of things his mind created while sleeping he was remembering parts of his life...recent parts. Parts that he hadn't remembered until now.

A hacker? The USB drive. Mitchell. Breaking his watch. A vampire...staring at him intently? Damien picking him up and jumping out his window? Flying out to Tinker Air Base. Argh...too many pieces. His head hurt.

He crawled out of bed and slipped on a robe. The sunlight hurt his eyes. Coffee may help. He went to the bathroom and grabbed a bottle of headache formula. Acetaminophen, aspirin and caffeine mixed together in one tablet, supposedly helps with everything from migraines to hangovers. Three pills and a cup of coffee for breakfast. Walking down his stairs, he glanced at the family portrait hanging in the hallway. Images of him throwing his phone and shattering the framed copy in his office came racing back...his headache spiked. Franklin stumbled on the stairs, yet he held on to the pills.

He walked into the kitchen and flipped on the coffee maker. He waited while it brewed and glanced out the window. It was a dreary day. Overcast skies, but at least, no rain. The two cup maker gurgled and perked and Franklin removed the mug, added Half & Half from the fridge and took the pills. He had no idea what day it was, or even the date. He glanced at his watch. His Rolex sat perfectly on his wrist, right where it should be. It looked newer to him somehow. Then his mind saw it with a broken crystal and him handing it to the jeweler for repair, and his headache spiked again. Franklin doubled over and grabbed his temples with both hands. It felt like someone was driving a hot poker through his skull.

Feeling nauseous, he went to the drawer and re-moved a towel and wet it in the sink. He wrung it out and put it over his face. He glanced at his watch again. It was almost 7AM. If this pain didn't subside, he'd be of no use today. He went to the wall and tried to see the date, his eyes having trouble focusing. It was a weekday according to his watch. He should be in the office. *Damn.* He picked up the phone and di-aled the office. He'd leave a message for his secretary and let her know his circumstances. She could rear-range his schedule. His mind flashed to him yelling at her to do just that, then of him not remembering that he had, and those pieces fell into place too…and his headache spiked again. Franklin almost dropped the phone and the nausea rose to another level. He held himself against the counter, cold sweats break-ing out against his skin as he waited to leave the message. When he was done, he hung the phone up and stumbled back to his coffee. It suddenly didn't sound so good.

His mind flashed to Damien laying him in his bed and pulling the covers over him. Was he tucking him in? "Soak in a warm bath when you wake up. It will make it all easier," he told him. "Don't be surprised if you get a little sick. It will be a lot like motion sickness." The pieces fell into place and Franklin's stomach lurched. He barely made it to the kitchen sink before he heaved.

When he was done, his legs felt weak. He reached for the coffee to rinse his mouth and spat it into the sink then rinsed it all down the drain. He took a long pull from the now cool coffee and staggered up the stairs to the bathroom. Franklin drew a bath and slowly stripped while the water filled the tub. He turned to the mirror and was shocked at the dark circles under his eyes. *You look like death, old boy.* His reflection agreed. He turned and looked at his profile. He sucked in his belly a bit and then smiled to himself. Who was he kidding? I'm too old to worry about such things. *Not like you're going to turn the head of some pretty young thing.*

The image of a beautiful redhead hit his mind. Her round hips and full breasts. His eyes widened as he remembered her eyes. Those exotic emerald green eyes that he found absolutely enchanting. Franklin found himself feeling aroused and excited and holding his breath at the memory. Who was she? He kept replaying the memory of her in his mind, getting more and more excited as he did, then the piece fell into place and his headache spiked again.

Franklin was brought back to the present and turned off the water. The tub was almost over full when he realized what was going on around him. He caught his breath and stepped into the tub. It was warmer than he intended, but he slowly lowered himself into the water, letting his skin grow accustomed to the heat. He lay with a washcloth over his eyes in the semi-gloom of the room and rested. He remembered the red haired beauty and found his body responding to the memory. He remembered her servicing him with her mouth, and he touched himself. He remembered the feel of her breasts in his hands. He remembered kissing along the cheeks of her ass. He remembered watching her walk into the bathroom and how her ass moved. He remembered how her cock swayed back and forth when she came out of the bathroom…his feet slipped against the end of the tub at the realization that his 'dream woman' had a penis and Franklin's head went under the water. He came up spurting and gasping, spitting and sucking for air, his washcloth having fallen over his mouth and nose, in effect waterboarding himself.

She had a what?! The piece fell into place and Franklin's headache spiked once more. Each time it spiked, it took a little less time to drop down to a dull thud, but the spikes seemed to get worse. When he recovered, he replayed the memory in his head. Yes, she had a penis. But how? How could such a beautiful, enticing woman have…? He shuddered. He didn't want to think about it anymore. He replayed the entire event and was assured that nobody knew of the indiscretion. She had called him Stewart and had no clue his real identity. Whatever had occurred the night he spent with her, nobody would ever know of it.

Senator Franklin sighed, replaced his washcloth, and lay back again. Let the memories continue. And continue they did. One after another until all the pieces of the puzzle were replaced and Senator Leslie Franklin's memory had been completely restored. When enough pieces of the puzzle that had been his displaced memory were put back, the bathwater was cold, the headache mysteriously lifted and the fog that he had been living in was lifted.

Franklin stepped from the bath a new man. One might say he had been reborn of the water that day. He had a renewed purpose and a restored vision.

He would stop at nothing to destroy Colonel Matt Mitchell and his damned Monster Squad. He had to for Damien's sake…he was all he had left.

22

Rufus sat at a round table with delegates from the *Beastia Conventio*. Many had taken great risk to slip from their territories and attend this meeting. Their weariness showed in their collective faces. Many were more than nervous, and some appeared quite shaken at the numerous empty seats at the once full table. Murmurings of the missing and rumors of how they had fallen to the many human hunters and their military teams across the world were hard to miss.

Rufus allowed them to hold their casual conversations and delayed calling the meeting to order while the attendees gossiped among themselves. *Let them stew in their fear. It will only make selling Mr. Thompson to them easier once they're worked up a bit more.*

Natashia appeared through a doorway and Rufus gave her a slight nod. She slipped back and went to Jack's room where Nadia and he were speaking of the coming moon and their plan to test his theory. Natashia knocked lightly at the door and stepped inside. "Jack? Rufus requests a favor of you, if you can spare a few moments of your time, please," she said softly.

Jack smiled at his new mother-in-law, "Sure, *mom*." He once enjoyed grating her with the unaffectionate term, but now, it seemed to grow on her. She looked barely old enough to be Nadia's older sister, yet… "What does Rufus need?"

She withdrew his uniform and tactical vest from a wicker basket. It had been cleaned and pressed. She held it out to him. "He has delegates from the other families here. Soon he will be telling them about you and your agreement to go back to your people," she explained. "He feels that if you make your presence known, it will drive the importance of what you do home to them. It will make it more…'real' to them."

"He needs their permission?" Jack asked.

"No." Natashia smiled. "Not at all. But many are planning on taking matters into their own hands. They are wanting to take the fight to your people on their own terms, and Rufus is hoping to stay their hand a little longer. By making your presence known, they will see that what he says is real and perhaps save many lives in the process. Both human and vampire."

Jack realized then the true importance of what Rufus had requested. If the vampire families came together and staged an attack against the Monster Squad on their home turf, a lot of innocent civilians and military personnel at Tinker would be put at risk as they slaughtered their way onto the base to get to them. The squads could lock down underground and wait them out until dawn, but those trapped above…it would be a bloodbath.

"Yes, of course," he said and removed his robe and began dressing. Natashia took his robe and Nadia folded it and laid it aside. Natashia then held open his underwear for him to step into and Jack paused. It took him a moment to gather himself.

Nudity among the wolves was natural and it was taking him time to get used to it. Especially around the natural beauty of their women, but he hesitated only a moment before stepping into his boxers, and then his BDU pants. Nadia pulled his undershirt over his head, then he sat and Natashia helped him into his socks. "I'm not used to having help to get dressed," he told them, blushing slightly.

"We don't mind." Nadia smiled at him, giving him a wink.

Natashia handed him his boots and stood. "I shall go to the chamber and wait for Rufus to signal for us. When he does, I shall open the side door and you may enter there. Please, go to the front of the room and simply stand there until you are addressed." She said. "Please, Jack...try to ignore the comments that any of them make, or any threats that are said so long as they are seated, okay?"

Jack's face twisted in confusion. "Okay? But why?"

"One of their rules is that they may say anything while seated. But if they stand, that is considered taking action. Then, and only then, can the others *re*-act. Do you understand?"

"So they can say anything...call me names, threaten my family, et cetera, and it doesn't count unless one of them stands and does it? Then all bets are off and I can beat his ass?"

"Again, no. Rufus is the host. He will handle all indiscretions," she warned. "Agreed?"

"I'm not sure I can do that, mom," Jack said with a soft smile.

"You must, my son." She smiled back. "Do it for Nadia."

He turned and gazed at her for a moment and his heart melted all over again. "Damn, but you drive a hard bargain," he muttered. "Okay. Deal. I'm the puppet. Don't speak unless spoken to."

"Thank you, my dear." She planted a less than chaste kiss on him and then walked from the room.

Jack followed her out with his eyes, wondering if her intentions toward him were motherly or not, then tossed the idea. It was ludicrous, right? She was Nadia's mother...

"Let's finish preparing you, Jack," Nadia said, holding out his BDU blouse. He stepped over and she helped him slip it on, buttoning it up for him and then kissing him when she reached the top.

"Hey, what's the deal with your mom?"

"What do you mean?"

"Did you not see the way she kissed me just then?"

"Yes, so?" Nadia replied. "I think she likes you, Jack. You showed real heroism when you stood your ground against her Halfling form."

"So?"

"My mother also likes your sense of humor."

"But the kiss..." Jack pleaded.

"Was just a kiss."

"Well, it felt like more."

"Only because you find her attractive, Jack," Nadia stated.

"What? I do not. I love you!" Jack tried to defend himself.

"There is no harm in finding my mother attractive, Jack. She is a very attractive woman. I take after her in many ways. In fact, many have said that I get my form from her." She ran her hands down her sides as if to indicate so. "Besides, my love, Mother is mated. You and I are mated. There is no harm." She smiled.

Jack was befuddled. "No harm? She practically ran her tongue down my throat." Nadia gave him a smirk. "Well, it wasn't exactly a *friendly* kiss."

"Jack, you were holding her by the breasts only a short time ago. Was it a caress?" Nadia smiled at him.

"It was in *self-defense!*" Jack sputtered. Nadia laughed.

"You read too much into small things, Jack." Then to aggravate him more she added, "Wait until she *really* gives you a kiss. You may well forget all about you and I being mated. My mother can be quite persuasive when she wants to be." She wiggled her eyebrows at him and Jack paled. "I am teasing you, Jack!" She slapped at his chest. "Now relax and finish dressing! Rufus is waiting for you!"

Jack pushed his foot the rest of the way into his tactical boots and began lacing them. He pulled his BDU pants down over the tops of the boots and cinched them over the lace knots. Nadia handed him his vest and he began checking his pouches and satchels. All of his gear was still inside.

He thought surely that Rufus would have disarmed him...she handed him his duty belt with holster. His pistol was still in the holster. He pulled it and checked the magazine. It was still loaded. He slammed the magazine home and checked the chamber.

"Be careful in there, Jack. Those are silver bullets. The representatives will all be allergic to silver," she said, still adjusting his uniform for hm.

Jack simply nodded and replaced the weapon in its holster. He patted his BDU pants pockets where his P90 magazines would have been. Empty. He looked around and Nadia had her back to him. She turned and presented the basket. At the bottom sat his P90 carbine and the spare magazines. He took the P90 and attached it to the short sling on his vest, then stored the magazines in the mag pouch that was sewn into the side of his pants. He did a quick check of everything. Nadia handed him his sunglasses. He glanced outside and shook his head.

"Take them. They won't be able to see where you are looking," she said. Jack slipped them on. His eyes quickly adjusted to the extra tint. She then placed the boonie cap on his head with a satisfying tug. "There. You look absolutely terrifying," she said with a giggle.

"Yeah, that laugh really sells it, sweetheart." He leaned down and kissed her again.

"Come, I'll show you where mother wants you."

"Ooh, mother *wants* me," he teased.

She punched him in the arm. "Be careful or I'll let her have you, mister." He smiled down at her as she led him down to the great room where Rufus had convened the meeting. She found her mother listening to the representatives argue on the other side of the door.

Her mother held a finger up to her lips as they approached. Nadia held Jack back in the shadows and they waited. Natashia listened intently as Rufus spoke with the attendees.

"We have been too idle for too long and I know that many of you wish to combine your peoples and take the war to the humans. From what we have gathered, the *Lamia Humanus* have already done so and are laying the bread crumbs to make it look as if it were we who attacked their hunters." A murmur rose from the group and Rufus allowed them to make their assumptions. "However, we had infiltrators in the *Humanus* group closest to us. It took us a long time, and unfortunately, it cost us the lives of too many wolves to accomplish this, but eventually, we were able to infiltrate their ranks."

Rufus stepped away from his seat and slowly walked around the table, "During their attack of the American hunters, one of my wolves was able to *capture* a live hunter." Gasps and more murmurs came from the assemblage. Rufus raised his hand to silence them and garner their attention once more. "He was badly injured during the attack, but we provided him with aid and succor."

"Why?!" an attendee yelled. "The hunters would have gladly removed your head from your shoulders given the chance!"

"Or staked you in the sand and let the sun do their dirty work!" another yelled.

Jack started to enter, but Natashia held him back with her hand. She shook her head. "Not yet…wait for Rufus." She whispered.

Rufus held his hands up again, "Please. Please. Hear me," he said. The attendees calmed slowly and he continued. "The man was injured and needed our help." He said softly. "And he needed to be informed of the *truth*."

"The truth does not matter to a hunter!" a voice called out.

"Ah, but it does!" Rufus answered. "When the hunters are in fact, *wolves* themselves!"

The room exploded with arguments and exclamations and disagreements and vampires hissing in disbelief. Rufus allowed a moment for the noise to die down then continued. "They are, in fact, werewolves, however, they do not know it." He turned to the doorway and motioned. Natashia waved at Jack who snapped to attention and marched into the room. He heard the vampires roar to life and for a moment, his desire to open fire was almost overwhelming, but he continued on and followed Natashia's instructions. He marched to the front of the room and stood at attention.

Rufus nodded a thanks to Jack then turned to the crowd. He waved them down then continued once more. "As you'll notice, the American hunter did not enter with guns blazing. He did not toss in a phosphorus grenade and let us all burn in the sun's light. He did not make any effort to attack." Rufus paused to allow his words to sink in. He stood in front of his chair and placed his palms on the table and leaned in to his attendees speaking softly. "He now knows what he is. He now knows the truth. He now knows of the war between us and the *Lamia Humanus* and above all other things…he has agreed to assist us in taking the truth of our plight to his people." Rufus allowed his words to reach his people, but some would have none of it.

"His people will never suffer a single vampire to live!" one shouted. "We're all monsters to them!"

"If we are all just monsters, then why would they purposely inject their own warriors with the very same virus of the wolf?" Rufus asked.

"Only a means to an end!" another shouted. "There is no way that they can compete otherwise!"

"Untrue," Rufus countered. "Our kind have been hunted for centuries by these *mere* humans, and many have come close to making us nearly extinct." Rufus stood to his full height. "*Non*. If they truly believed that all of us were merely monsters, they would never have created their warriors with the very same curse that created the werewolf."

"It is too risky, Thorn! Once they know where we are, they will surely—"

"They will never know where you are. They will only know where *I* am. Of that, you have my word," he said. "And I will tell them all that I know of the *Lamia Humanus*. If we are to direct them to the true enemy, then we must try."

"Why would this human help us?" another asked.

Rufus turned to Jack and nodded. Jack assumed a formal 'at ease' position. "To answer your question, sir," Jack began, "Rufus already explained, I'm not human. I'm wolf. I just didn't know it until they tested my blood."

"But why would you help us?" he asked again.

"For one, I owe Rufus for saving my life," Jack said. "Two, he is allowing my mate to come or go with me, as we see fit. And thirdly…" Jack looked at Rufus and smiled, "he's my friend. And that's what friends do for each other."

Jack turned back to the group of vampires and gave them a good hard stare. He began a slow walk toward the table. "I don't blame you for not exactly trusting me. And to be honest, I don't know you, so I don't trust you. But I trust Rufus. If he trusts you enough to allow you into his home, then I'll just have to accept that. But the fact of the matter is, I gave Rufus my word that I would do my absolute best to convince my people of the war within the vampire families. How the *Lamia Beastia* have sworn off feeding on humans and only feed on livestock. How the *Lamia Humanus* have gone about redirecting the Monster Squad into attacking you and setting you up to be their fall-guys." Jack stopped when he reached Rufus' side. "I can't promise that I can make a difference, but I swore on my life that I would give it everything I had. And my life means a lot more than it used to now, because it's tied to my mate as well.

"If you insist on going through with your attack on the squads, I can guarantee you two things, a lot of your people will die in the attack, and a lot of innocent human lives will die in the attack, but you will never reach the Monster Squad. They are buried under ground so deep, you couldn't reach them with a nuclear bomb. All they'd have to do is wait 'til sunrise then come out guns blazing. Those who didn't run with the sunrise and tried to find a dark place to hide would be sniffed out and staked or…well, it wouldn't be pretty.

"The point is…this plan of his? It's the easiest and least bloody way to save the most lives. You can either get on board or you can get out of the way. But an all-out assault? It's suicide. I can guarantee that."

Most of the vampires were silent during Jack's impromptu speech, and very few said anything now. One, very large and very old looking vampire at the end of the table stood and Jack almost went for his weapon. "It would seem, Monsieur Thorn, that you have chosen your emissary well." He turned and walked away from the table. Jack looked at Rufus and then stepped back out the way he came.

Natashia greeted him in the hallway again. "I hope I didn't overstep," Jack said.

"I think you performed splendidly," she said.

Nadia hugged him and led him back toward their room

Rufus milled about to answer questions and discuss secondary options, and the whole time, he hoped and he prayed that Mr. Thompson was up to the task at hand. Without him, the civil war would soon be over and the *Lamia Beastia* would be forever extinct. The *Lamia Humanus* would execute their plan to use humans as livestock and rule the world. Rufus sighed and then continued the terrible task at hand…politics.

Franklin searched like a madman. Of all of his memories, he could not recall any of Mitchell and his group of idiots actually finding his USB drive. They discovered a virus in their computers, but they didn't actually search his person. He dug through his carry-on luggage. Finally, he found the suit pants he had worn that day. *Please be there, please be there, please be there...Aha!!* Franklin's hand felt the familiar shape of the USB drive and slowly withdrew his shining jewel from his trouser pocket.

"You're going to go down in a ball of flame, Mitchell. You and that half-blood bitch you have working for you," Franklin growled.

He marched to his closet and got dressed. His head still ached, but nothing at all like it had before he crawled into the tub. He glanced at the alarm clock on the bedside table. It was barely 10:30AM. If he hurried, he could get it in the afternoon express back to the hacker. Franklin quickly dressed and found a small manila envelope to fit the USB into. He slipped the envelope into his breast pocket, and after taking two more headache formula and swallowing the rest of the cold coffee, he left to overnight the package.

As soon as he was on the road, he called the hacker and told him the package would be en route. Be prepared for it. Use the email address he finds on it and the data on there and make it public ASAP. Send it to every news agency, every internet blog, every tabloid, anybody who might possibly take it 'to the people' as quickly as possible. The hacker laughed and assured him, for what he was paid, he'd hack the president's email and send it to him if he wanted.

"Just get it to the press. The president will get wind of it soon enough." He smiled.

Franklin ran into the nearest express shipping office, scribbled the PO Box address on it, kissed the manila envelope good bye and paid for overnighting it. He walked outside and headed for a coffee shop and one of those gourmet coffees all of the interns are so wild about.

This was going to be a good day. He could feel it in his bones.

23

After much soul searching, Laura decided that it must be her that was changing. Maybe she just wasn't cut out for this line of work anymore. She had talked herself around in circles and kept coming back to the same conclusions…she just didn't agree with her boss' tactics. It had happened at the company and she left, and now it was happening here…except she really didn't want to leave the Monster Squad.

She went back to her office and reflected on her time with the team. She knew that they provided a necessary service and had saved a lot of lives over the years. For the most part, people didn't know about the monsters, and those who had seen things, dismissed what they had seen to an overactive imagination. In reality, people didn't want to know what was out there. It distorted their perception on reality. And recently, Laura's own perception on reality was being distorted. She had been asked to do things that went totally against what she thought was right.

She stood and went out to Evan's lab. He was busy working on something small, using a magnifying glass to see the miniscule object under an intense light. She tapped on the table as she approached to get his attention.

"I heard you walking across the common area toward my lab space, Laura. What can I do to help you?" he asked without looking away from his project.

"Evan, I'd really like to speak with you, if I could."

"Of course, Laura. What would you like to speak about?" He reached to his side and picked up a small soldering iron and touched it momentarily to the object then smiled, his attention still on the tiny object.

"Evan, this is important. May I have your attention, please?" she insisted.

He laid the object to the side and turned off the intense light behind the magnifier, pushing it aside as he turned to her, his smile unwavering. "My attention is entirely yours, Ms. Youngblood."

Now that she had his attention, she wasn't exactly sure where to start. She decided to jump right in and hope to iron out wrinkles later. "Evan, I know you've been out of it for a while…"

"I was imprisoned, Laura. Let's not mince words," he said.

"Er, yes. You were imprisoned for three years. So, you weren't exactly privy to Colonel Mitchell's behavior during that time." She paced in the small space of his lab area. "But from the time before and what you remember of the Colonel and from the time since you've been back…does his behavior seem…" she searched for the correct word, "*off* to you in any way?"

"Define 'off', Laura. I'm not sure that I know where you're going with this."

Laura sighed. "Does he seem to be acting less like himself?"

Evan swiveled his chair side to side for a moment as he thought about her question. Suddenly he looked up at her and said, "No." Then turned and picked up the tiny object again. "Are there any more questions you'd like to ask me?"

"Evan, come on!" she pleaded. "This is *me*! Talk to me."

He spun back to her and practically glared at her. "You come to me and ask if your boss seems 'off'? You never so much as came to visit me while I sat in that silver-plated cell and rotted for nearly three years," he said through gritted teeth. "*Three years!* And now that I am out, you've barely spoken to me, but you're concerned about Matt. Fine. Let's just talk about him. I'm sure the two of you got real cozy while I was locked up, eh?"

She stepped back, shock registering as she realized that Evan was not only jealous, but hurt. Here she was, waiting for him to come to her to express interest in resuming their budding relationship, and he was wondering…God only knew what he was wondering, all the while he was working away and gong about his business as if nothing was wrong. "Evan, I don't…I didn't know," she stammered.

"Didn't know? Didn't know what? That I was alone? Or that I was starving in the darkness?" he seethed. "Didn't know that my heart was breaking for you every moment of the day?"

"Yes, of course…I mean, NO!" she stammered. "I had no idea that you ever thought that Matt and I had something going on. That idea is ludicrous!"

"Is it now?" he barked. "Then why the sudden interest in how he's acting?"

"It's complicated. I guess I can't expect you to understand, you—"

"I'm what?" he growled. "Just a vampire?" His words dripped with venom.

She suddenly turned angry. "No. That wasn't what I was going to say at all." Now it was her turn to get angry. She stepped toward him, hands planted firmly on hips. "I was going to say that you've been gone too long to notice the subtle changes in his behavior." She took another step toward him, this time with a finger pointed in his face, "I was going to say, that if I'd had any clue that you still cared about me, I would have been *man enough* to make the first move the moment you got out and tried to rekindle what we had!" She took another step, jabbing the finger more pointedly. "I was *going to say* that had I known you were going to just throw yourself into being Matt's butt-buddy and shadow puppet, I wouldn't have risked my career and possibly prison time slipping you blood and then busting you out!" Now she stood directly in front of him and he was leaned back against his workbench, her finger directly in front of his face. "I was going to say, that had you been around, that maybe you would have noticed his behavior changing and could help me identify it so that I could know if it was him or me!" Then she stepped back and made an effort to calm herself. When she looked back up, there were tears threatening her eyes. "Because, if it's me, then I can't do this job anymore. And I really don't want to leave, but I will if I have to."

She turned and left as quickly as she gracefully could before she lost control in front of him. Evan sat quietly for a moment contemplating what she had just dumped on him, and he felt like an idiot. Even before he was made into a vampire, he wasn't very good with reading women, much less dealing with relationships. This only went to prove that being an immortal didn't improve one's charm with the ladies. He shook his head and in his frustration, swiped his arm across his workbench tossing everything across the floor. If he really gave two shits about his work, he would have cared about the damage he'd done, but honestly, the only thing he cared about just left in a huff. If he had a functioning brain cell left in his head, he'd take off after her and try to fix it, but for the life of him, the only words he could think to say to her was, 'I'm sorry' and somehow, he doubted that would fix this.

Screw it. I have to try. He ran after her, trying to follow her scent, but he lost her near the ventilation intake. The facilities air intake sucked up everything and he was left standing alone, wondering which way to go. He closed his eyes and tried to imagine, if I were an upset female, where would I go? The lady's room?

It sounded as good as any other place, so he tried. He went there and placed his ear to the door. He heard nothing. He opened the door slightly and had no idea what to expect. Rather than the plush interior with feathered fans and perfume bottles, lotions, and stacks of every conceivable tissue known to man, he found a sterile looking white tile restroom that appeared, for all intents and purpose identical to

300

the men's restroom…minus, of course, the stand-up urinals. Which would make sense, since women don't normally stand to urinate. Unless, they weren't…he was thinking too much. "Laura?" he said softly.

"She's not in here," another woman's voice said. "And you shouldn't be either." Judging by the slight accent it was either Sanchez or one of the other Latino women who worked at the facility. He prayed it wasn't Sanchez. That woman scared him. If he were smart, he would simply say, excuse me and slip out, but…he really felt the need to find Laura.

"Any chance she came through here?"

"Nope," said the disembodied voice. "Now get out before I stake your ass, bloodsucker."

Holy shit! Evan thought. Whoever it is, knows I'm a vampire. But… "Sanchez?" Surely she was the only one whose senses were sharp enough to be able to tell.

"I swear to God, it's bad enough I have to shower with all those swinging dick smartasses, but if I can't take a dump in peace, I'm gonna give you a swirly so bad you're gonna look like the singer for the Stray Cats, you got me, lab rat?"

"Yes, ma'am!" Evan said, and scooted out the door. He turned quickly and bumped into Laura. "I'm sorry!"

"For sneaking into the Lady's Room?"

"What? No. For…us," he said. "I'm sorry. I know that doesn't fix anything, but it's all I have." He sighed, sounding defeated.

Laura gave him a stony look. Evan knew he bought exactly zero points with his comment. "Laura, you know me. I've never been exactly good

301

with the ladies." He pleaded. "I'm sorry. I shouldn't have exploded like that on you. You came to me looking for a sounding board and I unloaded my insecurities on you and..."

"And maybe I could have been a little more sensitive with your situation as well," she said, not meeting his gaze. "Evan, I can't say that I'm exactly good with people either. Nor am I that experienced with relationships. At least, not successful ones."

"Do-over?" he asked, a lopsided grin breaking across his face.

Laura smiled at him then threaded her arm through his. She pulled him toward her office. "Let's see if we can work through *both* our problems and our insecurities in my office, shall we?"

From within the restroom Sanchez yelled out, "Thank God! I never thought you two would leave! Get a room already!"

Mitchell scanned the activity reports that came in from the field. With the full moon almost upon them, the activity level was picking up and the action reports reflected everything from possible zombie outbreak in the middle of Mexico (unconfirmed), to goblin activity in lower Canada (single sighting confirmed, awaiting secondary confirmation), to a possible baby vamp attack (single confirmation, awaiting secondary confirmation) in California. Matt sighed. If either of the single confirmations got a secondary confirmation, he'd be sending out Second Squad. If the other gets confirmation while Second was in the field, they could have simultaneous ops running. He really didn't like that possibility but they always ran that risk when the full moon came about.

And the worst part was, the night of the full moon, he'd be out of commission. Again. Just like *every* full moon. He needed Laura more than ever at that time, and the possibility that she may be coordinating two operations at one time? She was up to it. He knew she was. That was why he hired her. He double checked the date on his watch. Two days to go before the full moon.

Matt could feel his ability to keep everything in check slipping. Sometimes he even questioned his ability to continue his command. But every time he questioned his ability to lead, his hubris rubbed that doubt to ash. So many times he wanted to bring Laura in and tell her the truth, but...how would she react? Would it change their working relationship?

Matt, found himself drinking more. And feeling it less. He poured himself a scotch. He clinked a chunk of ice into the glass and swirled it around a few times before swallowing the drink back. He waited a moment for the familiar burn. Nothing. He could taste it just fine and he relished the flavor. He just couldn't enjoy the slight buzz that it once gave him.

He looked out over the training grounds that his men used and sighed. If they knew the truth...if they only knew the truth. They'd probably turn their weapons on him. Then each other.

When he questioned what they had done, he thought back to his wife Jo Ann and daughter Molly. They never stood a chance. Neither wanted to go camping that fall weekend, but Matt insisted. The weather would be perfect, he told them. The moon would be full, they could build a huge campfire and make s'mores. It was supposed to be a new beginning, but instead, it was the end. It was the end of Mitchell Mathews – the lone survivor of the attack. When Major Mathews discovered the full extent of his injury and his miraculous recovery, plans were put into place. It didn't take long to discover *why* Major Mathews recovered so quickly. But *what* Mathews became every month...that was a topic of much debate. The few who were in the know quickly decided that if Mitch Mathews was attacked and survived, then his attacker was still out there. And if there is one, there are more. So, a new unit was created to deal with just such a threat and Major Mathews was put in charge of it. Except Major Mathews was erased, his records destroyed, and Matt Mitchell was created. A perfect example of oversized government and the glory of computer records. If you aren't in the computer, then you no longer existed. It worked easily enough for Matt to simply swap his surname for his first name, so why not try it for Evan Peters? Dr. Peter Evans had raised no eyebrows when he was brought on staff. Those who did know were smart enough to keep their mouths shut.

Good for them. *They'll live longer if they keep quiet.*

Matt shook his head. Why would he think such things? That wasn't like him. Matt sighed. He poured another drink and considered once more of bringing

Laura in on the truth. She *was* his XO. She should be privy to all things that had an impact on the operation.

He made an executive decision. He picked up his two-way, "Laura, can you come to my office?"

It took her a moment to respond and when she did, she sounded breathless. "On my way, sir."

When Laura knocked and entered, her lips looked red and swollen and her shirt tail was untucked. She was still trying to put her hair back behind her ear and make herself presentable before she entered, and failed to catch the details. Matt assessed the situation and jumped to his own conclusions. "Did I interrupt something, XO?"

"No, sir." She adjusted her collar then looked him in the eye. "I was just going over some…results with Evan."

Matt smiled. "I'm glad that you and Dr. Peters have worked things out." He offered her a chair. "Laura, we need to talk."

"Okay, sir. Is something wrong?"

Matt sat on the edge of his desk, contemplating where to start. "I need to come clean with you about a few things, XO. Especially if I'm to expect you to pick up the reins once I'm…gone," he said solemnly.

Laura was not expecting this in the least. She never expected Matt to consider leaving, much less to leave her in charge. And *could he* leave her in charge. She wasn't military and this was most certainly a military operation. As far as the service was concerned, she was a civilian contractor, yet…

"Matt? What are you talking about?"

"I need to tell you a story about a young major who lost his family. A major who was, himself, attacked by a werewolf and survived." He finally met her eyes and sighed. "I need to come clean with you about who I am and why I'm so adamant about ridding the human race of these damned creatures."

24

Nadia had packed them a light picnic lunch and they ate along the shore. With the forest behind them and the salty sea air blowing in on them, Jack felt like he could conquer the world. They watched the waves come up and make small crashes on the rocks, sending sparkling droplets into the air and sea foam along the surface of the water. A seagull cried out above them and Jack threw a piece of sourdough at it. It failed to catch the offering, but the gulls on the ground scrambled and fought for it.

"I could stay like this forever." He sighed soaking up the sun and breathing deeply of the clean air.

"So could I," Nadia said. She sat next to him and sliced hard cheese into small bite sized pieces. "Perhaps when you have fulfilled your obligation to Rufus, you will return here and we can stay?" It sounded more like a plea than a question.

"You mean retire?" Jack laughed. "I'm a bit young for that, don't you think?"

"You will not age now, Jack. You've been made wolf. Remember?" Nadia reminded him.

He hadn't thought of that. It had only been...what? Maybe five years? Six? How much does a man age in that time?

"What would you do then? Go back to hunting our own kind?" she asked him.

"I don't know," Jack said. "I don't even know if they'll have me back." He propped himself up on one arm and watched her. She looked sad. "What would you have me do, Nadia? Would you have me come back and whisk you away to see the world?" he teased her.

"*Non*. I would miss my family too much," she whispered, tears threatening her eyes.

"Then what? Come back here and do...what? Lay around all day, eating cheese and grapes and making love to you?" he asked defensively.

"Would that be so horrible?" she asked, the tears flowed freely now.

"Nadia, that sounds *wonderful*, but there has to be more. For me, anyways. I need to be doing something productive."

"And loving me is not productive?" she asked. She placed her hands upon his chest, "It could be if we tried enough."

Jack was taken aback with that one. She meant children, didn't she? So soon? And...holy Christ on a cracker...he wasn't expecting that. "When I said productive, I meant like...a 'job'. I need to be working."

"You could be security here, Jack. Rufus has security, but none of them are truly warriors like you." Her eyes were practically begging him, and he could feel his heart breaking.

"You don't want to see the world? Even for a little bit? Leave the island for a Honeymoon?" he asked. "Go to Paris or London or...shit, even

Detroit? Not that there's anything in Detroit worth seeing except maybe a Tigers game, but nothing says we have to stay. Just go be by ourselves for a little while, then you could come back and we'd have those memories forever." He gave her a smile, but she was shaking her head.

"I cannot leave my family," she said flatly.

"So my bargain with Rufus…it was for nothing? You wouldn't leave if he threw you out, would you?"

"No. I would find a way to stay with them," she said, her eyes downcast. "And I would hope that you would come back to me."

Jack stood up and stared out to the sea. He had made his bargain with Rufus to save her from what he perceived to be slavery, only to find out that it wasn't really slavery. At least, not the way he thought of it. He made the agreement with the idea that they could leave whenever he was done and then he and Nadia could make the decision together where they wanted to go and what they wanted to do with their lives. That it would be a mutual decision…but she never intended to leave. He tried to remember if she ever alluded to leaving. Or if she ever made a comment about staying there forever, but no matter how hard he tried, he couldn't remember. He continued to stare at the ocean, arms crossed over his chest and Nadia sat behind him. She said nothing, but the tears ran freely and he knew.

Jack turned and without saying a word to her, he walked back to the castle and to his room. He had packing to do. It didn't matter now about the experiment. It didn't matter whether she could control her wolf during the pull of the moon or not. He had given his word to Rufus that he would deliver the state of their plight to his people, and he intended to live up to his word. Nadia may be his mate, but she made up her mind. Her pack meant more to her than her mate. So be it.

Jack disrobed from the beach gear and began putting his uniform on. As he was dressing, Natashia passed by in the hall. Jack called to her from his room. "If you see Rufus, could you ask him if I could speak to him please?"

Of course Natashia was puzzled. She knew that Nadia and Jack were supposed to be enjoying a picnic lunch on the beach, but she didn't mention it. "Rufus will be sleeping at this hour. But as soon as the sun sets, I will let him know of your desires."

"Thank you, Natashia." Jack went back to dressing and packing his gear.

Natashia only raised an eyebrow. He did not call her 'mom'. Perhaps there is trouble in paradise? If so, Nadia would be needing her. She slipped down the hall and out through the dining hall door.

When Jack had finished, he realized, it took far less time than he expected. He still had hours left before sundown. He went to Rufus' study and waited. As soon as Rufus could arrange for transport back to the mainland, the sooner Jack could begin his journey back to Oklahoma City and get his obligation over with. Depending on how the team accepted him (or not) this could be a very short, one-way trip.

Jack ran through his plans continuously in his mind. Playing and replaying every possibility until he had all avenues of recourse panned out in his head.

Before he realized it, the time had passed and Rufus entered the room. "Good evening, Mr. Thompson."

"Rufus." Jack nodded. "How soon can you arrange transport to the mainland?"

Rufus was somewhat shocked at the abruptness of Jack's request. "Is there a rush?"

"Let's just say that I'm ready to fulfill my obligation to you." Jack was unreadable. Rufus studied him a moment, then nodded.

"I can have the boat ready within the hour. Once you reach shore, I shall have a vehicle standing by at your disposal."

"It would really help if I could get something with government plates. Or is that asking too much?" Jack asked.

"*Non*, that should not be a problem," Rufus said. "I believe black SUVs are the norm, *oui*?"

Jack smiled. "Oh, yeah."

"I believe we can fill that request." Rufus turned then asked, "Anything else?"

"How far south are we? I need to get to Oklahoma City and I wasn't carrying cash when we were on the op." Jack blushed.

"I shall see to it that you are adequately seen to for your journey." Then he stepped out of the room.

Jack stepped to Rufus' bar and checked out the different decanters. He purposely stayed away from anything with a red tint. Amber looked good. He pulled the stopper and sniffed. Smelled like alcohol. He poured himself a small glass and knocked it back. "For luck."

Franklin's phone rang and he glanced at the screen. Blocked number. *Must be the hacker,* he thought. "Franklin," he said, answering the phone.

"Right. Look, *Senator.* I got your package."

"Great! Send it out! Send it out, *now!*" He practically jumped up out of his chair as he stood.

"Seriously? Do you have any idea how much shit is on here? What *kind* of shit is on here? And you want me to send this out? Who are you, *really?*" the hacker asked.

Franklin went past mad and straight to infuriated. "Does it really *matter?* You've already been *paid* haven't you?!" he practically screamed into the phone. "Just do as you're fucking *told!*"

The hacker almost lost his temper, but decided to take the high road. He was a world-class destroyer in the digital world. It didn't matter if the victim was an internet forum troll or a leader of the free world, he really didn't like being spoken to like this. Still...he had already been paid. Handsomely. And, whether the voice on the line truly was the 'Distinguished Gentleman from Illinois' or not, if he truly wanted this data released to every media source tonight, then so-fucking-be-it. Still...

"Hey, man, I don't want to be the one to piss in your Post Toasties, but do you have any idea what is on this flash drive?" he asked.

"Of course I do, you idiot!" Franklin hissed into the phone. "It's exactly what I need to destroy the son-of-a-bitch who has made my life a living hell since I met him! It doesn't matter if you believe it or not, it's all true! So for the love of God, just do it! Release it! Send it out! Send it out, now!" Franklin screeched.

The hacker shook his head as if Franklin could see it. "Okay, man. It's your funeral." Franklin could hear the clicking of keys and the hacker said, "Hold on, it's uploading to the main server now." Franklin was practically shaking in anticipation. This time tomorrow, Matt Mitchell would be no more! "Okay, man. Last chance. I can just as easily delete this and…"

"No! Don't you dare! Send it out. Please. I beg you. Just do it and I'll leave you alone forever," Franklin pleaded.

"Okay, man. Whatever." A few clicks later. "It's done, dude. Data is sent," the hacker said. "But remember, dude. What's been seen, can't be *un*seen. Later cocksucker." And hung up.

Insolent little shit. Franklin started to get angry, but then realized…it had been done. Mitchell was done for! By this time tomorrow, every news agency, tabloid, internet blogger…every single media source in the world would know about the Monster Squads and Colonel Matt Mitchell!

Senator Leslie Franklin had won! He actually whooped aloud and pumped his arm in victory.

Laura sat patiently while Matt told her his story. She would nod when expected and gasp when it was appropriate, but the whole time, in the back of her mind she kept telling herself, *why didn't I see this? It makes such perfect sense. Why didn't I notice the little signs?*

Once Matt explained who he was, how he became a wolf, the fact that the bane only helped to curb the urges, but didn't prevent the shift, all of the pieces fell into place. Matt then told her that something big was coming. He didn't know what, but he had been feeling it build up for some time now and he feared that whatever it was would come during a full moon, when the squads were the busiest and he was 'preoccupied'. He also told her that he expected her to pick up the reins and take over when he was no longer able to.

Laura sat patiently and listened. She debated for some time on whether to interject her own opinion a few times, but decided prudence was the best policy. Until the end when she asked for permission to speak freely, and he foolishly granted it. Laura expressed her opinion, but at least she did so calmly and professionally. She told Matt that she had respected him for many years, however, recently, his behavior had her questioning whether she was cut out for the position any longer. She also told him that she had come within a hair's breadth of turning in her resignation letter because of it. To his credit, Matt listened carefully, and after a long discussion from both sides, Laura agreed to add a new position to her job description…as the good Colonel's moral compass.

She accepted that the more often he shifted, the more the wolf was exposed and the more influence it had on his attitude and behavior when he was human. A side-effect, he called it. The bane helped, but it could only do so much…and after years of shifting, the wolf had recently begun to have much more influence on his aggression and competitiveness. Laura claimed to understand, but she couldn't really know what he was going through. Still, she agreed to act as his moral compass for as long as she could. And Matt agreed that when the day came that he could no longer effectively lead, to step down and let Laura take the reins. Both felt a certain amount of 'cleansing' had taken place when they were done, and Laura felt a lot better about resuming her position as XO. But she told Matt, if he gave an order that she felt went beyond what was right, she may have to call him on it publicly. If the wolf caused him to ever try to retaliate or to try to embarrass her…and Matt assured her that as long as he had *any* control left, that day will never come.

Laura hoped he was right.

25

Jack made landfall a lot sooner than he expected. The Monterey open bow craft had skimmed the surface of the water at sixty knots, and apparently the island was a lot closer than he had expected. A group of men were waiting at the dock and threw a line to the approaching craft. Jack grabbed it and pulled them in alongside the floating dock. The boat's pilot never moved from behind the wheel, but he handed him a satellite phone. "When you're ready to return, I'm speed dial pound-sign-one. I can be back within the hour," he said and shot Jack a wink. Jack took the phone, but wasn't sure if he ever would return.

He walked to the rear of the craft and one of the men extended a hand to help pull him to the floating dock. "Your car is waiting outside the gate. Fully fueled. Government plates, as requested." He reached inside his bomber jacket and retrieved an overstuffed envelope. "Travelling money."

Jack felt the heft of the package. Good grief, he wasn't travelling Europe, he was just travelling up the state of Texas and into central Oklahoma. "Overkill?" he asked.

"Rufus takes care of his people," the man said. "Besides, you may need to hire backup or acquire more firepower, or…whatever."

"This isn't a raid," Jack explained. "It's a...diplomatic mission."

The men raised eyebrows and shot him quizzical looks. "Good luck with that."

Jack considered their disbelief and realized that he was going to need all the luck he can get.

He grabbed the bag that Rufus had provided him and walked to the car they had provided. If he didn't know any better, he'd swear it was a government vehicle. Black SUV with government plates, just as requested. He glanced at the windshield and noted that it even had a base sticker from San Antonio. *Nice touch.* Should make entry a lot smoother.

Jack tossed his bag into the passenger seat, unhooked his P90 and laid it in the floor next to him and started the truck. He turned to the man in the bomber jacket. "Tell Rufus I'll do the best I can, just like I told him. I'm going to drive straight through if I can."

"Full moon's tomorrow. You should have enough adrenaline pumping through you to make it," he replied. He leaned against the window and added. "I meant it when I said good luck. There are a lot of us on the ground whose lives depend on your success."

Jack nodded and put the truck into drive and pulled away. He took the first highway he found heading north and started working his way toward I-35. Thankfully, the wolves had put a Garmin GPS in the SUV to make the trip a bit easier. The hardest part was keeping the cruise control set at the speed limit and not flooring the accelerator. He was in for a long trip. He longed for a good cup of coffee like the wolves made back at the island. Somehow, they knew how to make it so that it tasted good, unlike any other cup of coffee he had drank since the augmentation. His taste buds had changed, but his desires hadn't.

Jack turned on the radio and flipped through the stations until he found one with old time rock and roll and settled back into the seat for the drive. Although he was as tense as he ever was prior to an operation, he did his best to try to relax. He may be going home, but this was no homecoming.

Franklin was practically giddy when he returned home and walked through the door. He was actually whistling to himself as he came in through the kitchen entryway. He should have noticed the breeze blowing back through that slowly shut the kitchen door, but he didn't. It wasn't until he stepped into his study and saw Damien sitting behind his chair, his feet propped on his desk, that he even noticed the study window open. Franklin paused and set his briefcase next to his desk, then hung his suit coat on the coat tree in the corner.

"You have a key to the house, Damien. I don't see why you insist on using the window."

"Keeps my skills honed, father," Damien said, scraping his nails clean with his father's letter opener. "Somebody once told me to find my skill and exploit

318

it." He paused his nail cleaning and glanced at his father. "I think that somebody was...*you*?!" He chuckled to himself.

Franklin sighed. "Why must you be this way, son?" he asked. "Didn't I provide for you? Send you to the best schools? Give you everything you could ever want?"

"Give it a rest, father. The things that I truly wanted, you didn't have time for," Damien stated. "But we've been down this road far too many times to rehash it now." He took the letter opener and stabbed it into the desk while sitting up. "Look what you do to me, father! I'm a fucking vampire with daddy issues!" He burst out laughing.

Franklin hated it when Damien got like this. His outbursts were so unpredictable and with his strength and bloodlust, the violence was palpable. He bordered on insanity when he was human, but now that he was undead...he was completely unmanageable.

"But, father, there is one thing I've learned since being turned. Do you know what that is?" Damien asked, jumping up onto Franklin's desk and squatting down like a gargoyle. "Never make the same mistake twice!" His maniacal laughter echoed out through the hallway. Franklin felt his hand begin to shake so he placed it behind his back in order that Damien couldn't see it. Never show him fear, it only feeds his dementia. "But with you...now, with you, father, I make the same mistake five or six times. I just can't help myself. You bring out the worst in me."

"Why are you here, Damien?"

Damien instantly sobered. His hysterical laughter squelched. "How is your mind, father?"

"Clear as a bell," he said honestly.

"You're welcome."

Franklin nodded. "Yes, thank you."

"And Mitchell?" he practically spat the name out.

Now it was Franklin's turn to allow his features to twist into an evil smile. "The wheels have already been put into motion. It seems that while the son-of-a-bitch may have screwed with my memory, during his interrogation, he forgot to ask one tiny little question. And that question is coming back to bite him in the ass."

Damien turned a skeptical eye to his father. "What question is that, father?"

"If I still had the USB with the virus on me." Franklin smiled. "You see, it not only held the virus that would try to connect their secure computers to the internet, but it also downloaded all of their data onto its flash-drive."

Damien hiked a brow. It seems his father wasn't a complete idiot after all.

"They were so busy trying to secure their computers again and drilling me with 'why would I do this' that they forgot all about the device I used. It was still in my trouser pocket when I returned home."

"Where is it? I want to see it," Damien demanded.

"Already sent to the hacker and released to the news agencies," Franklin said with an evil smirk.

Damien's eyes bugged out. "What?!" He jumped down from the desk and grabbed his father's tie, pulling him closer to him. "Did you at least *check* the data first?!"

Franklin stuttered and stammered, "N-no! It was encrypted! I couldn't have checked it even if I wanted to!"

"You fool!" Damien threw him across the study to crash into his mother's armoire. "They could have compromised the drive and put anything they wanted on it!"

Franklin struggled to regain his footing. "They couldn't. There was no way for them to access it. It was encrypted…"

"They have the best people on the planet working there," he hissed. "There are no secrets to those who hold all the keys."

Franklin was on his hands and knees. "You'll see, son. You'll see…" he gasped. "Tomorrow. Mitchell will be destroyed. He'll be pulled out of the dark and into the light of the public eye. You'll be safe my son. He won't ever be able to touch you…ever." Franklin lifted his eyes to plead to his son…but he was gone. A breeze blowing softly through the study window the only indication he had ever been there.

"Jesus, Apollo, I think you could bench a friggin truck!" TD said, spotting for Apollo in the gym. The bar was so loaded that it curved in a distinct 'u' shape and Apollo stared intently at the ceiling, huffing and grunting as he pushed out the last rep.

321

TD helped him place the bar back on the rack and listened to the metal stress as it took the load, the clank of the Olympic plates a welcome sound. Apollo sat up and Jimmy handed him a towel to wipe down. "I wish they would find something to give us a better work out besides this old stuff. It's getting to where it's barely a challenge anymore and we can't fit anymore plates on the bar."

"I'm telling ya, man. There's a nice Toyota Tundra out in the parking lot!" TD joked.

Marshall stopped with the arm curls and turned to him, "I think that's Spanky's truck, dude. He may not appreciate you pressing it."

Jimmy got a gleam in his eye. "Hey. Let's go pick it up and move it!" The others groaned. "No, seriously. Let's go stick it in between something so he can't get it out!" he giggled. Marshall hooked his chin toward Jimmy and then pointed over his shoulder.

Jimmy turned around to be eye to sternum with Spanky. "Not a good idea, Tango. That truck is my baby."

Jimmy looked up and smiled. "You know I was just messing around, right, Spank?"

"Mm-hmm. I'd say that too if I got busted."

Apollo walked by and snapped Jimmy with his towel. "Busted!"

"Hey, I'm just trying to cook you up a better workout, Jolly Black Giant," TD joked.

"Maybe we could find you something else to lift?" Marshall asked. "I think there's a Humvee around here somewhere." He laughed.

Apollo stopped and struck a pose, mocking the bodybuilders they'd all made fun of so many times before. Catcalls and whoops from the other guys in the gym echoed through the room and Apollo ate it up. Changing poses and flexing his muscles for the crowd. He had just assumed the 'crab' position when he felt a pinch on his ass and he jumped, propelling himself forward into Wallace's arms. Wallace, being so much shorter than Apollo, looked up at him, then abruptly dropped him to the floor to a roar of laughter. "Sorry, buddy, I don't swing that way!"

Apollo quickly looked around for the offending pincher only to find Sanchez standing in the doorway smiling at him. "Looked too good not to," she quipped.

"Girl, you're gonna get it now," he said, scrambling to his feet.

She squealed and ran out of the gym with Apollo hot on her heels.

Jimmy stood there a moment staring after them. "Well, damn," he said, disappointed. "He was supposed to spot me when I got through spotting him."

"I have a feeling he's going to be 'spotting' her," Marshall quipped.

"Dude, how is it you can make *anything* sound dirty?" TD asked. "Seriously. Somebody ask you to change the oil in their car and you could make it sound dirty as hell."

"It's a talent." Marshall grinned.

Sanchez ran by the door again squealing with Apollo hot on her heels. TD walked to the door and watched them go down the hall. "I think he's gaining on her."

"She could give him the slip if she wanted. She's slippery that way." Marshall wiggled his eyebrows.

323

"Dude!" TD exclaimed. "Seriously? Again?"

"Tell me you haven't thought about changing her oil…come on, tell me. We've all seen her naked," he said. "Hell, I got a woman at every base I've been assigned, but I'd still use my dipstick on her and check her oil level!"

"TMI!" TD said. "Come on, man. She's Apollo's woman for crying out loud."

"And you're telling me you wouldn't do her?"

"Well, no. I mean, if she were single. And interested," he admitted.

"Oh my God. You're intimidated by her!" Marshall teased.

"For shit's sake," TD sighed, "I'm not intimidated. I like strong women."

"Bullshit, man. You're intimidated by her because she's a hellcat. You're scared she'd rip your balls off and wear them on a necklace."

TD laughed. "Actually, dude, you couldn't be more wrong. I'm more scared that *Apollo* would rip them off and flush them down the toilet!"

Marshall simply nodded. "Yeah. Okay. Good point."

26

Colonel Mitchell and Laura were going over the intel on recent activity. Laura checked for recent confirmations on the reports, and so far, none had been reconfirmed. The tension levels were high and the upcoming full moon had a lot to do with it. She knew from experience that the closer they got, the more the activity level would increase.

Matt slipped a flask from his front pocket and poured the contents into his coffee cup. Laura pretended not to see, she knew from their talk that the scotch would have little effect on his performance, but it would help calm the nervous tension building in his system. Rather than sip it, he tossed it back in one swallow and set the cup aside. The command center was basically empty other than a couple of technicians who were preparing the equipment for the next operation. They, too, knew how the activity levels seemed to follow the lunar cycles.

The moon may only seem to control the werewolves, but it also gave the predators better light to hunt by and humans seemed compelled to act like complete and total idiots as the moon came closer to being full. Combine it all together and you have a recipe for disaster that they had to contend with.

Laura looked over the feedback reports from the crew monitoring the police reports and their field spotters for monster activity. They had geeks who did nothing else but scour the web and news reports for key words and patterns. Her gut told her that a shit-storm was brewing, and she was waiting for it to break. She could tell by Matt's nervousness that he shared the sentiment.

All they could do was wait and prepare for a long night.

Jack made good time. He counted down the miles as the signs rolled by, mile marker by mile marker. He tried his best to stop for fuel at smaller stations with the fewest people present. He caught fewer stares in his tactical gear at the smaller stations. It wasn't easy driving all the way up from south Texas and keeping a low profile, but he was doing it. Keeping his speed at the posted limit and staying to the slow lane helped.

He had stayed on I-45 until he hit the Dallas metropolis, then worked his way across to I-35 and pointed the black SUV north again. It was too dark to be distracted by sites along the way and concentrating on driving was enough to drive him insane. He glanced at his watch and figured he had about three hours left before he hit the gates at Tinker.

Jack played out the different scenarios in his mind over and over, trying to imagine how it might actually go down when he reported back to his unit. But he knew as well as anybody that no matter what contingencies he might plan for, it all goes out the window once his boots hit the ground. As far as he knew, the squad assumed him dead.

Jack chuckled to himself. They had called him Phoenix once after a particularly hairy incident with a pack of vamps in an abandoned school building. The squad had cut the gas line feeding the old building and let it fill with gas, then just before the building was set to be popped, the perch where Jack had been sitting overwatch to snipe any who attempted to escape broke loose and collapsed onto the decaying roof. He fell through the rotting boards of the roof and into the top story of the building. He knew he only had moments to get out of the building before the whole thing went up in flames and made a mad dash for the doors. The building went up in a fire ball just before he made the doors. It had blown him out of the open double doors and Jack was able to tuck and roll then come to his feet and walk away, but to his team, it appeared as if he simply walked out of the fire ball. The name Phoenix had stuck with him ever since.

"Well, if they think I'm dead and I come walking back in now, they'll *really* think I'm a fucking Phoenix," he said to himself. He ripped open a beef jerky he got from the shit-n-git and stuffed it in his mouth. He kept thinking about the team that he went into that op with. Rufus told him that none survived but him. He truly hoped that Rufus was wrong.

327

Jack patted the arm pocket on his BDU shirt. The satellite phone was still there. He considered calling Nadia, but…what would he say? What could he say? He didn't even tell her good-bye before he left. He hated leaving that way, but he was hurt and didn't know what to say. All he knew was, no matter what the squad might think or do, if they go on the defensive, he had to stay alive. For her sake.

He truly didn't expect that they would fire on him, but he didn't expect that they would accept him back with open arms. Best case scenario, many, many hours of debriefing, most likely followed by chemical questioning, and if he was lucky, they might not imprison him. In his mind, he technically turned coat by mating with a werewolf. And he agreed to help a vampire clan; albeit one who saved his life, and seemed completely non-threatening.

If he could convince the Colonel that Rufus was the real deal and that the squad was being used, then perhaps maybe…just maybe he could accomplish his goal. Then they could toss him *under* the prison. As long as he could get Mitchell to listen to him.

That's the key, though. Getting the Skipper to listen to me.

The night turned out to be uneventful. Laura spent the evening taking catnaps in her office when she could. Matt checked in on her and even spread a blanket over her one time in the wee hours to keep her from catching a chill. He pulled the shades over the window in her office and switched off her desk lamp before he slipped out and quietly shut her door.

The adrenaline coursing through him had kept him from sleeping, but was leaving him feeling ragged. He almost looked forward to shifting at the full moon just to give his system a reset. His nerves were almost shot. Evan came up beside him with a foul smelling brew and handed it to him. "It will help, sir," he said, offering the steaming cup.

"It smells like boiled assholes," Matt said, handing the cup back.

"Probably tastes like it, too." Evan smirked. "Just drink it. It will ease the nerves. May even ease your shift tonight as well."

"Tonight? I lost track of time," Matt said as he took the cup and, while holding his breath, drank it down.

"It's nearly dawn, sir," Evan said. "I'm about to head to bed myself."

Matt stifled a belch, hoping dearly not to have to taste the concoction a second time. "Bed? I thought as long as you were down here, you didn't fall prey to day/night cycles?" he asked.

"Usually, I don't. But I've been going for days, and my mind could use the rest."

"Roger that." Matt looked into the cup and saw the black residue. "Bane?"

"Among other things, yes, sir."

He nodded and handed the mug back. "Thank you, Evan. I do appreciate it."

"You're welcome, Colonel."

"I think I'm going to go topside and watch the sun come up. Maybe help the squad pack some of the gear. They pretty much know that something will happen tonight. Always does on a full moon."

"Roger that, sir." Evan smiled at him.

Senator Franklin waited impatiently by his television in his office. He wanted to see the first broadcasts from whoever had the nerve to report first about the Monster Squad and its illustrious leader and their wasteful appropriation of government funds. He was practically shaking with excitement and actually found himself biting at his fingernails...a habit he had spent years breaking himself of. He had arrived at his office in the wee hours of the morning and frantically switched from CNN, to FOX, to ABC, to MSNBC back to CNN and kept switching channels hoping to be the first to catch the breaking news.

Surely someone would see all of the CCs in the email and realize that *everybody* was being sent the information. Surely somebody would risk running the story first thing based on the official looking documents rather than trying to validate each one through some fact-finding fiasco? He was beginning to become impatient when he finally got to MSNBC and saw the footer that read, 'Breaking Story' and he turned up the volume, "This just in: In an apparent mass e-mailing to nearly every news agency from Senator Leslie Franklin's private e-mail address comes this full-length video of the Senator confessing certain crimes to an unidentified male prostitute. We want to warn our viewers that although the video has been blurred out, you may want to remove your children from the room."

Franklin dropped the remote to his television. "NO!" he screamed. "This is wrong! That's not right!" His eyes focused on the red haired woman from New Orleans with the green eyes that he was sure nobody knew of…and although the image was blurred, it was obvious that he, Senator Franklin, was on national television, sucking on her manhood. It cut to another image that, although blurred, showed Senator Franklin on all fours with the red haired woman behind him, obviously giving it to him from behind. Her breasts and organ had been blurred out, but his face and the look of pure pleasure wasn't. He watched as his form snuggled next to the redhead, his head resting on her ample chest and he saw his mouth moving. The sound came on and he heard his own voice. "Of course I killed my wife. I had to. She was the one with all of the money." He looked up at the redhead with desire and kissed her breast. "Took the old bat forever to finally die. She probably would have survived her cancer if I hadn't been poisoning her medication."

Franklin fell to the floor of his office and felt all the blood leave his face. He could hear the reporter talking, but his mind wasn't registering what was being said. His entire life flashed before his eyes and he wasn't proud of what he saw. He felt his body begin

to shake and he wished it was an earthquake, opening up to swallow him whole and remove him from this nightmare. Scrambling across the rich carpeted floor, he scooped up the remote. Perhaps the other news agencies had more tact and refused to run it? Perhaps…no. There it was. He changed the channel again. There he was, admitting murder to his male lover. At the bottom of the screen, it read 'For the unedited version go to our website…'

Franklin screamed and threw the remote at the flat screen, but it refused to break. One corner of the screen glowed blue with tints of green, but the scene jumped to the redhead giving it to him from the rear. He curled up in the fetal position to cry just as his cell phone began to ring. He ignored it. He had to. People couldn't know already. There had to be a way to take it back. To deny it. He could claim it was all faked in order to discredit him…that was it…maybe people would believe it.

Franklin slowly made his way to his feet and looked at his watch. It was early. Very early. Surely nobody else was here yet. He could slip out of the offices and go back home. He could hide there until things blew over. Surely they'd all forget in a day or two. What was the name of that one senator who got caught screwing his au pair? Right?! Nobody remembers. It was old news.

The image of him and the redhead flashed in his mind again, his voice repeating, "Of course I killed my wife…" and he retched in his trash bin. He had to leave. Now.

Laura woke with a start. She actually jerked awake, knocking the blanket to the floor. A knock at her office door snapped her back to reality. She sat up and flicked the light switch on the wall. "Come in," she croaked.

A bleary eyed technician stuck his head into her office. "Ma'am, you might want to check the news-feeds this morning. We just picked it up a little while ago, but I can't find Colonel Mitchell."

Laura glanced at the clock on the wall. Nearly dawn. He was either asleep, or, with his condition, trying to burn off the extra energy his body was creating. "I'll find him," she said, sounding like she had just gargled with gravel. "What channel?"

The tech frowned. "Pick one, ma'am. They're all running it."

Laura had an 'oh-shit' moment, thinking the worst, fearing the storm had finally broken and this one was big enough that the secret they had fought to keep hidden all these years was finally out. She scanned her desk for the TV remote, then finally stood and pressed the power button. It was on FOX news, and the first thing she saw was a screen shot of Senator Franklin on all fours with the redheaded transsexual behind him. Parts of the image were blacked out, but she knew exactly what was going on because she had been there. She felt ill as her eyes

333

scanned to the bottom of the screen and the 'Breaking News' banner. She turned up the volume and listened while the reporter explained that nobody knew exactly 'why Senator Franklin would e-mail the video to every major news outlet, internet blogger and tabloid, but according to sources, the man in the images shown here was confirmed to be Illinois Senator Leslie Franklin with an unknown transsexual prostitute'...Laura turned off the television.

She practically fell back on the couch. *He did it. He actually did it.* Laura searched her side for her two-way radio. "Colonel, come in."

"Go for Mitchell," he responded.

"Franklin sent the package," was all she said. She waited for him to respond. It took much longer than she expected.

Finally, Matt came back across the radio, "I'm topside, Laura. Meet me in the hangar." She couldn't tell by his voice any emotion. She wasn't sure what to expect when she reached him topside.

Finally, she keyed the radio, "Roger that, sir. See you in twenty." She had just woken up and knew she must look a mess. She at least wanted to drag a brush through her hair and pour some coffee to take with her.

She stood and went to the small sink in the corner of her office and wet a paper towel. She wiped her face and flipped open the cabinet door above it. She looked like death, but had looked worse. Grabbing a brush, she pulled it through her hair a few times and pulled it into a tight pony tail. When in doubt, a pony tail hides a mess, and if you can get it tight enough, it can pull the wrinkles from lack of sleep out of your face. Even tighter, and the pain will keep you alert. At least, that's what she told herself.

Piping hot java juice and she would be right as rain.

27

Franklin had no sooner got in the door and his phone stopped ringing. Seventeen messages were left on his answering machine. He tentatively reached out and pressed the button and one by one the recorded messages played out. People he had long called friends, even though they weren't, left the most horrible messages for him. They told him how he needed to turn in his resignation, quit, save face while he could…before he went to prison. He needed to do the right thing for the party, regardless of how forgiving the party may be, this isn't the same as 'coming out'. The only friendly message of support came from an opposing party member who he had come through the ranks with as Freshmen…a damned boy scout who extended a hand of friendship and offered to be a sounding board during this obviously difficult time. How many times had Franklin scoffed at the man for being weak because he had offered his friendship in the past? Finally, he heard Damien's voice. "I warned you, father," he growled. "Now we will deal with Mitchell our *own* way. We will drown him in a sea of blood…and you will be the first in our path!"

More messages followed, but Franklin didn't hear any of them. He was shaking too badly. He stumbled to his bedroom and began ripping apart his closet.

Jack approached the main gate at Tinker with his ID in hand. His window was down and the gate guard only gave his vehicle a cursory glance. The inspection sticker on the truck was good, the plates were government, and he knew his ID was good. The only problem he may have was if Mitchell knew he was alive and had alerted the guards to be on the lookout for him. The guard glanced at the ID, glanced at his face and saluted him through. Jack pulled forward, navigated through the concrete barricades and made his way south and west toward the hangar. The rising sun to his left and the oncoming morning traffic felt like any other day of the week.

So why did he have this knot in his gut?

Oh, yeah. He was supposed to be dead. He'd lost track of how long he'd been gone. Surely Mitchell had replaced his squad by now. They may even still be in training. They may have even cut their teeth with some minor incident. Jack knew with the full moon tonight, shit was going to get ugly, fast. He also knew that Mitchell would find a reason to not be there and Laura Youngblood would have to command the operation. Mitchell was *never* there on the roughest night of the month. The rest of the month, you couldn't pull his ass away from the hangar, but on the full moon, he'd fucking disappear…

Jack hit the brakes so hard that the minivan behind him almost hit his SUV. A horn sounded and he could hear the minivan's driver cursing him even through the closed window. Jack hurriedly pulled the SUV into the parking lot of the Base Exchange and parked it across two parking spaces while the realization sunk in. *Oh my God. Mitchell is a wolf, too!* "Son-of-a-bitch!" Jack yelled and punched the roof of the SUV leaving a noticeable raised dent in the roof. "Why didn't I ever put two and two together before?" *Because you didn't know what you were before, dumbass!*

"Fuck me!" Jack yelled. He stepped out of the SUV and paced. This was significant, but he didn't exactly know how. *Think, Jack. Think!* He stopped and placed both hands on the fender of the SUV. His heart was racing and he was having trouble thinking. Between the energy rushes of the moon's pull and being separated from Nadia, he was having a lot of trouble focusing. He kept pushing her from his thoughts, but more than anything he wanted to turn the truck around and go home.

Home.

Home? Yes, home. As much as he hated to finally admit it to himself, *she* was home. Home wasn't a place, it was *her*. It didn't matter if he lived on the island or if he was working at the hangar, where Nadia was, he would be. He had to be *home*.

But first, he had to complete one last mission.

Laura entered the hangar and found Matt help-ing the squad pack gear into different crates and go-bags. They separated it into different areas for differ-ent threats and although the teams were always ready, in times like these, when threats were immi-nent, they would check and double check that everything was right. No soldier wanted to risk their gear failing them in the field. It was make-work, but it was a necessary evil.

She approached him tentatively, unsure of his reaction. When he noticed her, he stood tall, his face solemn. Matt seemed honestly troubled. He turned to Laura, away from the squads, even though they would eventually hear of Franklin's 'exposure' he hoped to keep their part of it from them. "I truly hoped that he wouldn't remember. I hoped that he would never use it," he said softly.

Laura looked away, shaking her head. "We shouldn't have left the USB drive with him, Matt. He eventually would have, you know it."

"Laura, we went over this," Matt sighed. "I had hoped he would have the sense to *check* it first and realize we had something on him. That he would back down…"

"We knew his psych profile suggested that he wouldn't do that, though. Evan even told us that his personality type would preclude such action," she argued.

Matt sighed. "You're right." He stared off through the open doors. "You're right. Whatever comes of this will be on my head."

One of Matt's butter-bar lieutenants approached him. "Colonel, you have a priority call. You can take it there." He pointed to a phone near a workbench.

Matt went to the bench and picked up the phone. "Mitchell."

Senator Franklin spoke quietly into the phone, "You aren't answering your cell, Mitchell. Is that your way of being insubordinate?"

Matt pulled his cell out and glanced at it. Dead. "Apologies, Senator. I forgot to charge it…"

"Doesn't matter now, does it, asshole?!" he snarled.

"Excuse me?" Matt tried to play stupid, but he knew he had it coming.

"Don't play coy with me, Mitchell. You may have won the battle, but you're going to lose the war. There's a blood bath coming and you will *drown in it*! Mark my words, Mitchell. I was the only thing that could have saved humanity and you just…" Franklin paused and Matt could hear something hit the phone. "You just caused the fucking apocalypse!" There was a blast across the phone line followed by another sound that Matt couldn't make out. The line didn't go dead, but he couldn't quite hear. The full strength of the shotgun blast that took off Senator Franklin's head wasn't carried across the line, but Matt knew a gun blast when he heard it.

He set the phone line down. "Trace that call and alert EMS to that address!" he yelled to his Lieutenant.

"Matt, what happened?" Laura asked.

"I think Franklin just shot himself," Matt said.

Laura paled.

This was their doing.

Jack pulled up alongside the hangar and noticed the double doors at the front were standing open. *May as well make a grand entrance,* he thought. He could see what appeared to be two full squads checking and packing gear. Just another day preparing for the muck.

The two guards normally assigned outside the hangar weren't posted outside the door. Normal when both squads are topside. Jack rolled up and inside the front area of the hangar. He stopped the engine and opened the door. He clipped his P90 back to his vest, grabbed his duffle and shut the door.

"Who does this clown think he is?" Wallace asked, nudging Spanky. They couldn't quite make

341

out the figure in the black SUV at the far end of the hangar, but they both knew he had made a huge mistake rolling up on their turf like he owned the place.

Spanky whistled to Apollo and gave a motion to the front doors. Apollo stepped from around the Humvee and instantly his hackles rose. Somebody was about to get an ass-whoopin! Apollo bowed up and started stepping toward the unknown intruder. The other squad members fell in.

Colonel Mitchell stepped out in front of the squads just as the door to the SUV closed and Jack turned around to face the incoming squads with the colonel in front of them. Just as he had figured, all of the contingencies he had planned on the island and during his drive here went right out the window. *The best laid plans of mice and men...and shit.*

Jack strode up toward the teams until they noticed who he was and they stopped. The new members had no clue, but he realized that the Colonel didn't seem surprised at all that he was alive.

"Chief Petty Officer Jack Thompson, reporting for duty, sir." Jack snapped off a salute.

"Who the fuck *is* this guy?" Lamb asked.

Apollo broke into a toothy grin. "Phoenix, you son-of-a-bitch!" He practically ran up to bear hug him.

Jack grunted as Apollo lifted him from the ground and the original Monster Squad members surrounded him to welcome him back. Colonel Mitchell held his ground. The new members of the Monster Squad surrounded the Colonel. "Who is this guy, sir?"

"A dead man."

When the original clamor was over at Jack's resurrection from the dead, he approached Mitchell. "You're not happy to see me, sir?"

"Thompson, we have to follow protocol. You know that." Neither man smiled.

Jack nodded. "I expected as much."

Mitchell nodded at the guards who quickly approached Jack. "Yeah, yeah. Give me a minute." He unhooked his P90 and handed it to one of them. "Careful with that. It's loaded. Might put an eye out." He pulled his FiveseveN from its holster and handed it to the other one. "Easy there, buster. That's a real one. No airsofting with that or somebody goes home in a body bag." He pulled his magazines from the various pouches and pockets and handed them to his squad mates. "Here, you guys can probably use these."

He looked up at Apollo again. "Damn it's good to see your ugly mug again, you brute." He punched him in the arm, "I can't believe looking at *you* would be refreshing."

"Believe it," Sanchez said with a smirk.

"Yours?" Jack asked.

"Damned straight, baby." Apollo grinned again.

"I'm nobody's'," Sanchez reminded him.

"That's right!" Apollo quickly corrected. "I'm *her* bitch," he whispered.

Jack laughed. "Sweet, bro."

"Ahem," Mitchell interrupted. "Protocol, Jack."

"Yes, sir," Jack said, sobering. "Lead the way. I live to serve. Ask and I shall obey. Waggle the carrot and this ass will follow. I'd say some more, but I've been driving all night and I really got to pee."

"Needless to say, we have a lot of questions, son."

"Oh, we *definitely* have a *lot* to talk about, *sir*," Jack said, giving the Colonel a knowing look. "A lot to discuss."

"It sounds like there's a few things on your mind, chief."

"You don't know the half of it, Skipper." Jack reverted to his nickname for the Colonel from the early days and Matt did a double take. Skipper being the Navy term for most boat captains and Jack being a Navy SEAL, he often called his CO that as a term of affection. This time, Matt knew it wasn't meant that way.

"Anything I should know offhand before we get started?"

"There's a war, sir. And we're stuck in the middle of it. We're all being *played*, Skipper... by both sides."

"Really?" Matt said disbelievingly.

"Oh, yeah," Jack said. "There's a shit-storm coming. A war like we've never seen before and God Himself only knows how many people will pay because of it. What you decide today may very well tip the scales of that war."

The elevator doors opened and Matt dismissed the guards so that he could address Jack alone. "Just what do you know, soldier?"

"Everything."

From the desk of Heath Stallcup
A personal note-
Thank you so much for investing your time in reading my story. If you enjoyed it, please take a moment and leave a review. I realize that it may be an inconvenience, but reviews mean the world to authors…

Also, I love hearing from my readers. You can reach me at my blog: http://heathstallcup.com/ or via email at heathstallcup@gmail.com

Feel free to check out my Facebook page for information on upcoming releases: https://www.facebook.com/heathstallcup find me on Twitter at @HeathStallcup, Goodreads or via my Author Page at Amazon.

The Monster Squad Series

Mankind always suspected that he wasn't alone at the top of the food chain. Since time immemorial, he has had an innate fear of the dark, a fear of the unfamiliar, a fear that something evil lurked just outside his field of vision. Once the sun set and the moon lit the sky, an unfamiliar snap of a twig or rustling of a bush could make the deadliest of men's blood run cold. Something was out there.

Humanity had spent its time enjoying a peace that can only be had through blissful ignorance. For centuries, stories of things that go bump in the night had been told. When creatures of the night proved to be real, the best of America's military came together to form an elite band of rapid response teams. Their mission: to keep the civilian populace safe from those threats and hide all evidence of their existence.

Caldera

For years, the biggest threat Yellowstone was thought to offer was in the form of its semi-dormant super volcano. Little did anyone realize the threat was real and slowly working its way to the surface, but not in the form of magma. Lying deep within the bowels of the earth itself, an ancient virus waited. Recently credited with wiping out the Neanderthals, the virus is released within the park and quickly spreads. Can mankind prevent a second mass extinction? Can humanity survive the raging cannibals that erupt from within?

Whispers

How does a sheriff's department from a small North Texas community stop a brutal murderer who is already dead and buried?

When grave robbers disturb the tomb of Sheriff James 'Two Guns' Tolbert searching for Old West relics, a vengeful spirit is unleashed, hell bent for blood. Over a hundred years in the making, a vengeful spirit hunts for its killers. If those responsible couldn't be made to pay, then their progeny would.

Even when aided by a Texas Ranger and UCLA Paranormal Investigators, can modern-day law enforcement stop a spirit destined to fulfill an oath made in death? An oath fueled by passion from a love cut down before its time?

Forneus Corson

Nothing comes easy and nothing is ever truly free. When Steve Wilson stumbles upon the best-kept secret of history's most successful writers, he can't help but take advantage of it. Little did he know it would come back to haunt him in ways he'd never have dreamt... even in his worst nightmares.

With his life turned upside down, his name discredited, his friends persecuted, the authorities chasing him for something he didn't do, Steve finds himself on the run with nothing but his wits and his best friend by his side. When a man finds himself hitting rock bottom, he thinks there's little else he can do but go up... unless he's facing an evil willing to dig the hole deeper. An evil in the business of pitting men against odds so great, they risk losing their very souls in the attempt to escape...

Flags of the Forgotten

What do you do when you've devoted your life to working for the government, then that very same government turns on you?
You take the fight to them.
It's just another day at the office for Bobby Bridger and his cohorts when they are used as scapegoats. Follow along as this rag-tag group of operators attempt to stay one step ahead of their pursuers.
From the heart of Texas to Pakistan to the very bowels of the CIA, these boys know how to play hard, fast and dirty.

Hunter Trilogy

Born of Viking stock, careered into the Swedish Navy, Sven Ericsson finds himself in the fabled New World. Away from the restraints of society, the young Northman is dragged into long nights of debauchery; nights that lead him into the waiting arms of a dark beauty that will change his very nature forever.

Fighting his new unnatural status, Sven steers clear of humanity, skulking along the fringe of society, and filling his inhuman need with the blood of the outcasts or the easily forgotten. A shadow among the shadows...until extraordinary events, centuries later, force him to emerge from the dark. A mishap of his own making pits Sven Ericsson into a moral quandary that will remind him what it means to be a warrior.

He is a killer. A fighter. A Hunter of his own kind.

Sinful

Charlie Johnson is your average American teenager. He's a good student, he's a good son, his girlfriend is the love of his life. He's a nice kid. Charlie also murders people for their sins. A serious car accident leaves Charlie comatose and when he comes to, he suffers from visions of unspeakable horror that keep him awake at night. He soon discovers that when he touches people, he can sense their evil and see their greatest sins. Some crimes are too terrible to describe. Some crimes are too terrible to go unanswered. Some crimes can be averted...but only if you're willing to step into that world.

For a refreshing change of pace, check out JJ Beal's exciting Young Adult Zombie thriller.
Lions & Tigers & Zombies, Oh My!

The cold war has heated up again. This time the battle will be fought in every street of America.

Trapped in a major city, hours from their small town country home, a team of young girls find themselves cut off from everyone they know and left to fend for themselves as the world spins out of control.

With nothing but their wits, their softball equipment and their friendship to hold them together, they face incredible odds as they fight their way across the state. Physical, emotional and psychological challenges meet them at every turn as they struggle to find the family they can't be sure survived. How much more can they endure before reaching the breaking point?

ABOUT THE AUTHOR

Heath Stallcup was born in Salinas, California and relocated to Tupelo, Oklahoma in his tween years. He joined the US Navy and was stationed in Charleston, SC and Bangor, WA shortly after junior college. After his second tour he attended East Central University where he obtained BS degrees in Biology and Chemistry. He then served ten years with the State of Oklahoma as a Compliance and Enforcement Officer while moonlighting nights and weekends with his local Sheriff's Office. He still lives in the small township of Tupelo, Oklahoma with his wife. He steals time to write between household duties, going to ballgames, being a grandfather and the pet of numerous animals that have taken over his home. Visit him at heathstallcup.com or Facebook.com for news of his upcoming releases

www.devildogpress.com

Indian Hill Series

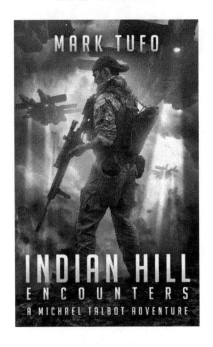

All That Remain By Travis Tufo

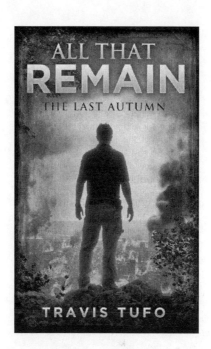

Prey By Tim Majka

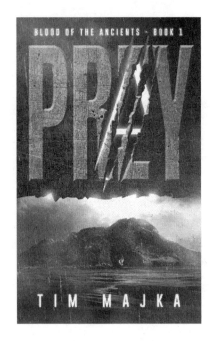

Vodou by Brandon Scott

CUSTOMERS ALSO PURCHAS

SHAWN CHESSER
SURVIVING THE
ZOMBIE APOCALYPSE

WILLIAM MASSA
OCCULT ASSASSIN
SERIES

JOHN O'B
A NEW WO
SERIE

ERIC A. SHELMAN
DEAD HUNGER
SERIES

HEATH STALLCUP
MONSTER SQUAD
SERIES

MARK T
ZOMBIE FA
SERIE:

Made in the USA
Las Vegas, NV
23 October 2023

79602459R00215